BEYOND THE LEDGE

CHERYL BLAYDON

North
Country
Press

Beyond the Ledge

ISBN 978-1-943424-27-6

Library of Congress Control Number: 2017955905

North Country Press
Unity, Maine

Acknowledgments

There are many people involved in the making of a novel. My heartfelt thanks to my early readers—Ruth Alley, Hilary Bartlett, Chip Griffin, Melanie Howe, and Lynne Nicoletta, whose thoughtful input helped shape BEYOND THE LEDGE.

I'm also grateful to Joan Dempsey, editor, teacher, and friend, whose generous encouragement and guidance throughout the manuscript has been invaluable. Thanks also to Patricia Newell of North Country Press whose careful eye for detail keeps me on my toes.

And to Sarah and Sean, thank you for your faith in my dreams.

Chapter One

A Romanian woman gave birth at sixty-six that year. Prudence, at thirty-five, had failed twice, each before the first trimester. After reading that article, Prudence had concluded that she and Nick were undeserving. But then, her self-pity had become a tour de force, swaddled in twenty-three consecutive days of cloud cover thick as cotton batting. He had called it brain fog and she had said that even her syntaxes suffered from mold, and both were probably right if not equally unhappy. Forecasters shook their heads and strange fronts collided. A nor'easter hit its stride, heading up the coast with Maine in line for possible hurricane-force winds. Ahead of the system, Oyster Cove had been painted with a broad brush that melded sky and sea into one. Insipid pigments of gray coughed out continuous fog, enveloping the inherited house, while below the second-story window a colorless sea roared its displeasure. Nothing could alter Prudence's foul mood, not even the letter containing the wishes of her late great-grandmother, revisited whenever hyperbole of the Maine sort was called for. Tempers were short, wood was at a premium, and still, chimneys spewed smoke with abandon, leaving the air acrid and thick.

The clapboards reverberated with the rat-a-tat of a loosened shutter. "Dammit-to-hell, Hannah," Prudence said. The crinkled stationery floated a moment and then landed on the bedroom floor. "This is not the time for more problems." In response, the house groaned against the increasing wind, which now wheezed damp air through unseen cracks. Warts, her intrepid ancestor had called such things, just as she had called the old house an opinionated dowager holding court on Thatcher Lane. A quaint characterization spun from Hannah's repertoire of choice expressions, and a description that would come to fit Hannah Ellison herself.

Prudence refolded the letter and tucked it into her nightstand. Great-gran had a way of making a point, even from the grave. Toughened by life's burdens, and joyful from its blessings, Hannah's words were as true now as they had been five years earlier. But the very same letter had also emphasized: 'meet a good man, settle down in Oyster Cove, and fill the house with a passel of little ones'. Prudence had in fact found the man, but according to Nick, the house, having taken them hostage, had become a needy mistress. The coast was pockmarked with similar types—leftovers from the shipping era—that evoked a certain romanticism with their widows' walks and wide verandas—until they needed updating. At least once a year, Nick pushed to put it on the market, and with each push, Prudence hauled out the letter in resistance to her husband's attempts to sell. Hannah would roll over in her grave, she countered, and he would roll his eyes as always.

This morning had been no different, except now the topic of sex or lack thereof had been brought into the equation and their queen-sized bed more of a drop-zone for free-falling emotions than a place to make love. It had been another morning of teary beginnings that never ended well. She looked at the empty bed. Nick's presence lingered in the twisted sheets and hollow of his down pillow, and the simple words that had started it all, punctuated the air with disdain.

"Mm, you smell good," he'd said. Familiar pillow-talk—her husband's intention obvious, her reaction ungenerous. A hormonal fugue, she'd insisted, predicated by her second miscarriage, but that hadn't been entirely accurate. In truth, she couldn't explain it even if she tried.

After showering, he'd taken his frustration to the kitchen, no buss on the cheek, no comment. Banging and slamming had echoed upward, his consternation meant to hit its target. And now, dancing attendance on the coming storm, a colony of gulls mocked her with their screams and lightness of being, while she stood at the window anchored in place.

Hannah had referred to the seabirds as gatekeepers of the harbor. Today, they were just one more annoyance. A small coastal oasis, Oyster Cove had been swallowed by monotony, the sodden filminess muting the royal hues of fall. It was a time earmarked as a pilgrimage for tourists, but they would find little to laud this September. Neither could she.

A young look-alike of Hannah stared back at Prudence from the glass. "Get your butt out of this house," she demanded of her spitting image—the lavender-gray eyes that were now shadowed by sleepless nights, and lips set in familial stoicism. Having made friends with the photos boxed-up in the attic, Prudence identified many of her New England relatives in the lines and angles of her face. Of course there was more to it than that. She'd met her true self here, found both kith and kin in a sleepy, understated village edged up against the sea.

By all accounts, Hannah had been a doer, not a dweller of problems like her great-granddaughter, and the dusty old house with its cranky past, was meant to have been filled with happy, rambunctious kids. Though proud of her Ellison-Stone lineage, this morning she was overwhelmed by self-doubts, craving the reassurance of her studio, the time alone if only for a few hours and even to rail at the gods. Ever since she had been introduced to art as therapy for her childless condition, she had come to rely on the little one-room shack as one clings to a life-preserver. More so today, she thought, given the atmosphere emanating throughout the house and the short window ahead of the storm. Maybe it was the danger involved in hiking the ledges instead of driving that would shake up her listless body, allow her to be present and immerse herself in the look and feel of canvas and paint instead of here, choking on remorse. Anything, she thought, to de-clutter her mind and get the creative juices flowing, and break the mysterious hold on her spirit. Then, she might be more inclined to make it up to her husband later.

Prudence wriggled into her paint-stained jeans, each tug a reminder of the too-hot dryer with the broken timer. Not that anyone would notice she'd left her jeans unbuttoned, but still she slipped on the oversized ragtag sweatshirt Nick had worn to paint this room. Even with many washings, a little of the pearl tone paint remained in the fibers, along with the touch-up latex for the guest room, a delirious yellow picked a long time ago by Hannah and adored by Prudence. She adjusted the new toile drapes and finished making up their bed, tearing up without provocation as she was prone to do. "Stop it!" Hadn't she shed enough of those, she thought, struggling once more with the damn button before heading to the kitchen?

Taunting her, a whiff of Nick's after-shave—subtle, with a hint of bergamot—hung in the air, draping the breakfast nook where he'd more than likely glowered at the day ahead. A rubber band lay on the crumb-spattered counter next to the leavings of his meagre breakfast. As a result of Nick's haste, the cupboard door with the broken clasp yawned open, exposing the jumble of boxes within. The odd tableaux was reflected in a rectangle of glass where farther out to sea, a curtain of rain hung from the pewter sky as if from an invisible rod. At once, a lone herring gull sounded a shrill and repetitive *KEE-AH,* a warning to the image teasing in and out of the mist, a ghostly outline hinting at the real thing: a bow sprit here, stacked traps there, a lobster boat headed into port. Borne out of a hurricane somewhere in the tropics, and like the small number that had made it this far north, this type of storm was not to be trifled with in open-ocean—even the gull understood.

Prudence rummaged the corridor off the kitchen for her rain gear: tall rubber boots, a floppy canvas hat, and a time-worn jacket yellowed from linseed oil. Items more closely related to her heart than mere necessities for coastal living. The boots and hat were Hannah's, but the jacket had belonged to Great-gran's lover. The reliable slicker, sized for a large fisherman, and a small stash of prized letters, were all that remained of Hannah's relationship with Timothy Parker, the man who had triumphed over her young widowhood, and whom she had loved long after

4

he'd been lost at sea. Prudence had marveled at the bravery and tenacity she had discovered in their written words, and clung to the idea that she had inherited more than the house from such a wonderful woman.

The letters had been tucked away from greedy eyes, and in the most unlikely of places—under sofa cushions and inside shelved books—and always within Hannah's reach. She had been thirty-five at the time they were written, the same age Prudence was now. And the Thatcher Lane cottage—where Nick had proposed—continued to echo Hannah's existence through a mircpoix of humor, tenacity and sorrow, the basic recipe for life by another young woman on the brink of change. Prudence winced. She and Nick had been skirting each other for days and something had to give.

"Damn it, Hannah," Prudence yelled. "What am I doing wrong?"

Her only response, a contemptuous wind that pushed against her as she exited the creaky kitchen door. The same hard driving gusts that muted all other sound. Before she had taken another step, she was enveloped in the scent of brine. It rode the air, tangy and sweet and redolent of the tropical island she had once called home, but with enough similarity to tether her to this craggy place. It was exactly right. And so was the jacket, though it dwarfed her five-six frame and the shoulders felt off-kilter with her own, and commanded her to hug it tighter to her body. For once she was glad for the empty stretch of ledge ahead—no chatty types tide-pooling and exchanging recipes—as she picked her way across the slippery rocks, the tall green 'wellies' her only defense against wholly slick surfaces. In truth, she was never alone out here. The lovers walked with her, their embrace as palpable as their presence within the walls of the old house. They had taken this trek many times to reach their favorite spot near the modest lighthouse, moments documented in snippets within the precious letters: legendary seas, curly waves tapping the coast's rocky shoulders in greeting, boulders holding back the tides, and Tim's green peapod dory. And the fog. Always the fog—that one consistent in this coastal clime—that now began to blur Prudence's vision. Gauze-like mist festooned the length and breadth of granite and schist, a thickening banner prepared to hide her yellow-clad figure and leave only the dark bonnet of that small landmark peeking through. There were long moments when she would be isolated from both land and sea. Hormonal or not, she thought, you are one crazy lady.

Walking through the front door of Pelletier Realty, Nick was struck by the tomblike quiet—none of the usual bantering since his staff of two were both on vacation. Lucky them, he thought, the stillness invoking the building's prior use as a funeral parlor on a morning that smacked of ill-winds and a brooding sky. "This place still gives me the willies." His words echoed around the bland, chilly space, causing him to shiver. Don't be such a girl, he thought, heading to the back. He had often questioned his reasoning for setting his sights on this building in the first place. If he ever had the nerve to admit such thoughts, his wife would be more than amused. Pru, with her carpetbag of island lore, believed in spirits while he had always eschewed the notion. But this was not the morning to remind her. His day had started badly from the get-go, Pru's remarks and off-handed response to his needs had left him out of sorts and confused. Thinking he had long ago surrendered any hope of understanding a woman's moods, here he was roaming his back office, coffee going cold on his desk, trying. This whole baby thing had him twisted up inside. He didn't know if he was depressed like his wife or if it was guilt giving him heartburn. The dehumidifier whirred and he popped a Tum's. He was behind schedule and sleep-deprived, and had a lot of ground to cover for his first appointment. Scrambling through the files for the right listing, he lunged for a falling folder, and banged his knee, hard. "Damn!" It was only eight-fifteen and the day already sucked. Sourly, he reached for the ineffective windbreaker—he'd left a heavy-duty L.L. Bean jacket on his boat—and knocked askew a framed Goethe quote, 'Character is formed in the stormy billows of the world'.

An avid seaman, Nick understood the confluence of coastal weather during a nor'easter, but not the condition of converging emotions. He was inept when it came to Pru's reactions from one day to the next and this morning was a perfect example. She had shut him down again, but he didn't have time to go back home before she left for work; that is, *if* she even bothered with the bookstore today. Invested as she'd become in her paintings, Pru was now looking for someone to buy out her share of North Sky Books, a business she and Vivien—never to be called Viv—Sanford had built up through grit and hard work. To this day, he marveled that they had come to him looking for property. Prudence's decision was baffling—the business was going well, but he also felt sorry for Vivien who had become a good friend. Yet, as he reminded himself, Vivien didn't seem to mind the current change in plans. Had women always been this complicated?

"Oh fuck!" He'd also left his hat on the boat. Naturally. And wasn't she moored all the way out in Salt Harbor, exposed because he hadn't taken the time to put her in storage! Too early, he'd said, a few more days to enjoy her still. His wife had been right, he thought, his mood fouling like the weather. The *Mystic* would be sitting high in the water by now, the yawl's classic lines buffered by the ugly oversized fenders bought at a Rotary auction just last month. It pained him to think of the way they could mar her wooden hull if things went wrong. His fault—either push the speed limit on Mason Road or worry the rest of the day. Another bad idea—Dickie Bronson's on patrol this week. Friend or not, if Nick got caught speeding, an expensive ticket would follow and he'd never hear the end of it from Dickie—or Prudence. He changed his mind—he'd call the yard—one of the boys would check on the yawl. This was the first significant storm of the season, and one that local armchair meteorologists had bets on. Listen in on just about any conversation and talk of the weather was right there, front and center. He had never known a group of people so mesmerized by atmospheric conditions, but then he had never lived near the sea before coming to Maine. Now he had become just like them.

Pelting water danced on the pitched roof, its tempo growing louder as the big hand on the clock kept time. He made a run for his Jeep through a wall of rain. Cold slapped the back of his neck as water plastered his thick, dark hair against his collar while the flimsy windbreaker puckered and clung tenaciously to his solid torso. Taking the keys from his pocket, the cold metal resting between his fingers registered a moment in time—Hannah's silver locket—Pru's touchstone. It was back around her neck again, worried like silent algorithms between her long fingers. The sadness was almost too much to witness. He inserted the key, his anger turning to something else. Distracted, he revved the car a little too long as he vowed to make it up to her later.

Chapter Two

Prudence Stone had arrived in Maine on a June day torn straight from the Chamber of Commerce brochure. Even her painted toenails had reflected the brilliant sky, a different shade of blue than the one left behind in that other place she had called home. For so long, she had sunned under a tropical sky, bathed in the warm sea and eaten the fruit of the mango tree, that she had no idea what to do with the unexpected inheritance located at the end of a knobby-fingered peninsula, nor an inkling of how she would adapt. Poor Byron Thayer, Hannah's attorney, old by then as well, had been left the task of setting her on the right track, and had subsequently gone on to become an advisor and trusted friend. And back then, trust was the dominant word in her vocabulary. The disappointed dreams of a romantic poised on the verge of marriage, Prudence had never believed she'd be happy again, that she would find the likes of a Nick Pelletier, dark-eyed, handsome, and solid. Or the depth of feeling he evoked, promising to cherish her forever. The rub, of course, was that like many new couples, their fledgling relationship had been challenged and then nearly detonated by a meddling mother-in-law—and worse, her views on grandchildren. The old harpy had quickly ordered up three—as if she had an *In* with the Man himself. The woman wouldn't have cut it in Hannah's world, but, like it or not, Rita Pelletier was now a card-carrying member of Prudence's family. Marriage was more fragile than she had expected, and though she hadn't always had the courage to counter Rita's snobbery, Prudence was honor bound to find the proper cloak to place over her thin skin.

She was halfway to the studio when the heavy fog simply vanished—into thin air. A shiver went up her spine. A title of a book Vivien had recommended. Prudence had only read a back cover blurb; 'mountaineers moving step by step'. Haunting words, she thought, given where she stood. She changed her pace. Surf hammered the rocks and stinging nettles of salt pricked her face. Years of island living had taught her to respect the sea and yet here she was, taking chances to once again prove she was as strong as her Maine clan. Insane. A great *WHOOSH* blew up in front of her and turning to avoid the spray, she was for a heart-stopping moment on the edge. She stepped back as the water surged and churned up the shoreline, leaving soapy foam to clean the aftermath. If only the suds could clear away the detritus of her mind, the left-behind litter of all the things she might have done wrong during her pregnancies. And yet, Dr. Gordon, afflicted with a sage-like countenance and anointed with a newly minted license, had made it clear that she was healthy, that these things just happened, and she should not give up hope. He also didn't feel it was soon enough to inflict fertility drugs into her system. But, against her will, the echo of his sound reasoning dissipated with each crashing wave. It was high tide and the ocean spoke with an even louder voice than the one in her head. It was a certain music associated with Oyster Cove and its working harbor, magical notes for anyone willing to listen. Steeped in history, the waterfront was a cache of the curious and cantankerous, a place that prided itself on its resistance to change, and a location she had chosen never to leave.

Cocooned as she was by the sounds, she missed her foothold and her boot caught the edge of a striated boulder. They were ominous and darker when wet and the glaze of water had disguised the rift that sliced through this one. Thrusting her hand out for balance, she lost her footing again and groped for purchase in a mucky heap of seaweed. The locket shifted beneath the heavy jacket. Her fingers had scraped something sharp. Probably a shard of sea glass or shell, she thought, gingerly righting herself. It had not broken the skin, but her wrist hurt like hell, and the locket was safe. Leaning into the wind, it caught the floppy edge of her hat and sent it toward a watery grave. Mother Nature was having some fun with her. Like a soggy Frisbee, the hat wobbled mid-air before sinking beneath the surface. Vivien had always referred to it as Prudence's Linus blanket, albeit a grown-up version. It was gone in the blink of an eye and before she could mourn, her dampening hair molded to her head like one of Hannah's old brown hairnets.

Of all the practical items left behind by Hannah, Prudence had also inherited a plethora of knitted tea cozies and pot holders, crocheted antimacassars and frilly aprons. Many had been made by Hannah's friends, whose graves Prudence still visited. The gifts had become a symbol of a sisterhood of the strong women of Thatcher Lane, all widowed young, and all enduring hardships far greater than anything Prudence had suffered. Though two of those women had been childless, as if to give voice to some of Prudence's own fear, Hannah had one daughter who had never given her any peace or much joy.

Prudence had for a time worn an apron or coddled a teapot in one of the cozies as a way of absorbing their personalities, but now the various materials, once useful to their crafters, were cosseted in memory and neatly packed away in the attic. Homegrown therapy sessions had come out of their daily burdens, and a safe place to relinquish their words for posterity had been created.

The neighborhood had since changed. Between attrition and rising property taxes, the residents were becoming younger and seemingly more sports-minded, jogging and biking throughout Thatcher Lane and adjacent streets, and not particularly interested in the coffee klatches of Great-gran's generation. Thanks to her relative's foresight, Prudence and Nick would not have to be concerned about that tax expense for at least a few more years, but she knew that her passion for painting was at present an indulgence that might become another sticky wicket in their marriage. How could she explain what had morphed from emptiness and longing into a possessive need to create art?

As she neared the harbor, the fog swept in again, but this time more ethereal with the appearance of colorless veils embracing the wind. In between its layers, she spotted her beacon—the cabin's metal stovepipe. A tentative drop of rain touched her cheek, followed by a few more that meant business. Without caution, she jumped the nearest rock, leaving the ledge for pebbly flats and muddy weeds, running as fast as her clumsy boots would allow. As she reached the cabin, the bloated sky emptied its contents, bore down hard on the shingle shakes and drenched her at the threshold. Water spilled from her lank hair, down the slicker and onto the floor. Removing the jacket, stale air re-adjusted around her shaking form. Raw, wind-spewing damp had by now crawled deep into her bones where for the rest of the day it would take up residence like an old crone. Beyond that, the storm would render the village altogether colorless, its trees stripped bare by the wind's assertive and final indignity. Left in the storm's stead, a slick sheen of leaves, the former red, gold and green allure trampled upon, ridden over, and gutter-strewn. Soggy and unglorified, a few stragglers lay at her feet, a leafy postscript to the precarious hike.

Vermillion—having surpassed her need for the rich transparency of Alizarin Crimson—screamed at her from the far wall where she had tacked a large, experimental ink pour. The color red was steeped in meaning and by now matched Prudence's emotionally charged circumstances. As a result, she had become a collector of red paint. The latest batch—Cadmium light, Venetian Red, Cobalt Rose and Pozzuoli Earth—names both regal, foreign on the tongue, and viscous on the brush. No matter where that particular piece ended up or what medium she chose in the future, flecks of red would stain the floor, silent, silly provocations to help squelch her fears and spread her artistic wings. It was another reason to have a room of her own, she thought, channeling a recent tome on Virginia Wolff that had made it into her permanent collection. Having a bookstore had not only provided an income, but it fed that other well of curiosity, the one that had unknowingly burned within her from childhood. The only obvious difference between home and studio, was here the reading material was art-centric. What she sought creatively was easier than dealing with that uncomfortable place—the earlier discontent shrouded in empty words. Or comforting solicitations from friends about loss and trying again, even her husband's inability to understand or if he did, to voice it. Maybe that was normal too, and maybe she had lost the ability to care. The chaos of her thoughts led to the disarray in her surroundings, the pungent odors of oil and varnish, and even unsold work. Six small canvases painted last summer depicted the riotous gardens of a nearby cottage. They showcased the varietal blossoms that spilled down the frontage like a floral waterfall tumbling toward the sea. Of the six, four 8 x 10s were lined up like yesterday's leftovers, apparently unpalatable to the usual customers. Archie Carmichael, her mentor and coveted-award recipient, had encouraged her to push her boundaries, to shake up her preferred style in oils and use different mediums. And she had, and then like a child with a good report card, she had boasted some of Carmichael's comments to Nick. His reaction had been unexpected. Perhaps it was from feeling he'd been replaced by something intangible or just that he hadn't believed she had the talent, but it had come across as if he'd presumed she would never aspire to being more than a 'Sunday painter'. They'd had their share of arguments, mostly resolved, but there was still an underlying current running through them like static electricity. Of course, there were hobbyists in the community, and while not disrespecting them, she had finally cut a narrow swath into the more established stable of local talent and was determined to be taken seriously. It wasn't difficult to make the connection that she needed to give birth even if only to a good piece of art. Thank goodness Vivien understood her need to grow, she thought, checking her watch. Where books had always been Prudence's salvation, they had opened a door on this new passion, and Vivien had stood by that, even when it inconvenienced her. And when she thought of Vivien, she also suffered a twinge of guilt.

Vivien had been in love with Nick from the moment she saw him. But Nick had made a play for Prudence and Vivien had stepped away without ever giving voice to her disappointment. Instead, she had done everything to champion her friend's marriage. Prudence's appearance at the store today was necessary on every level, but it too was dependent upon the length of time it took for the winds to peter out and head offshore.

Droplets of water beaded up and then slipped without rhythm onto the floor where she'd hung the jacket—cattycorner from the finicky, boot-black stove. Prepared to wage wills with the small iron tyrant, she grabbed up short lengths of apple wood and bits of kindling from their bin, and a matchbook from the metal box on the sill. The edges of the tin were beginning to rust from salt exposure, and prying it open she broke a nail. Nick often made admiring comments about her hands, but now she couldn't remember the last time he had done that or even complimented any part of her appearance. Stifling the urge to hunt for an old emery board, she eased her baggy sleeve out of harm's way and with an orchestrated move, struck the match to paper. For once, she was rewarded without excessive smoke, by the glow that swallowed the dry wood. This time, a curly plume shot upwards and out the stack that poked through the mossy roof. The flames sputtered awake and grew loud as they changed colors. Maybe she had shoved too much wood in at once, she thought, hearing her father's caution. Had Ben Stone lived, he would have pinned a schematic not only for the stove, but for life, to the wall for her to follow, anything to keep her safe. The studio was in direct contrast with Ben's love of modern, clean lines, and he would have taken her to task for using a questionable shack, a relic really, even with its modicum of charm. A thought-provoking architect, he had often planned out his projects at the large walnut drafting table set up in his study while she quietly passed the time seated on the floor with a box of Crayons and his discarded paper. It was only as a result of art therapy class that she realized she had inherited his artistic bent, and while she had grown up following her adventuresome whims throughout the Caribbean, the seed of creativity must have been planted long before she had moved to Maine. To heed her true path was paying homage to the man who'd set it all in motion and opened her eyes to the world and its beauty. Beyond her marriage and her desire for motherhood, her need for self-expression was long past her control.

Everywhere she turned, the modest cabin revealed the wear and tear indicative of harsh Maine winters. Endurance—a synonym for life, she thought, as she blew the dust off the cubbies purposed for blank canvases, and flea-market finds used in still-life paintings. She grabbed a tube she had forgotten to cap and dabbed at the wall. The paint had filmed over, but with pressure, a trickle of red leaked under the crust, just enough to mark the perfect spot for an extra shelf. Books on Klimt, O'Keefe and Vermeer crowded the existing one. Robert Henri's book had been handled so much that its edges curled in resistance to her touch. Before turning over the cabin, Nick had updated the fixtures in the closet-sized bathroom, plugged old holes to preserve heat, and added caulking where needed. The cabin had previously been used by renters who'd sought a retreat in the quiet village in summers—writers in particular—before rustic had flown out of fashion. No question, it was stark. And, yes, in her present state of mind, Nick's magnanimous offering had managed to lose the giddy wrappings it had come with. His barbs aimed at Carmichael's teaching ability had poked her tender spot—vulnerability. Who knew where blame could be laid, she thought, or if it mattered, but perhaps the walk, and talk, with Hannah on the way over, had done some good, maybe make her less defensive with Nick. Grabbing a pencil, she scratched out a grocery list for later and along with a menu idea, decided that while she was here, she might as well make a few changes.

Stoking the wood for good measure, she moved the spindly stool from in front of her easel and placed it in front of the window in order to chalk-mark the floor, laying out the placement for furniture that would make the room homier. Prudence was always cold and by nature, a nest-maker, even here, so rearranging furniture would create warmth and help organize her thoughts to better put them in perspective. It was apparent that the pieces inherited from the previous tenancies had succumbed to time, especially the wicker chairs, which had been left outside in the rain too many times to count. With the storm warnings dominating the news, the decorative trappings normally left till Columbus Day had been put in storage last week. Around April and the final snow melt, buoys were tacked against the shakes blackened with age, creating multi-colored patterns to disguise the building's exterior shabbiness. Wooden lobster traps that would grow weedy near the side door by summer's end, became snapshot-worthy vignettes and the whacky souvenirs forgotten by previous occupants were left for display on the only windowsill on the street side. By early summer, the little shack breathed new life into the crooked row of similar buildings, becoming happy and carefree and luring tourists off the beaten track. As calculated, the playful bait also brought them through the door to see her latest endeavors. Across the room, the wobbly wicker settee with unraveling back legs was another matter altogether. It needed to be replaced, and soon, by some sort of daybed or anything to provide a sense of comfort. Or even as a backdrop for new work. At another suggestion from Carmichael—a master of figurative paintings— she considered hiring a male model from the life-drawing class he ran in the village. Not that he really had a vote, but Nick's was still out. His face had changed before her eyes as he wrestled with his idea of what that might entail. But that was a concern for another time, she thought, setting that thought aside. Picking up a number-six spatula, she scraped the crusted paint from the nondescript dining table, giving it the needed elbow grease because the surface had taken on the look of a Jackson Pollock. Like the settee, it wobbled, especially under the weight of heavy pottery or the jugs she preferred for her set-ups. The containers and subsequently the paintings were filled with enticing broad-leafed blooms or voluptuous fruit and found objects, in ways that would tell a story. The rocker with its original chipped (Chinese red) paint had been a different matter from the onset—an item to be lovingly preserved. She had rescued a holey, sneeze-provoking—but beautifully patterned—wool blanket and turned it into a cushion for the hard seat, often sitting before the fire to peruse supply catalogs.

Nick wouldn't have paid attention from an art perspective, but the cabin's best feature was the windows. On one side, north light, indirect and cool, allowed control over color contrasts and subtle changes as she painted. The other faced southward, taking in the expanse of the sea and the waterfront where plein air painters often planted their easels in hopes of nailing the perfect little painting. With the long spate of bad weather, even the die-hards among them had given up. From the onset of summer, they folded into the tapestry of Oyster Cove, eventually finding their way to Thatcher Lane. They set their easels along the ledges and rendered their focused subjects with brisk strokes, always angling for shadow and tone. With the season came the motor bikes, the cyclists and ubiquitous car-topped kayaks. It was a village rife with the chatter of explored sites and daily accomplishments. For the artists, it was their group critiquing and shared techniques and an appreciative audience to gird them on. Prudence had tried plein air, often, but found painting outdoors less to her liking than studio work. Here, with no one watching, Mozart, Bach and Vivaldi could accompany her at high volume and paint flew from her brush as though from a conductor's baton. In her self-contained world, she could paint for hours, become one with the subject on her own terms and reinforce the joy of creating. This is why she needed to be here today even though the light was all wrong and not even Mozart could override the ensuing noise. To the south, there was nothing but a churning ocean, miles of slate-colored water that stretched toward infinity. It really was going to be worse than she had anticipated, she thought, with an involuntary quiver. Not up to tropical island standards, but bad enough, especially here.

Squinting, she groped for the colors Carmichael—before relocating to Florida—had claimed existed even in a foggy landscape. She had paid attention when they stood side by side in early morning fog, her eyes peeled for the great reveal. But whatever was supposed to be there now had vanished within the foreboding sky as the brunt of the nor'easter clawed at the edges of her sightline. Unseen, but rising, the tenor of the growing gale, a violence breathing down on her that charged her to pay closer attention. Loud, demanding and seemingly weighted with the rage, the type that had rained down on her by her late mother. Prudence had long-ago locked up that part of her childhood and thrown away the key, and the provocative wind was forcing it all back like an overdue tide. The woman had been a monster, and every base and demeaning word she had ever hurled while Prudence was growing up promised to take the air out of the room. Victoria Stone had succumbed to her cocktail of pills years ago, and her marriage to Ben had been usurped by her previous marriage to the vodka bottle. Frozen in time, Prudence was faced with impossible feelings and thoughts that had clouded her judgment and lowered her self-esteem, emotions she had stuffed down until they'd nearly choked her. Had she been fooling herself all along? Could it be less about her biological clock and more about trying to prove she would be better at mothering than Victoria? Had Prudence been looking in the wrong places for gratification? Was that at the crux of her conflict with Nick, compounded by out-of-control hormones? If so, something had to change; this was eating her up inside.

The room filled with a pent-up wail. It rose from that deep well of self-pity, the wallowing place that had become her secret friend. Pacing along with her sobs, the wind ratcheted to a new level while all she could do was crouch on the floor with her back to the wall as she expected the worst. Rain pounded harder, and then blew sideways and beat at the latched door; she expected it to buckle at any moment. Just when she thought it couldn't be any worse, the force tapped into her emotional DNA—an auto-response caused by years of coping with tropical hurricanes—the scent of fear as the cabin quivered against the intrusion and rising water pounded the pilings beneath its rickety deck boards. And, then, like her crying, its power was spent, unsustainable over colder water, and she had hopscotched miles of memories, excising Victoria's hold bit by bit until it no longer mattered. She was safe; the building had held. In the new lull, her father's voice, the man who'd collected globes, the prophet of her childhood, was as clear as if he'd been in the room. In truth, at the pinnacle of the wind, she'd had her doubts, even pictured a search party looking for the woman who'd been washed offshore as the tiny building was pulled from its pilings. And as everything quieted, she had waited for Ben's words to embrace her because she instinctively knew what he'd say—that this little building she cherished had not only held, but flaunted sturdiness like a pensioner flirting with time. It was what he'd always said about Hannah. Something that had made him proud of his Maine heritage.

Prudence stood and wiped away her tears and added another log to staunch her chill. A day begun as a way to spur her forward had turned inward, invoking the past, a remarkable cleansing. Her biological family were gone and the death of Byron Thayer a year ago was the last chapter in the story of her surrogate family. He had been both friend and counselor and like her ancestors, a true stalwart of the coastline, the storied survivors. Emotionally exhausted, she closed her eyes and whispered her goodbyes, knowing that no matter what, they would all be listening.

In spite of being dumped on by rain and battered by wind, Nick had managed to tie up the sale of the two-hundred-year-old farmhouse located off River Road. Tree limbs had threatened the power lines, but he'd finalized as much as necessary before the worst of it had swept through. The property bordered Vivien's swath of prime land adjacent to her farm, which is how he had found it in the first place. He had wanted to include both parcels, but she had made it clear that she would never part with hers. Throughout the storm, he hadn't had time to worry about his own house or Prudence. She was smart in weather like this, had even been through a lot worse. So he did what was necessary and focused on the client, a man who gesticulated his ideas with a fat cigar and was short on both attention and stature. To Nick's good fortune, the guy was no fool when it came to a bargain. Once inside the building, he had been unable to find fault with anything significant, except for his realtor. Nick had been nitpicked over every strip of chipped paint, each creak in a floorboard, and even grilled on his expertise and the length of time he'd been in business. Now, seated in his Jeep, a cloud of cigar smoke clung to Nick like a bad omen—his next client had canceled. Stressed, he re-checked the documents nestled in a thick waterproof pouch. His stomach grumbled. Why not grab an early lunch, he thought, turning onto Middle Road. His paltry breakfast was long gone and though the wind had diminished, the rain hadn't, and the best fish chowder to be had was within a few miles of Stonycroft. He swung the car left, a shortcut to Route 1, and passed the small strip-mall with its defunct stores and a pizza parlor recently closed. The restaurant's Italian-style awning was lopsided, and the building needed paint. Already in realtor mode, and fully soaked, he jumped out of the Jeep for a quick look around. There was evidence of neglect on the outside, but peering through the window, he saw thoughtful details. A photo of the owners in the kitchen of their Tuscan home before they had come to America, was thumbtacked to the glass-enclosed menu next to the doorway. Mama, wrapped with a white apron, was proudly placing a bowl of pasta on the table. The lacy cloth could have been an heirloom, and sunflowers stood proud and alive in a pottery vase. Papa and three young men, presumably the sons, held their glasses in salute and grinned for the camera. "I'll be damned," Nick said to the smiling Castelanos in the photo. The reason for stopping flew from his mind; he had unintentionally dusted off an archived dream. One he wanted to immediately share with Prudence. Getting back in his car, he headed the other way, travelling fast on the slick roads. Fifteen minutes later, he pulled into a space in front of North Sky Books, the Jeep's tires throwing up standing water as the wipers strained to take the excess spray.

Like an agile athlete, he jumped a huge puddle and sprinted through the door, weaving in order to avoid the runoff from the drainpipe and then cursed because it hadn't as yet been fixed. Both Vivien and Prudence expected him to take care of it, but his handyman, Lloyd Tucker, had put that chore on the back burner saying there were more pressing repairs. It was a pain in the ass to pull him away from the harbor before the first snow fell. God forbid, Lloyd might miss a tidbit or two among the summer people and the grand boats they brought to Maine. Or the charter boat gossip when the tall ships made port. Nick could only hope that with this lousy weather, Lloyd's boredom would provide the necessary incentive and this little matter of the drainpipe would go away.

Vivien was behind her desk, showcased by the warmth of the painted wall. Her bright green sweater, shelves of colorful book jackets and that particular paint were the perfect antidote to the gloomy day. "Hey Vivien, where's my girl? Her car's not in its usual spot."

"She called earlier and said she had something important to take care of. Everything okay?"

"I wish I knew. These last weeks have been hard on her, but then you probably understand that stuff more than me."

"I know you guys think we're all hormonal, but I've never experienced what she's been dealing with."

The terra cotta backdrop for Vivien's desk, a color Pru had chosen, invoked warm fields, ancient ochre buildings and love. "I should take her to Italy," Nick blurted.

"Wow! Where'd that come from?"

"Believe it or not, it came from a pizza place. When I saw their 'For Sale' sign, I figured there might be a business opportunity in that building and all of a sudden, I was back in Italy. You didn't know I'd once basked in the vineyards." He didn't have the words to explain that he was worried about the direction his marriage was headed.

"Well, look at you, the world traveler."

"Okay, I had that coming. It was after college, but I do have great memories, and we never had a real honeymoon. And I think a change of scenery would be good for her. I'd like to surprise her so I thought I'd stop at the travel agency and pick up some brochures to help make my case."

"Don't worry," she said. "I can keep a secret."

Nick grabbed the phone book.

"Are they open during lunch?" he asked.

"Hang on, I know the number," said Vivien. "My friend Jodi works there."

While he waited for the women to catch up on small talk, Nick wandered to the window. Traffic was slowed by a turning 18-wheeler. A cop in a bright yellow coat and white-edged black hat appeared out of nowhere like a giant bumble bee, and with expert hand signals, maneuvered the behemoth around an electric pole.

Nick checked his watch; Vivien was taking her sweet time. He only needed a simple answer, he thought, turning to see that she held up her index finger…a minute more. The two women were obviously covering more territory than office hours. He smiled in spite of his impatience. Vivien had been their friend from the beginning, never meddling, but always a shoulder to cry on.

"She's there till four," Vivien said.

"At last. You're terrific, by the way." He gave her a peck on the cheek.

"You owe me, and *please* don't forget that drainpipe or come winter, we'll have an ice dam for sure."

Relishing their lighthearted friendship, he said, "Pushy broad, aren't you, Viv?" He stifled a laugh on his way out—she hated the nickname.

Across the street, Fred Stanton stood at the entrance to his pseudo-pub, his girth made even larger by a caricature in the overhead sign. The bar was supposed to have been modeled after one in London, but from what Nick had seen, the only things English were the bulldog kept as a mascot and dark beer on tap. Nick waved, but Fred was too busy arguing with a passerby, obviously drenched, who wanted out of the rain and maybe a beer to warm his blood. Fred didn't open until three and, as everyone had found out, Fred never opened even one minute early. Absurd, Nick thought, heading for his car. He let out a long whistle as he climbed in and waved the man toward the bookstore. The guy would not only find refuge inside, but the company of a red-haired beauty to take away the rainy-day blahs. He might buy a book or be fortified by a cup of hot coffee if Ms. Sanford took a liking to him. Nick recalled the early days in this neighborhood with ease. When he had purchased his building, most of the small storefront businesses were mom and pop types. Now, the former dance studio was an office supply store and a ladies' clothing store had become an arm of a large gift emporium in Portland. All that remained of the familiar was a corner café—closed today—serving only breakfast and take-out sandwiches, and a gas station-convenience store down the block. Fortunately, the bookstore business had remained consistent throughout and most of the credit had gone to Vivien for her innovative ideas.

Eleven o'clock and the diner—another of the last monuments to

23

another time—was half full. Nick added his damp jacket to the peg rack and grabbed an end stool. As usual, he shooed away the proffered menu and ordered the chowder.

"Be up in a minute," the waitress said. Her heavily made-up eyes fastened on his face until they slid to his wedding ring.

She was new, and too young to be an experienced flirt—nothing like Vivien—but Nick twisted the gold band for good measure. The warm inscription encircled his cold skin, the word 'Always' a testament to their vows. Maybe with this travel plan, he could bridge the growing chasm, be able to talk things through as before. He said he had always wanted kids too, but—and it was still a big but—would it be so terrible if it were just the two of them? Was that so selfish?

On the day Prudence and Vivien had chosen his building in which to set up shop—when they'd met to discuss the details—Vivien had done all the talking, tossing about that flame-colored mane, coming on strong, but it was Pru who had captured his full attention. The first real conversation they had shared had been the day she had been painting that particular wall a fiery shade of earth—the very day he'd known he would return to Italy, as he'd sworn to do with someone special. Pru had resisted every request for a date, and Vivien, recognizing the fait accompli, had championed their union to no avail. Then in a strange twist of fate, Hannah's dearest friend Aurora died, and Nick not only showed up at the funeral to support Pru, but brought a potted plant to the gravesite. He'd been viewed in a new light after that. It hurt him now to accept that while he hadn't been paying attention, that light had begun to dim.

"Here you go." The waitress placed a substantial white bowl in front of him. Blushing profusely, she slid the requisite oyster crackers—plus an extra pack—across the countertop and rushed away. His eyes followed her as she batted those same long lashes at a man closer to her age, seated at the other end of the counter. Given her body language, it appeared she had found a satisfactory place for her flirtation. It had been a while, but Nick still remembered what it felt like to be that age. With a shake of his damp hair, he took the contents from two of the packets and crushed them into the bowl. The third went into his shirt pocket for later on. As he spooned up the creamy mixture, he thought about a piece of pie to take back to the office. Then remembered the brochures and the food that awaited them in Italy, and changed his mind. Maybe he would get some flowers on the way home tonight to set the stage.

Chapter Three

The deluge had become a thin drizzle, and the wind turned lighthearted again, the way a fall breeze was supposed to behave. Prudence was too drained to continue what she had started and had pulled the rocker closer to the stove in an attempt to dry her jeans, still damp from jacket hem to boot tops. The heat had a soothing effect and she might have even closed her eyes for a while when a muffled thump signaled the end of her musing.

"What the…"

"You in there Prudence?"

"Oh God." Lloyd Tucker was the last person she wanted to see today; there was nothing left for him to put in storage. And she was not in the mood for his quirky nature. Nick found him useful, but he overlooked the fact that his handyman was a total busybody who had grown on her only in the uncomfortable way of a bramble bush that called for a wide path. One of the peninsula's true old-timers, vivid storyteller and outright gossip, it was purported that Lloyd could fix anything. It was well-known too that the man's habitual tales and his nickname 'Bones' had been passed down the line from each generation, slipping comfortably over the heads of all Tucker men as easily as their orange hunting caps.

"Hang on." She unlatched the door, and he charged in waving a white paper bag like a surrendering soldier.

"Brought doughnuts."

"That was nice of you." She forced a smile and dropped the bakery bag onto the chair. Maybe that would discourage him from 'sitting a spell'.

"Goddamn it's soggy out there." He slapped his wet hat against his leg and made a bee-line for the red color that pierced the dank room. "Was at the general store trying out today's special and saw the smoke. Figured it must be you, so I told them

I'd like two of their doughnuts to take to my friend, Prudence, and didn't that get their ears perked up." His nose practically touched the painting. "What's it supposed to be?"

"It's called an ink pour, and it can be whatever your imagination tells you." She was surprised by his interest. Then again, she suspected the gift, as well as his question, were bedded in his resolute desire to know all and tell all. The store, known for its take-away lunches, many-layered burgers, and homemade baked goods, was also the hub for waterfront gossip. She could just imagine what the store clerk was saying after that little encounter with Lloyd.

"Hmm," he said. "Guess I'll have to think on that." He turned his attention to the stove.

Willing him to refrain from one of his long-winded anecdotal yarns and still be polite, she moved toward the door, "thanks again for bringing those," she said. "Nick will appreciate your checking, but I won't be long now."

He stirred what little was left of the embers. "Looks like you don't need any help, so I'll just be runnin' along."

He was out in a flash, a wiry caricature of small town Maine, and as soon as she had latched the door, she realized something she had never thought of—he would make the perfect subject for a painting—if she could contain his nervous energy.

The bag was crinkled from the damp, but not soaked through. It was an unlikely gift from an unexpected visitor, but the heavenly aroma had her salivating. She could stall no longer. The wafting sweetness awakened long-forgotten taste buds. These were no ordinary doughnuts. Puffy and with a jewel-toned filling, they were culinary works of art. She plucked out one of the soft confections, freeing it from a square of wax-paper. Biting down tenderly, reverently, powdery white flecks spread over her teeth and lips and onto her sweater. Like a woman starved for joy, she lapped up the rich blueberry filling, licking the spill from her fingers where the jelly oozed from both ends, and then reached for another. God, they were good! Savoring the second, she felt a pinprick of guilt; she should have saved at least half of one for Nick.

Returning from lunch, Nick spotted Lloyd waiting, dozing in his battered Ford. It was parked as always—askew at the curb in front of Nick's office. Wrapping his knuckles against the window, Nick mimed for him to roll down the glass. "What are you up to?"

"Not so much as I'd like," Lloyd said. "Prudence is down at the harbor in case you're looking for her."

"That so?"

"Yeah, I was hoping to catch up with my brother-in-law over at the deli. Just thought I'd check the cabin for you while I was down there. You know, with the rain and all."

"That was mighty nice of you." Nick had accentuated his old Denver twang for good measure. He'd had an inkling she'd go there, but thought she might have waited out the storm. Pointing to the sky, he said, "Looks like we dodged a bullet after all, right?" He wasn't about to discuss his wife's whereabouts with his maintenance man. "Find some time please for that leaky drainpipe at the bookstore before Vivien has my head. And check on the Edgewater cottage too; I'm still worried about that roof."

Lloyd tapped the brim of his cap. "Sure thing."

With the truck turning away, a prominent bright red and white slogan stuck to the cab window came into view. There was no mistaking that it was a political jab. That would be Lloyd all right, he thought, shaking his head. Other stickers featured coon cats, moose heads, and references to drivers from down south, all of them on the bumper and each scraped or tattered from run-ins with immovable objects. Nick had never been able to bring himself to call his helper by his nickname, but he remained faithfully fascinated by Lloyd's audacious persona and his need to know everything happening in his harbor domain at all times.

As far as Nick was concerned, all that really mattered was that Lloyd did a good job maintaining Pelletier rental properties. With a roar, a billow of exhaust and the rattle from the beleaguered tailpipe, Lloyd left Nick engulfed in fumes. As he caught his breath, it dawned on him that Lloyd had been checking up on the widows again. Five middle-aged women from Boston—a consistent income for the past three summers—rented the big cottage on the road near Pru's studio. "So that's what you were up to, you horny old dog."

He was still laughing as he walked through the office door, and then he noticed the flashing light on the answering machine—an angry pulse in bright red. His client calling to say he'd changed his mind about the farmhouse? Nick wouldn't put it past him, not after the mental hammering he had given Nick. Before punching the button, he tackled the residue of his hasty departure—the scattered papers, opened files, and the few leaves that had blown in on the heels of his discontent. Righting the tipped wastebasket, he returned the folders to the cabinet, checked his watch and made coffee. He wanted a dry run for his presentation to Pru before leaving for home. Jodi had compiled everything she thought he'd want including a brochure showing a tantalizing farmhouse B & B where they would use as a base for at least the first two nights. As he spread the brochures out, the beauty of Italy came flooding back. It had been a memorable after-college trip taken with a fellow graduate, traipsing the countryside, sampling local foods and cheap, but terrific, wines in out-of-the-way taverns. And, flirtatious infatuations with women more beautiful than he'd ever seen, a small nugget he hadn't shared with Vivien. Anyway, at forty and married to Pru, he rarely looked back on that aspect of his youthful escapades. Maybe the young waitress had indeed triggered the unmistakable melancholy. "You're too old for this." He laughed at his reflection in the front window.

If he hurried, he could make it to the co-op market at the edge of town before they closed. Flowers would be good; Oyster

Cove had been leeched of color. Whatever he could find would do the trick as long as it brought a little brightness to the table. The list grew: a little cheese to go with one of his favorite reds, chocolate in case they were out of flowers and a baguette of French bread. Knowing his wife, it would serve him well to set the stage and broach the situation in a way that would allow her to take her time weighing both sides of any issue. She had at times called him obtuse, and she wore the badge of a Libra. Those damn scales had often tried his patience, but he was learning. He couldn't imagine why she had been compelled to be at the studio on such a day, but he would hold his tongue. Anyway, if it helped alleviate whatever struggle she was dealing with on this particular day, he would be satisfied. He missed her, an odd thought since they were together each morning and evening. Strange as it sounded, she had been absent in some obscure way, and he wanted her back. Scooping up the colorful pamphlets, he strode for the door with far more hope than he'd entered with that morning.

Outside, Prudence yanked the cabin door until she heard the hard click; in the womb of a timeless structure, the nightmares of her youth had been purged and her beloved ghosts put to rest for the day. How she would deal with this new self-discovery was another matter. She had always been reticent about sharing the traumas of her youth, so she wouldn't be leaning on Vivien quite yet. Maybe after a new partner was found, she thought, but not today. Too many balls in the air to deal with and she needed to shake out the day with a walk. Not the ledge this time, but the long way home, a chance to untangle her brain even though it meant walking through what had to be a mud hole by now. And it was. The ground was fully saturated so her footfalls made a strange sucking sound as she made her way to the intersection that would take her onto wider paved streets. It was a comical performance—one foot at a time, being careful not to lose a boot in the thick substance that acted a little like quicksand underfoot. But the air had cleared, and if not for the pooled water on this tucked away path to remind her, evidence of the storm had vanished. When she arrived in Maine on that first summer day, this route was bone dry and used as a way to acquaint herself with the town and its many hidden homes. Eddy Lane—the pretty street known for its flame bushes, was just up ahead, but the plantings were massive in comparison to that first time. These same bushes now hid many of the welcoming porches, and like Thatcher Lane, unfamiliar names had sprouted up on mailboxes or over doorways. Except for one, recognizable by the painted rocks at the end of their driveway. Back then, this family had owned a pharmacy with an old-fashioned soda fountain in the back. One could fill a prescription and satisfy a sweet tooth at the same time. All of Oyster Cove had been a surprise back then. Especially the two-lane bowling alley. Sadly, the pins have long since been silenced and that space divided into two separate shops: one selling tee-shirts with assorted logos, the other a gift shop featuring all things shells—lamp bases, jewelry, night lights and even napkin rings. A lot of changes and not all of them newsworthy.

As she turned the corner, it was obvious the nor'easter had left its mark on the exposed street sign at the intersection of Eddy and Thatcher Lane. The signpost now leaned in, much the same way as Hannah's ancient hydrangea bushes bent toward the road in front of her house, obvious even from a distance. The worst of the bunch drooped, beaten and bedraggled in the aftermath, similar to how she had felt when she left the studio. There was evidence of new mold on the house —a freeform darkening stain was creeping up the white trim surrounding the door and windows, something that she hadn't noticed before. Just one more item to add to Nick's 'honey-do' list. He was not going to be pleased, she thought, walking directly to the car path— Hannah had never wanted a paved driveway and Prudence had respected Great-gran's wishes. The keys were in the glove box as always; theft had never been an issue in this neighborhood, and she was hopelessly forgetful about keys of any sort, something that drove Vivien crazy. Thank goodness she had been forgiving of Prudence's many absences these last months. While she owed her partner much, and the walk had done a great deal of good, she still needed to hurry if she wanted to beat Nick home later. Pressing the accelerator, she steered the rusting VW Beetle through roadside runoffs, creating a v-shaped spray of displaced water that hid the tiny auto within. Laughter emerged from that darker space as she sensed a resurgence of energy and the affirmation of her abiding love for her Maine family.

Prudence followed the sound. Vivien was in the back room, humming along with the radio, and keeping time with her hips as she waited for the coffee maker to stop. The woman exuded femininity, Prudence thought, taking in the green so suited to Vivien's coloring. Today, she looked like spring itself.

"Well, look who the cat dragged in," Vivien said. "Are you ever going to find a jacket that fits?"

"I love Tim's jacket—it's so perfectly retro," Prudence said. Compared to Vivien's appearance and feeling even more bedraggled than Hannah's hydrangeas, she placed the slicker around the back of the extra chair and plopped with a thud onto the cushioned seat.

"Maybe so, but I hope you realize you look like a skinny waif in it."

"I don't even care. Today was a good day, even if I thought I was about to become a statistic when that gale blew over. But it felt so right being back in my studio."

"It was nasty up here too—we lost power for a half hour, but from your appearance, not half as bad as Oyster Cove. What were you thinking?"

"I'm pretty sure I wasn't. More like acting on impulse but without rehashing all the motives, suffice it to say the time was well spent. We might be eating by candlelight, which might actually be good, but I was in such a rush to get here, I didn't check the house.

"I really needed to tell you in person that I know my absences haven't been easy on you, but you have been wonderful through it all. And, I promise that I'll do my best to spend more time here until we can find someone to buy me out." Prudence said.

"I only just got off the phone with a woman I think has potential. I didn't want to get your hopes up before, but she just *might* be the person we're looking for."

"Tell me everything…who, what, when?" Prudence leaped to her feet.

"Sit, have some coffee." Vivien handed Prudence a mug and a couple of tinned biscuits. "You could use these too," she said. "Let's see…her name's Ursula, she's stylish, fifty-ish, I guess, and she'd come by looking for a specific dictionary, *Everyday Spanish and English,* to be exact. We don't carry it, but I asked if she was learning and she said, no, she taught Spanish and was going to help a friend. Well, you know how much I've always wanted to learn the language. We've been talking every few days or so since, and somehow I got the idea that we could hold classes right here after closing time—with your okay—and she loved it. Anyway, she's dying to make new friends and with the winter looming, wouldn't it be great to have something like that to look forward to?" Her green eyes flashed their excitement.

"Now I know why it's going to be so hard letting go of this place. This idea is so *you.* You will absolutely be in your element, probably even baking your decadent chocolate things to help lure in the students."

"Triple chocolate truffles! Like you couldn't afford some of those calories right now. The best part of this whole idea is that she's looking to invest in a project she can sink her teeth into— her words—and your time frame for phasing out could allow that to happen. What do you think?"

"I'm speechless." While Vivien turned to refresh her coffee, Prudence curled the biscuits into the napkin and tucked them into her jacket pocket to be savored later over tea.

"I'm excited. And you're going to want to look at these figures, see how they work for you. If they do, I'll set up a meeting with Ursula." Vivien set her cup down and pulled the account book closer to Prudence.

"Can I take this home with me? Nick and I had a small row this morning, and I need to make it up to him tonight."

"Feel like talking?"

"What can I say? I've been a bit of a bitch, but it's not just that. Frankly, I'm worried. I've spent the day sorting myself out at the studio. Let's call it mental acrobatics and that Nick's worth the effort," Prudence said. "Hopefully, I'll get home in time to do something nice to make it up to him."

"I told you a long time ago he was a keeper."

Prudence knew she'd been bested the moment Vivien became their matchmaker, and she had always known that Vivien—without ever voicing it—had wanted to be the one Nick would fall for. "I hate it when you're right."

"I like gloating…there aren't many men in this little burg worth getting all worked up about."

"Are you sure it's that you don't want to be bothered with a *real* relationship?"

"Don't get me started on that. Love 'em, leave 'em, that's my motto."

"I thought you always said bed 'em and leave 'em?"

"I did, didn't I?" Vivien said. "You have a memory like a steel trap, but I love you anyway. Now go, and give that sexy husband of yours a hug for me." Vivien had, in fact, educated Prudence about her beliefs early on. Considered independent and sassy, she enjoyed relationships until she tired of them. Not quite a Phoenix risen from the ashes, but a wiser woman free from the shackles of a cheap and controlling husband.

At home, Nick found Prudence sitting in her favorite nook. She had a mug cradled in one hand, a half-eaten cookie poised for dunking in the other, and a scrunched teabag bleeding a brown stain onto a paper napkin. "Did we lose power?"

"The entire neighborhood. They're saying an hour before we're back up and running. At least we have gas and an abundance of candles." Unlike the way he had left it, the kitchen was orderly and lemon-fresh. Then, from the light of a hurricane globe on the counter, he spotted onion slices soaking in milk, "Are you making onion rings?"

"*And* a big juicy steak with a small salad on the side." She watched his smile broaden. "I've been running on sugar all day, and this is the least I can do after the way I behaved this morning. Forgive me?"

He reached over and pulled her off the cushion. "How's this?" He kissed her like a man starved for attention, yet gentle enough to draw her in so she would respond the way she used to.

"I'd say that was kinda hot." She felt her color rise. "Are you hungry? This won't take long to put together."

He was more than a little hungry, but not the way she meant. After this morning, he knew better than to rush into sex. Besides he wanted to build to his surprise. All that stuff written about how men are from Mars and women from Venus had already infiltrated their household. It was all about the timing. "How about I open this wine?" Nick said pulling the bottle, the fresh bread and small block of cheese from the bag.

"What's all this?" Prudence sat back down, amazed. He'd had matching ideas about their evening. "Hang on." She leaned over and grabbed hold of the plate holding a large pillar candle. "Just let me light this so I can see what's happening."

Nick had blocked the brochures with his body and as he placed a glass of wine in front of Pru, he spread them out like a deck of cards on the table.

"What on earth?"

"I know you'll want to think this over with everything that's on your plate, but I thought we might take that belated honeymoon to Italy. I sold the farmhouse today."

"That's fabulous! You've been showing that property for almost a year now. But when did you come up with this idea for this trip, and when would we go?"

"Let's say I had an epiphany today, and I think we deserve it. As to when, I'd like sooner than later and obviously before the weather gets too cold. What about the first part of October?"

Prudence was too flummoxed to speak. On cue, the electricity came back and light flooded the room. Landscapes rich with groves and red-roofed buildings on hazy hills lay in front of her like a menu with too many choices. He'd brought eight different brochures, each as beautiful as the first. She went back and forth like a child selecting a new toy. "I don't know what to say."

"Don't say anything just yet," Nick said, topping her glass. "We have good people to run things while we're gone." He brought the bread and cheese to the table and slid in next to her. Picking up his favorite pamphlet, the one that had first caught his attention at the travel agency, he said, "Chianti, in Tuscany, sounds romantic right?"

"I'm overwhelmed...I never dreamed..."

"We could both use this, and the doctor said you're physically okay. I just want us to feel right again. Is it too much? Am I going too fast? God knows, I'm not equipped with sensitivity, but I am trying."

Chapter Four

Nick slept peacefully beside her, his left arm flung over his head, contentment obvious in his slackened facial muscles. Perhaps dreaming of Italy, she thought, watching the involuntary twitch of his eyelids. Sleep had eluded her. There it was again— expectations. They foiled her every time. Nick had stirred her with all that talk of Italy and romance and then fallen asleep as soon as he was satisfied. He worked hard, and yes it had been a particularly stressful day, but geez! What about her needs? Maybe she had become less attractive or too shrill. Or he just didn't understand anything.

Daylight beckoned her to the window. Slipping from the bed, she reached for her robe and the thin-soled slides she preferred around the house, having long ago given up the barefoot joy of warm sands. It was chilly nearest the window, but yesterday's grainy texture had been replaced by breaking sun that offered up a new day, replete with the comings and goings of the local fishermen. As though snuffing out a candle, the wind had blown away the gloom and everything had returned to normal. Like a bullseye, the obvious red hull of the *Alice Mae* had been targeted by the early morning sheen. The rays had zeroed in on her bold lettering as well as the bulk of her owner, Jake Nolen, at work on his traps. Rugged and handsome, he'd made a splash in the local paper just last month, arguing over mooring fees and fishing rights. She and Nick had often sailed past the sheltered coves where many of the local boats were moored. And having become adept at identifying hulls and markings, there was no difficulty this morning in spotting the white-hulled *Mariah* with its telltale numbers idling in a field of green and white buoys out beyond the rocks. It was a scene that on any other day might have filled her up, make her take to her paints, but now she was just plain cross. And maybe just a tad selfish, she thought, as she heard Nick stir.

"What's it like out there today?" Nick said.

"Come see for yourself."

Rubbing his eyes, he came up behind her, "Want to come back to bed?"

"I thought you wanted to see what the day looked like." She turned to face him and his obvious erection.

"I'd rather see what you look like," he said, slipping the robe from her shoulders.

She didn't want to plead a headache, that had never been her style, but her head was filled with all the things left unsaid the night before, so instead she tried to avert his attention. For some reason, she couldn't find her footing since she hadn't exactly been his poster girl for the last few months. "I'm afraid," she said, using the one thing she thought wouldn't foster an argument.

"Of me?"

"Don't be silly; it's the long flight."

"Just because you had a traumatic experience…and may I remind you that was six years ago, before I even met you. We can't just put our lives on hold because of some jerk who didn't know how to fly a small plane."

"Easy for you to say." Nick traveled to Denver at least twice a year.

"I don't force you to visit my mother, but I'll be damned if I'm going to let irrationality stop us from having the trip of a lifetime!"

"What's so irrational?"

"I give up," Nick said, slamming the bathroom door. Prudence had carried that old story in her head from when she lived on St. Thomas and she knew it about drove him crazy.

Okay, so she'd spoiled his mood, so what? After all that romantic talk, he hadn't even noticed how she'd changed in these past months, the disharmony with her body and the ensuing insecurities, the needs she had but could not articulate. None of this was easy and as she realized what she had done with just a few words, the impending trip mattered a great deal.

Even between pregnancies, she drank little and hadn't taken anything medicinal, but he didn't have time to be more sensitive. "How about I just get you drunk before take-off?" Nick retorted, re-entering the bedroom. Of all the things he thought he'd have to counter, this hadn't been one of them. "Look, I'm sorry, Pru, but let's not spoil this; hash it out with Kate later on. After all, they fly all the time and maybe she has some pills that would work. I've gotta run...call you later." He pecked her forehead.

Thank goodness Kate was back, Prudence thought, rummaging through her dresser drawer before heading to the shower. Within weeks of moving to Thatcher Lane, she and Kate Newcomb had become fast friends, and a lot of that had to do with their mutual outlook on life. It didn't hurt that Kate had a wicked sense of humor as well as the ability to dole out her hard and fast rules for the way things should be. They had, in defense of their youth, promised never to become like the embittered crone who had lived down the street. Those of Hannah's world were all gone now, Prudence thought, the storytellers, the legend-makers and the hearts-of-gold, like dear Aurora.

Kate, who religiously accompanied her husband Michael on every business trip, had just returned from their second stint in India where, according to Kate, she'd had more than her fill of curry. Prudence tossed her night clothes and grabbed a pair of jeans. She was expected at Kate's at eleven, but right now the smell of fresh coffee beckoned—Nick had taken time to put on the pot.

Reflected off the water, opalescent light stippled the kitchen cabinets. Their semi-gloss finish had held up nicely against the sea air. The *Mariah* was no longer in sight, but a ferry to Monhegan Island pottered along in the distance. Out on the water, it was just another day at the office.

Her husband had also left her favorite mug beside the coffeemaker, a far cry from the previous morning...and yet. Maybe Dr. Gordon was right, she just needed time to let all those emotions sort themselves out. Taking honey from the cupboard and cheese from the fridge, she pushed a piece of the leftover baguette into the toaster, and opened her account book. Within minutes she lost her focus to the brochure lying open at the end of the table. No matter the dreaded flight, this trip really was an opportunity of a lifetime: the food, the architecture and the art, all waiting to be discovered. Down deep, she also wanted to discover the couple they had been, the lovers before loss, anger and frustration. Even, silly as it seemed, the same two people Vivien had stepped aside for in order that they could all remain friends.

A visit with Kate was just the ticket. Not only was she lacking in patience for anything that smacked of whining, or as she called it, whinging, but she would see right through and name whatever demon Prudence was fighting at the moment. Kate often reminded with her 'stiff upper lip' candor when making a point, that her English family had survived the wartime blitz. Not that any of that had a fig to do with the way Prudence felt about flying, but it was the way in which Kate approached life. Therefore, she would put the proper spin on Prudence's fears and expect that all would be well. Prudence, on the other hand, would then be too embarrassed to complain at all. Everything else was to be determined.

"Here we go." Kate draped a lightweight wool shawl around Prudence's shoulders. "This will coordinate perfectly with most anything you plan on wearing and it's just the right weight for this time of year. Speaking of which, poor Michael is really struggling with being back in the cold. For him, it's already winter and he's hauled out a heap of sweaters. Actually, he reminds me of you."

Prudence struck a model's pose, ignoring what could have been taken as a barb if she hadn't known better. The shawl's weave was luxurious to the touch. "I'm sorry he's miserable, but I'm glad you're back."

"I do love him, but it does get a little tiring, the way he goes on and on about Maine weather. He even referred to India as saffron colored, as if he'd ever seen the spice before. I just want to throw a book at him sometimes, but I wouldn't dare maim a book!"

"You are so bad, but at least the sun's out again," Prudence said.

"I don't really get upset. He just likes to complain, poor sod," Kate said. "So what has you so worked up? You didn't elaborate on the phone."

"It's the flight." She was reluctant to spill all. "It's the same with big storms and my angst over those horrific hurricanes, all the bad memories come rushing back. Believe me, I can't help it."

"I sort of get it, but you might be dwelling a little too much. Do you think this could have more to do with your body going through so many changes?"

"Maybe, I don't know. It's hard to explain. Don't forget, you always insisted that you never had a ticking clock."

"Let's just say mine's broken," Kate said. "I can still sympathize, but I hate seeing you beating yourself up. As for flying, it wasn't easy for us either after 9/11. And I know how anti-medication you are, but I have something you can take, if you like. I got them the last time I went to England—you know how progressive they are at the National Health. Just keep them in your purse in case it gets bad, okay?"

"Wow, that's really thoughtful."

"I won't be needing them anytime soon and sometimes just knowing you have them can ease the tension," Kate said. "Now tell me about this place you'll be staying at."

"Some kind of B & B the travel agent suggested. It's owned by a family named Bernoli and Mrs. Bernoli holds pasta-making classes for her guests…maybe a hint from my husband about my cooking?"

"You really are being sensitive, aren't you? I'm sure it's just part of the package and besides, you can teach me when you get back. And then we'd have to figure out a way to add lobster as a feature for the holidays. Just think of the fun we'd have."

"Whoa, you're getting way ahead of me…I haven't even had one lesson yet."

"Something else is bothering you, I can tell. Spill it."

This could get tricky, Prudence thought. It seemed so disloyal to Nick, and she rarely crossed that line between marital intimacy and fun repartee shared with girlfriends. Kate was similar, which is why they clicked. But it was now or never; she needed help. "Nick and I are out of sync, have been for months. At first I blamed it on the miscarriage, but lately…I don't know, our relationship is so *static.*"

"Are you talking about in the bedroom?" Kate said.

She'd underestimated her transparency. "Maybe it's me," Prudence said. "I haven't exactly been scintillating lately, but our sex life is lusterless for lack of a better word."

"Believe me, that's not unusual, at least not among couples I've known for years. Michael and I go through whole patches of time when sex seems to be the last thing on our minds. People get busy, or distracted and even a little bored. Maybe you're overthinking…you do that sometimes, maybe a lot. And I say that with love. Trust me, this trip will infuse you—"

"Infuse?"

"Let me finish. To paraphrase an American idiom, Italy will get your juices flowing again. Trust me."

"If you say so," Prudence said. She didn't push; Kate seemed so certain—as always—in her opinion. "Want to grab a bite to eat before I get back to work?"

"I was hoping you'd stay for lunch. I have a quiche fresh from the oven."

"Of course you do," Prudence cooed. It had been an ongoing joke that Kate was a typical type A. "You've always got your shit together."

"Not so." Kate maneuvered Prudence into the dining room where all her handiwork was difficult to miss.

"Right," Prudence said. The table, like Kate, was impeccably dressed. Even for a simple lunch, she'd brought out her granny's flatware and dishes she'd found abroad. A centerpiece of lucky bamboo with roots winding around smooth stones, filled a large glass vase. Soft music floated in from the kitchen and the aroma of baked cheese emanated from the sideboard, a piece from her late granny's estate in Surrey.

"I owe you anyway," Prudence said.

"Just have a great time over there, eat wonderful food, have tons of sex—and what do they say—get your mojo back."

"Another idiom, but with your accent, everything sounds possible."

"Ha, tell that to Michael." Kate pulled out a pie server and put a large portion on Prudence's plate. "He's picked up a bit of the delightful Indian dialect and insists we should leave our shoes at the door. I don't know what he'll request next, maybe buy a 'tuk tuk' to go about Oyster Cove."

A tiny bit of cheese caught at the edge of Prudence's lip as she nearly choked on the thought. "Wouldn't that be just grand? Michael chauffeuring you around the harbor."

"Ha, that's all we'd need. We would be the laughing stocks of Oyster Cove. Now, to change the silly subject, when do you leave?"

"October 10th. Nick's really fired up and says the weather should be perfect. And after what I saw in the brochures, I'm practically salivating for the artwork I have only seen in my books."

"Just think of all the fabulous paintings you'll do when you get back."

"From your mouth to God's ears my friend. But there's a ton of things to see and do once we're there. And I can't wait to see the art of the old masters besides all those I haven't even heard of before. I'm not sure when Nick picked out this location that he knew what he would be in for, and I hope it won't get too boring because I intend to drag him through all the museums and cathedrals. They even have a church and surrounding square with his name on it called San Nicolo, and it's not far from where we're staying."

"Well, at least he took the initiative; more than some men would do."

"I know and I'm grateful really," Prudence said.

"It's all been hard on you and no one is blaming you or Nick for anything. Now eat your lunch before the crust gets soggy."

"Your quiche is fantastic!"

"There's plenty more," Kate said.

"Maybe just a tiny slice, and then I have to run, the accounts call."

The quiche was light and creamy and filled with bits of bacon. "This'll add a pound or two so maybe everyone will stop telling me I'm too thin."

"You are thin and this bit of cream won't even show up. Italy will be good for you."

"You're the best friend ever and I'll take good care of that fabulous shawl, I promise." Prudence said. "And thank you for listening to my whining."

"What are friends for?" Kate began going over the tablecloth with a tiny handheld vacuum. "And speaking of friends, what's happening with our Julie? Last I heard from you, she was living in Amsterdam."

Prudence brought the dishes and cutlery to the kitchen, careful not to stack the delicate china. "Julie had a baby girl and she and Cooper are over the moon. They adore living near the canal and frankly, I don't see them coming back any time soon. We try to stay in touch, but babies have been a sensitive topic."

"They still have their cottage here, don't they?"

"Yes, but Nick rents it out for now." Prudence gathered up the Harrods' shopping bag containing Kate's shawl and a slice of wrapped quiche to take home for Nick. "It always meant a lot to me that you and Julie and I thought we would grow old together on Thatcher Lane, and even if I don't get that wish, I have to believe they'll want to spend at least the summers here, for little Addie's sake."

"Addie?"

"She's named after Julie's mom, Adele."

"You Americans and your nicknames."

"Don't go getting all posh on me...Kathryn Jane Newcomb!"

Kate put her hands up, "Truce."

"Gotta run, be nice to Michael. I'll call you. Ciao."

"Listen to you," Kate said. Kissing her on both cheeks, "See, European style."

"Talk soon." Lunch had been fun, a word that she had removed from her vocabulary lately. The mid-day glass of wine hadn't hurt either. Maybe she should relax like that more often.

Poring over the accounts, Prudence found they were in much better shape than she'd realized. Business had been good all summer, which shouldn't have surprised her. Vivien was a smart manager and all the latest non-fictions were well placed in the window alongside beach reads by favorite novelists. If Vivien was right, and Ursula wanted in, based on these figures, Prudence would get a do-able monthly payment from the buy-out.

"You look content," Nick said. Prudence was propped against a throw pillow in the windowed nook, reading.

If Kate was right, there was no point in bringing up a sexual discourse at all. There would be plenty of time for that when they got to Europe. "It's the only book we had on Italy." Turning the pages toward him, "I'll try not to be a pain in the ass about flying. Did me a world of good to see Kate, and don't get that smug look on your face."

"Sorry."

"Want to go out for dinner?"

"Sure. Whereto?" Nick said.

"I'm in the mood for simple, so how about the Lone Dory? We haven't been there since it changed hands and we can walk." New owners had come to town and while touting a different menu and a sprucing up, the restaurant had lost its ambiance and much of the local crowd. "I've heard the food's still good, but I doubt we'll see any of our old friends. They're all supporting the Lyman boy's bar because he has a band and doesn't mind it if the folks get a little rowdy."

"That's okay, I just want some fried haddock, and I wouldn't mind a little quiet tonight. Just let me freshen up." He tilted her chin up and kissed her. "Thank you."

"For what?"

"For everything."

"Hurry up before my mascara runs," she said. Tears threated to spill over; he was being so nice. Maybe Italy would infuse their marriage after all.

"You were right, this place is dead," Nick said.

"Let's order to go then."

"No, it's early, and I know you wanted to be out of the house for a while."

"Fine. Order me a white wine please," Prudence said, heading for the ladies' room, "And I'll have whatever you're having for dinner."

Pru was certainly being agreeable, he thought, as he accepted the menu from a young woman he didn't recognize until she said his name. "Is that you, Marabelle?"

"Sure is Mr. Pelletier. I've been working here since it changed hands, but I'm off to college in a few days."

"Whereto?"

"Bowdoin."

"Fantastic…I bet your parents are happy that you'll still be in-State."

"Yeah, they are. I'll tell them I saw you."

"Give them my regards, please."

"Sure will. Now what can I get you to drink?"

Prudence walked out of the ladies' room and saw that the menus had arrived and Nick had a pensive expression on his face. He was studying the young waitress who was heading into the kitchen.

"Do you know her?"

"She's the daughter of one of my clients, all grown up and on her way to college. Makes me feel old."

"How do I make you feel?" Prudence said reaching across the table for his hand.

"Are you flirting with me Mrs. Pelletier?"

"I do believe I am."

With just those little words, Prudence felt the balance tip again. She had to fully participate in this relationship if she wanted it to survive. Why had it become so difficult to be the way she was before the miscarriages?

"It's going to be a great vacation, sweetheart."

"I think so too." Prudence said as their waitress approached with the tray. "And now we're going to eat fresh fried fish and lots of potatoes and you'll be sorry you teased me about my thinness."

Their light banter continued throughout the meal, followed by strong coffee and a shared piece of pie.

"I'm glad we're walking home," Prudence said, checking for stars. "Do you remember how gallant you were on our first date?"

"Do you know how badly I wanted to kiss you that night?"

"Kiss me now."

They paused on the quiet road, and Nick wrapped Pru in an embrace that was both gentle and reminiscent. "It's what started it all," he said.

She tilted her head up and smiled, "Let's go home and talk about where those six years have gone."

The day before departure, the Thatcher Lane house bustled with last-minute activity. Sticky notes decorated the plant stands and a list of contact numbers adorned the refrigerator. The kitchen resembled a greenhouse as potted ferns were elbowed into corners between a *ficus* and a hibiscus tree. Prudence's orchids and African violets had pride of place to receive the most advantageous morning light, and a long-necked plastic watering can had been marked according to each variety's requirements. She had never lost the acquired taste for orchids and leafy ferns adopted during her stay in the tropics, but of all Kate's accomplishments, horticulture had not been one of them. She was, however, reliable and could follow instructions.

"It's like a jungle in here," Nick said.

"It's rather pretty, don't you think? I just might leave it like this and make you hack your way to the table."

"Aren't you feisty this morning?"

"Nervous energy."

"It's going to be fine, you'll see."

"So everyone says."

"I still don't know what I'm packing," Nick said.

50

"Don't go getting that hangdog expression. Don't I always come to your rescue when you visit dear Rita?"

"Do I detect a bit of animosity toward my sweet mother?"

"Yup," Prudence said, heading for the stairs. Never come between a man and his mother. Someone had told her that or she'd read it somewhere, but Prudence understood. If she had been hoping for a figure to fill the latent need for a mother, it hadn't taken long to realize Rita Pelletier was not going to be that woman. It was understood by now that her mother-in-law fostered great disappointment that Nick hadn't married his former girlfriend, Diana. Tough shit, she thought, yanking out the suitcases. Rita never swore. Prudence's father-in-law had been of a different ilk and they had gotten along famously. Charles Pelletier had loved it when she'd regale him with tales of the Caribbean, peppered with the requisite salty language. With him gone, she had learned to bite her tongue whenever Rita visited. Too bad, Prudence thought, neatly folding Nick's shirts. At least he never pushed her to accompany him to Denver when Rita summoned, always pleading some nonsense she couldn't handle on her own. A win, win for all concerned.

"Need any help up there?" Nick said.

"Ha, that's a laugh! You're spoiled and I'm to blame." There were organizational things that Prudence excelled at and packing was one of them. Her suitcase had been ready for a few days with the exception of toiletries. Nick would have literally thrown his clothes in at the last minute and sat on the case to close it and then hollered about items needed afterward. Since clothing worn in tropical climes was lightweight and spare, she had never encountered so much drama, especially from a man.

"Okay then, I'll head over to the office. There are a couple of things I need to do before we leave."

"Me too. I'm seeing Vivien this afternoon, and Kate's dropping by for a drink and last minute instructions around five. Unfortunately, Michael won't be back from Portland in time, but you can handle the jabbering of two women."

51

"I love jabbering," Nick said.

"That's what I thought," Prudence yelled from the closet. He'd be late getting home just to avoid it. The phone rang.

"Can you get that, Pru, I'm on my way out the door?"

Like she wasn't in the middle of something. "All right," she yelled, lunging for the phone. "Hey Kate, what's up?"

"After you left, I found a sweater set that you'd look smashing in. Want me to bring it over later?"

"Wonderful, see you then."

Instead of rearranging her case, maybe she'd wear the sweaters to travel in, she thought, provided they fit and she liked the color. It was hard to believe anything Kate had wouldn't be perfect. Prudence finished Nick's packing and left the suitcase propped open against the wall and changed into a fleece top and her 'better' jeans. Unlike her dear English friend, Prudence loved wearing jeans.

Passing the hall mirror on her way downstairs, she caught the image of a young woman with little makeup and without a lot of flare. Her hair was lifeless and suffered from indifference. She couldn't go to Italy looking like this! But who could she see on such short notice? Ginger, Vivien's hair stylist! She took walk-ins. Prudence raced down the stairs.

The woman who glided into North Sky Books later that day barely resembled the woman in the mirror earlier that morning. "Just look at you!" Vivien said. "Blonde highlights even."

"Ginger, who else? She convinced me and I love it. Reminds me of how my hair always brightened under the constant tropical sun."

"Waxing poetic, are we? Thank goodness for her then, because you look terrific!"

Prudence twirled, feeling for all the world like a new woman. "Amazing what a cut and color can do for one's attitude."

"Ain't that the truth," Vivien said, tossing her shiny mane. "I don't know what I'd do if she closed up shop."

"I know I've cut into our time by doing this, but we don't have all that much to cover, do we?"

"Not really. I just want to make sure you're happy with the order I'm ready to send."

"Pretty soon, you'll be making all the decisions, so maybe I should let it begin now."

"If you say so, but humor me this time, okay?

"Okay, shoot."

"There are some new authors among the usual roster, mostly in women's fiction, that I like. Also a couple of non-fiction best-sellers. I can't tell you how many times Danny Seralgo complains about all the 'chick-lit' we carry."

Danny owned a small antique store just around the corner. He had been divorced twice and spent most of his time among his dusty collection of vintage vinyls, accompanied by his Maine coon cats, Sasha and Munjoy. "I don't know how you do it, he's such a dour man. But I know he's been a good customer."

"That he is," Vivien said, handing her the list. "That's why I like to order all the books written about presidents and CEOs and political scandals that I know he prefers. There's a new book on Lincoln just out that will have him salivating."

Though Prudence had not had many dealings with Danny, Vivien kept a running dialogue with him and even dropped off some of her baked goods on occasion, sensing he was a lonely sort. Prudence never quite figured out if Vivien had a big heart or was simply an expert at marketing. "This list looks great, but since you've asked, don't forget to order that Michael Moore book for Mrs. Dougal."

"I don't know why she wants it; all she'll do is rant at me after reading it, but I'll add it."

"Good girl. Gotta keep the postmistress happy."

"So, are you all packed and ready to go?"

"I am, and of course, I've packed for Nick too."

"Lucky him."

"That's what I keep telling him."

"Don't worry about anything while you're away. The store will be fine and I'll be green with envy. Think of all that food and history—what I wouldn't give to be taken to Italy or anywhere for that matter. I haven't had a vacation like that in years. And that was with Paul, remember, the married guy you got so bummed about?"

"Well, don't forget, we'd hardly known each other when you told me of your escapades."

"It was all about the sex back then."

"I don't need to hear any more about him, he was such a jerk."

"He was, but like I said, I haven't been anywhere interesting since."

"I'll bring you back an Italian."

"If only; they are *so* sexy."

Seeing where this conversation was going, Prudence was ready to exit. "Be good and thank you from the bottom of my heart for clearing the decks for me these past weeks. If I can't bring a man back, I'll get you something pretty. Ciao."

"Don't forget your Berlitz handbook," Vivien said, giving her a big hug. "You'll need more than 'ciao' to get by."

Prudence opened the door and swung her head around so her hair swirled, imitating Vivien's classic move. Before the door closed fully, she heard the throaty laughter—her very generous and highly adventurous friend would be missed.

Kate tapped the glass and walked through the kitchen door. "Wow, don't you look lovely."

"I know I look better than I did," Prudence said. "Come on in, I've already opened a nice, crisp white just for you."

"None for you?" Kate said.

"I'm sticking to my red—much too chilly for me at this hour of the day for white."

"You'll love the Sangiovese, then, it tastes like dark cherries. Michael got some for our anniversary. Cheers," Kate said raising her glass. "I hope these sweaters fit, because with your coloring, you'll look like a million."

"Be back in a minute," Prudence said. She ducked into the small powder room off the kitchen to try them on. The teal shade brought out her highlights. "You know, I'm about ready to repaint these walls, what do you think?"

"Come out and let me see the sweaters first and then I'll give you my opinion about paint colors."

"Well?" Prudence posed in front of the doorway and then twirled in front of the table.

"Perfect. I knew they would be, especially since you're determined to bring your pearls. Just be careful not to leave your jewelry lying around in hotel rooms."

"Don't worry, it'll be fine."

"You're an innocent, Prudence, but at least you're going."

Prudence changed back into her fleece. "Come here, please, and see what you think of these swatches."

"I've always loved this little room. It was one of the first ones you remodeled if I remember correctly."

"Yup, but now I'm thinking it should be something that reflects the ocean, maybe the Caribbean Sea after all. Turquoise or a cool blue?"

"You're the artist, but I'd watch out for anything too cool. On gray winter days, the room could look like a walk-in freezer. I think I like this one," Kate said pointing to the deeper aquamarine shade.

"That'll work if I use lots of white trim and accent with my favorite color orange."

"See, that's what I meant. I never would have thought of that," Kate said. "You are a bit wound if you don't mind my saying."

"Just think, tomorrow I'll be off to Italy!"

"I'm excited for you. Oh hell, look at the time. I've got to put Michael's dinner in the oven. Don't fuss, I'll take care of the plants. Have a fabulous holiday and *please* try and relax," Kate said as she grabbed her jacket.

"Thanks for everything."

"No problem."

Prudence waved her off and then poured another wine. Might as well, she thought. Italy beckoned. And then, so did Nick as she heard the front door slam.

The scent of bacon curled around the stairwell and reached the landing. She was poised before the hall mirror, showered but dressed in the robe Kate had given her one Christmas, a token from her first trip to India. Kate called it a dressing gown, but it resembled a sari with soft folds. Last night had been a surprise. Nick had taken one look at her new haircut—said it made her look sassy—and pulled her up the stairs to the bedroom. While their lovemaking had been quick, it was on the right track. Maybe Kate was right, they'd just fallen into a rut. And just maybe, Prudence thought, losing two babies had impacted him more than she realized.

In the kitchen, Nick was ready for her. The table was set and a tall glass with an extra-large celery garnish rested near her placemat. "I didn't use too much vodka and I went easy on the hot sauce, but it is a celebration after all."

"Oh, this does taste good!" She could feel the warm slide of the drink's telltale heat. Her cheeks grew rosier with each sip. "What other surprise do you have for me?"

"I'm saving that for Italy," Nick said, cracking eggs into a bowl. "I hate to say this since you're in such a good mood, but I have to meet 'little Napoleon' right after breakfast."

"Why?"

"Some nonsense about a sump pump problem that requires my presence along with the plumber. I just knew he'd find a way to screw me out of a few extra dollars."

He plated the toast and bacon and set them on the table "I won't be long and you can take your time fussing over whatever gals like to fuss over," Nick said. "You really do look great, by the way." He made a point of kissing her as he passed the eggs.

The big breakfast helped absorb the alcohol, but it had a mellowing effect which was exactly what she needed. "I'll clean up, hon, you go ahead."

"It's good to see you like this," Nick said. "I can't wait for you to see the Italy I remember."

"Tell that to your pain-in-the-ass client," she said, waving her fork in the air. "I'm sure he's nice, but not today, okay?"

Nick laughed, and kept laughing all the way to the car. Prudence was such a lightweight and actually funnier when she had mixed drinks. His dad loved watching how expressive she became after gin and tonics on the deck. Her stories were animated and filled with island lore. Nick had always envied his wife's chameleon personality and had missed that aspect of her too. This trip wouldn't take away all her pain, but it could be a salve, he thought, turning the key.

She tidied the kitchen, tuning in to her classical favorites pumped at high volume, and sank into the window seat to finish the pictorial tour through Italy. There was still plenty of time before she had to dress.

Flipping the pages, it was obvious the layout designer was an artist of another type. There were plank tables set with cakes and pastries and another highlighting a platter layered with cuts of lamb garnished with rosemary sprigs. The herb looked so fresh she thought about rubbing her wrist against the paper the way she would perfume samples in magazines.

In one scenic backdrop, the sun played off the glasses filled with sparkling wine and in the foreground, decorative bowls were carefully arranged with colorful vegetables. A culinary page had been transformed into fine art.

The sky in the photos was bluer than she imagined it to be. Cameras played tricks like that, she thought, anxious to see for herself. Warmth emanated from the olive grove and through her body and the words blurred as sleep crept in and her eyes became slits.

"Ow." The book had fallen on her chest interrupting her chance to sample one of the sweet treats from the table that was so real in her dream. Checking the clock, she scrambled to her feet, but not before she heard the short honks signaling that Nick was home.

She rushed upstairs to put on her make-up, frantic now that she'd wasted the time reading. They were flying out of Portland and changing planes in New York for Milan. An early evening flight that would have them arriving at Malpensa Airport at 8:40 a.m. Weighing the costs of the non-stop ticket against the short length of stay, Nick had opted for the ticket, rationalizing that it would give them more hours on the ground.

"Pru, how're you doing?"

"Won't be long," she yelled back. "How'd it go?"

"Fine, but he sure is a pain in the ass, just like you said," Nick shouted as he climbed the stairs. "I need to change too." He grabbed his shaving kit and the fresh shirt she'd left hanging on the doorknob.

"I'm out, it's all yours," Prudence said. She ducked under his arm.

"I want to get there a little early just in case there's some snag somewhere. You look pretty by the way."

"You will too, as soon as you get your extra whiskers off." She tweaked his chin, "I'll be dressed in just a few minutes."

And there she was, in front of the marred mirror once again—Mrs. Nicholas Pelletier, about to go abroad, she thought, remembering back to those really early days in the Caribbean when anything was possible and fear was an imaginary word. "Come on honey, Tuscany calls."

Chapter Five

"Wake up, sleepyhead, you'll miss the scenery," said Nick.

Prudence had strapped herself in, prepared for the worst. Other than a few bumps and the occasional air pocket, the flight had been uneventful, and that was before he'd fallen under the spell of engine thrum and fallen asleep. She had not slept, with or without Kate's pills, obvious by the way she was conked out now in the passenger seat of their rental car.

"You'll have terrible jet lag if you don't wake up."

"How long have I been asleep?" She shifted positions.

"I'd say about two hours, right after the rest stop. You didn't even finish your *panino* so I had to finish it for you."

"I knew you would, but I ate enough. The peppers are already coming back to haunt. Guess my stomach is confused by the time."

"Well, I didn't want you to miss any of this."

Coined umbrella pines for their broad green canopies, Italian stone pines held the hilltop in balance between glaring sun and ripened earth. And the sky that she believed to have been photo-processed, was instead an artist's blue, an unforgettable color that might have been blended from tubes of rich oil paint.

In the foreground, flame-shaped cypresses created long shadows on walls the color of burnt earth. Fall had changed the landscape in Italy as well. Gone were the sunflowers and poppies displayed in her book, replaced by variant shades of green with hints of gold. Wide, fallow fields lay quiet in the distance where the horizon turned into a lavender haze. "It's like a dream," she whispered. "Unbelievable."

"Spectacular, right?" Nick reached for her hand, "I told you it was impressive, but these drivers! Cars zoomed past and he was already doing seventy. "They know we're tourists." He accelerated for good measure. "Watch for the Bernoli sign, please, I can't slow down right now."

"According to this, we're right on the outskirts of Radda," Prudence said, tapping the printed information. "There, up ahead, the sign with an arrow…"

Nick hit the gas in order to make the turn. "These guys are maniacs!" A yellow Fiat closed in, then quickly swung into the passing lane, narrowly missing the rental's bumper. As it passed, the driver mouthed something undistinguishable while raising a hand signal that clearly indicated his anger.

"I'm sure we can find easier roads for sightseeing; they're all madmen!"

"You've just gotten used to the slow pace of Maine."

"Aren't you miss world traveler," Nick said, giving her a loving poke.

"Touchè."

About a mile in, they pulled onto a quiet lane that opened up to reveal what the brochure had been unable to. "Feast your eyes on that!" said Nick.

"Oh my!" Under a red-tiled roof, walls of mottled stone secured the history of the Bernoli farmhouse to ancient land in the province of Siena. Off to one side and bathed in sunlight, a small outbuilding contrasted with the main house that had been shadowed by deep green vines. Clay pots filled with tiny blue flowers, marked the periphery and flat stepping stones drew the eye to a hammock at the rear of the main structure. The crunch of their tires had not disturbed a black and white cat languishing in the sunshine near a lean brown dog too lazy to bark.

Nick rolled down his window and sniffed the air. "It smells like pine, but sweeter."

"Wild rosemary, and there's a ton of it."

"Look. That must be Mrs. Bernoli."

Peering around the corner of the house, a handsome woman waved a pair of pruning scissors at them.

In full view, the woman dressed in a calf-length skirt and soft flannel shirt topping a plain jersey, was also carrying a small basket with a colorful bandanna tied to the handle.

Nick waved as he exited the driver's side. Prudence walked ahead as he unlocked the small trunk and retrieved their bags. Up close, she realized the lady of the house was nearer to seventy than sixty. Her skin glowed with good health and, Prudence thought, perhaps the after effects of their homegrown olive oil. She had read in a magazine that the purer the oil, the more beneficial to the body on so many levels, and according to the Bernoli brochure, their production would be high.

"You are the couple from America, Nicholas and Prudenza, no?" She put down her basket and gloves.

Oh lord. "Please, Mrs. Bernoli, call me Pru. That's what Nick calls me." Prudence held out her hand, but just like in the movies, Mrs. Bernoli kissed her in the Italian way—lightly on one cheek, then the other—in welcome.

"And, you, I will call Nico. That is good, no?"

"Si," he said. "I like it…grazie."

Prudence stared at her husband. Of course, she thought, he'd already learned the basics.

Inside, the space was homey and crammed with books and polished wood and in one corner, an ebony piano.

"I know we'll enjoy our stay, Mrs. Bernoli, this is even more than we expected."

"You will call me Lena, please, we are family here. *Signora Bernoli* is my mother-in-law. You will meet her on Sunday when she brings the pasta to our family dinner…mine isn't good enough for her."

Prudence picked up on the disdain. It was instant rapport—another woman who suffered a difficult mother-in-law.

"Our daughters say that Marco suffers from 'mammismo'—and he is too old to be tied to his mother. They are modern women but I say nothing. Wait until they find husbands…then they can talk to me."

Nick had been caught staring out into the distance in the direction of the grove, identified through the terrace doors by the glint of sun on silver leaves. "So, Nico, what do you think of our humble farm?"

"It's amazing," he said. "Just like I remember it. I came to Italy right after college many years ago, and I've never forgotten the Tuscan hills."

"Good, then you will enjoy."

Prudence yawned.

"I'm sure we will," Nick said.

"You will cook with me?" Lena said.

"Yes, I mean Si," said Prudence, stumbling as she tried to make a good impression. Good old jet lag was nagging, just as Nick said it would.

"We will put him to work too, "Lena said. "If he wishes."

Nick blushed. "I'd only get in the way."

"You can go with my husband then, to see the olive press."

"Now you're talking!"

"Come, I take you to your room." Lena led them along the terrace and stopped near a small table with an orange umbrella tilted to one side. "*Ecco,* this is your room," she said, handing over the key to a substantial wooden door. The dog had stayed back to lounge in the sun, but the cat had come to Lena's side, edging her way between the suitcases and her mistress. "I hope you don't mind the animals. This one eats the *topos,* the mice."

"Not at all," they chimed.

"Is the land always this fragrant, Lena?" Prudence asked as she scooped the cat into her arms.

"It is the rosemary," she said, her hand waving to multiple locations bordering the house.

The cat squirmed. Prudence had been turning too far from her mistress and she wanted down. "Okay little one." She set the cat on the ground, "The plants looks so hardy, nothing like the little pots I grow at home."

"We know the rosemary for its many powers, stories told through the generations. When you have time, I will tell you what my Nonna told me, but now you rest and when Marco is home we will have some wine." Lena opened the door to their room.

"This is beautiful!" Prudence exclaimed.

"Si, I like to think I'm...what do you call it, interior decorating?"

"It's perfect, you're obviously a woman of talent."

"Tell Marco's mother on Sunday," Lena said with a wry smile.

Prudence had found a kindred spirit, not only because of Lena's bouts with her mother-in-law, but in decorating. "What a wonderful woman," Prudence said as the door closed.

"Thank goodness her English is terrific because my Italian is really rusty."

"We'll both learn," she said, leading him toward the inviting bed that featured a headboard of barn wood. "Another fabulous feature; I can't wait to see the rest of the place."

He took her face in his hands and kissed her tenderly, "I've missed you more than I can say."

"I know, and I'm sorry."

"Hush," he said pulling her to him. "We'll have plenty of time to talk. Right now I just want to hold you."

"Then let's get comfortable." They rolled back the bedcovers and underneath the lavender coverlet were white, lace-edged sheets and a mattress looking much softer than their own. "This might be fun," she said as they gravitated helplessly to the center of the big bed.

Even as sleep threatened, they tried to explore the familiar contours of their bodies, once indicative of their lovemaking—their union a safe place to fall. But the time zones had taken hold. The scent of rosemary crept in wherever it could breach an opening. Their eyelids closed and beyond the ancient door, a lazy cat mewed with content.

"Pru...Pru, wake up."

"What time is it?"

"Eight, and I hear voices."

"Lena is expecting us to join them for a drink and I'm starving," Prudence said. The day was completely out of sync.

"Me too; let's get dressed and see if we can scrounge up some food. There must be a restaurant around here somewhere."

"Oh there you are," said Marco. "It is good to meet. We hoped you would join us for a drink. This is our neighbor, Aldo, he manages the grove."

Prudence instantly imagined a painting—Aldo in the field, his shock of white hair appearing like a handful of snow in the hot sun. In the flesh, the man's face was tanned, his blue eyes twinkly, his fingers gnarled, and yet his age was indeterminate. Halfway between the plane ride and the agreeable company, Prudence had begun to relax, really loosen the taut strings of tension that had been holding her together.

"Piacere," said Nick, shaking the man's large callused hand.

"Parla Italiano?"

"Only a little," Nick said, turning red.

"You will learn," Marco injected. "Lena and I will help."

"You're very kind." Prudence heard her stomach rumble. "Is there a restaurant nearby?"

"You will have a glass of wine and then you will follow Aldo. He passes a small *taverna* on his way home," Marco said. "There is no big menu, just plain food, and it is not far."

"Wonderful," Nick said. From the look of the unidentified dark green bottle, they'd gotten a head start on the wine. *Vino sfuso,* he thought, of course. Young wine you can take home in casks and decant into your own bottles. *La dolce vita!* The Italians really knew how to live.

Eating late was apparently de rigueur, Prudence thought, and then remembered that businesses closed mid-day and reopened late which made dinnertime later as well.

"Come with me," Lena motioned to Prudence. "Let the men talk a moment."

"What a comfortable looking kitchen," Prudence said. Copper sauté pans hung along one wall and gleaming pots filled a wide oak shelf. An oak mantel graced the kitchen hearth and was laden with painted pottery. Running her hands over the top of the island, Prudence asked, "Is this where you make your pasta?"

"Si, and it is where I will teach you. There are no other guests for this week, so you are welcome to stay, if you like. There is not so much to see in the village, but it is easy to drive to Sienna or Greve from here, where all the tourists go. It is nice to have young people around again. I miss my girls."

"Where are they now?"

"Milano, both of them. One in fashion and the other in law," Lena said. "What do you and Nico do?"

"I have a bookstore, but I'm a painter on the side...you know, artwork. And Nick sells real estate. We live in a really small town but it's very beautiful and the ocean is right at our back door."

"Do you have children?"

Prudence stumbled on her words. "We tried, but I lost them."

Lena took her hands, "*cara mia*," she murmured. "God will watch over them...and you," she whispered kindly. "He always has a plan, you will see."

"I hope so," Prudence said. She had never been a strong believer, but Lena seemed so certain.

"Come, we join the men and then tomorrow, after *colozione*—breakfast, I will show you how to make the dough. Perhaps by Sunday, you will be better than Marco's mamma." Then she crossed herself and whispered into the air.

Must not be a good omen to make such jokes, Prudence thought, as she was shepherded out to the men.

"Ah, here you are," said Marco. "Aldo's wife is waiting, but he will go slow and show you the road."

They bade the Bernolis goodnight, but she noticed as they drove away that Lena had stayed in the doorway. Pinpricks of light were breaking out across the vast expanse of sky, the backdrop for hills that looked etched in charcoal. "Let's stay the week," Prudence said as they got in the car.

"You don't want to go exploring other towns?"

"Lena said we're close to everything we planned to see anyway, and I really like her."

"Then we'll stay," Nick said. This week was all about happiness and Pru was beginning to look happy.

Ten minutes later, Aldo slowed down.

"I don't see a restaurant, do you?"

"No, but look, there's a large house over there."

"We'll soon find out." Nick pulled up behind Aldo and jumped out of the car with Pru right behind him.

"My Inglese, no so good," Aldo said. He led them toward the side of the house where a bright bulb exposed stone steps leading to what should have been a basement, and pointed. "Signora Guardino, she cooks like the angel," he said, kissing his cupped fingertips. No other comment required.

Aldo sprinted away, leaving them shaking their heads. "Oh boy," Nick said, taking her hand. "This should be interesting."

"It doesn't look like much, but I smell something really, really good," Pru said. They stood a minute, just breathing everything in. "Down we go, into the rabbit hole!"

Heads turned: an old man at a small table, his fork mid-way over a large bowl of spaghetti; another, a laborer of some sort, seated on a stool—sipping an amber colored drink—shouted to an invisible figure in a closet with steam pouring out; a middle-aged couple—vacationers like themselves perhaps—in rapt ecstasy, spoons poised over a shared dessert, a near-empty wine carafe to one side.

Signora Guardino—all four foot ten if Prudence gauged correctly—rushed from that little closet to greet them, her substantial countenance swathed in the aromas lifted from the pots and pans that held the meals yet to be discovered. "Buona sera," she said, plunking a carafe of red wine onto the only free table.

"Buona sera," Nick said.

La signora smiled broadly, "*prego*". She pointed them to the little board in the corner and left them to ponder.

"Can you believe this place?" Nick whispered.

"Si," Pru said.

According to their pocket Italian, they'd been given the choice of either beef tripe, or a *salsicce*—sausages with a serving of spaghetti in red sauce. They decided on the latter instead of something from the interior lining of a cow. "I can see the pounds adding up now," Pru said as Nick stopped at the kitchen doorway and called out the foreign words like a pro. "You're amazing," she said, as they walked the few steps back to their table.

"Keep that thought." He poured the wine into what looked like jelly jars. Rustic was the optimal word for their first Italian experience. "Cin cin," he said. They clinked glasses and she sniffed the air with approval. "The more you eat, the more for me to love."

"Not too much more, I can assure you."

Before he could sputter a word, their food was set before them. "Smells amazing," Nick said to the young man who closely resembled Mrs. Guardino, but taller.

"*Buon Appetito.*"

"Grazie," Nick said, and aimed his fork at a thick, pepper-scented sausage.

Prudence twirled her fork in the pasta and slurped it to her mouth, spattering droplets of sauce on her chin. "This is fantastic!" she said.

"Well, I'll expect you to be able to make it like this when we get home."

"I accept the challenge."

They had tried savoring the meal, but instead, appeared to have inhaled it. Their internal clocks would need resetting, Prudence thought, as the young waiter approached to collect their empty plates.

"Where you stay in hotel?"

"The Bernoli farm," Nick said. He would have liked to add more, but instead blurted out the rudimentary words that came to mind. "*Quanto lire*, for dinner?"

"Un momento."

"I hope he understood me, I only remember the basics."

The answer lay on the little tray carried back to their table. Two small glasses of clear liquid smelling of licorice, rested on top of a small piece of paper indicating the lira amount needed. "The drinks, no charge," the waiter said. "Lena Bernoli and mamma are many years, *amicas,* how you say, friends."

"Grazie molto," Nick said. "Thank la signora too, please."

Prudence leaned in and took his hand as they walked out under the stars in what was touted as one of the most romantic countries in the world.

The road back was dark and free of traffic and they rode in silence. A light had been left on at their door and one at the edge of the path to help guide them. Pru shivered as she got out of the car and Nick put his jacket over her shoulders and lovingly left his hand close to her neck. With this gesture, her heartbeat increased and she was overcome by a surge of passion, a feeling almost as foreign as the land they were in. As if he'd picked up the signal, Nick slid his hand from her neck to her back and pulled her in. "Look what you've done," he said pressing her to him.

He whispered what he intended to do to her. She'd almost forgotten how he could nearly bring her to orgasm in the telling. They'd lost the language of love in these last months, but with the sensation of a warm tide, those unspoken words suddenly washed over her body.

The moment the door closed behind them, he undressed her, slowly, taking pleasure in the small shudders as the air and his fingers touched her bare skin. "You're as beautiful as ever," he said caressing her hip and then the top of her thigh.

She unbuckled his belt and opened his shirt and pulled him to the bed. "I want you."

By the time he was fully undressed, she was feverish with wanting. "Come to me." Foreplay was not an option, her hunger was too great. It had been wrapped away in grief and now it called out for release. Nick eased himself down until she felt the full heat of his desire. She moved her hips up to meet him. There was a momentary edge of pain; her passion too quickly grabbed, but she didn't care. Her arousal was near peak. Relaxing her hold, she tried to prolong what she craved. Nick's breathing slowed too and he withdrew and began to caress her again, transporting her slowly to that moment she longed for. He was so good at this, she thought, as her body betrayed her and she cried out for more. He gave her everything: kissing her breasts, her belly, teasing her desire, then let his body speak until they were begging each other for the end they didn't want.

Satisfaction floated over them like a summer blanket. "We needed that," Nick said spooning her to him.

"I love you," she said.

"I was worried you didn't."

"Me too."

"Don't stop."

"I don't think I could. It was a bad time, that's all," she said. "Let's not talk about that now. Get some sleep and we'll see what Italy has in store for us tomorrow."

Nick rolled onto his back and Pru did the same. Within minutes, she felt the wetness of fresh tears on her pillowcase. In part they were a natural response, a release, and in part they were an affirmation of life, of the happiness they'd once taken for granted. Tomorrow she would ask about the rosemary.

The headiness of basil and sage comingled with the ever-present pine-scented herb. The aroma of fresh brewed coffee could barely compete. "Can I help?" said Prudence.

"Grazie, no," Lena said. She had laid out two different breads. She pointed—"*il brioche o il cornetti?*"

Prudence was prepared for the light fare—if you could call pastries of any sort light. No bacon or eggs and toast here, she thought. What a nice change. "Il brioche, per favore."

"Ah, you are learning already," Lena said. "We will work in a little while. Did you rest?"

"Si, the bed is very comfortable."

"I think our Tuscany is good for you. Cappuccino or espresso?"

"Espresso, please."

"You will need sugar, it is very strong."

"But delicious," Prudence said. She watched the cubes swirl as she stirred with the tiniest spoon she'd ever used. "Nick will be here soon—I left him singing in the shower."

"You have color in your cheeks, perhaps the rosemary, no?"

Maybe it was, she thought. "Please tell me more about it."

"This is legend. The rosemary is called the herb of love. In Latin we say dew of the sea, but always about love...*capisce?*"

Could Lena guess that only last night she and that mysterious commodity called love, had only just been reacquainted? "We

72

live near the sea," she said, feeling that heat as far as her earlobes.

"My Nonna said rosemary cures the sickness and even keeps the bad dreams away."

"That's a lot for one little herb to take responsibility for," Prudence said. Too bad she hadn't heard that in the months preceding this adventure.

"You have a sadness I understand, and if Nonna was right, you will find a way to be happy again."

Pesky tears threatened again and she turned her head. This wasn't the way she'd wanted the day to begin.

"*Cara*, it is all right, crying is good," Lena said coming to Prudence's side. "My brilliant daughter, Angelina, the romantic one, has poems about the rosemary. She thought my guests would like the history and the stories of Shakespeare. I will give them to you later and you can read them in *l'amaca,* how you say…hammock?"

"Yes, and you're very kind." Prudence wanted to absorb the mother/daughter relationship, to feel the balm that type of love must have produced.

"Buon giornoro," Nick hollered from the hall.

"We're in here," Prudence said.

"You sound like a true Italian," Lena said, pouring him a cup of coffee. "And like a man who is ready for a breakfast."

"I don't know how I could be hungry after last night's dinner, but I am." He downed the mini-cup of espresso. "By the way, Mrs. Guardino gave us complimentary drinks afterward."

"My oldest friend is very generous. Lucia's husband died two years ago and now her sons help her in the kitchen."

Prudence wondered what it would have been like to be bound so completely to the land like these generous Italians. What her life would have been like with a mother like Lena. "We're going to begin my lessons after breakfast," Prudence said.

"Then I'll take a nice long walk around the property and work off last night's *salsicce!*" said to the delight of their hostess.

"This is good, Nico, perfetto!

"Show off," Prudence said.

Nick laid a kiss on top of Prudence's head and picked up a cream-filled pastry. "Grazie, Lena, I'll leave you two to your work."

"There is a trail out back that leads to the upper grove. It is a good walk. Maybe Luigi will follow."

"Luigi?"

"The dog, he looks like Marco's old uncle who lives in Montecatini."

"I see," said Nick, shaking his head as he exited. He really didn't. Maybe the dog wouldn't follow him, he thought, as he approached the sleeping canine who'd set up camp outside the door. Luigi may have been old, but his nose still worked and he rose to the whiff of spice coming from Nick's hand, taking up the pace alongside. "Okay, boy, hope you're up to it."

"They make a good pair," Prudence said, peering through the kitchen window.

"The dog hunted the truffles, but not so much now. He is old and very stiff, but he will come back when he is tired, you will see." Lena busied herself with the clearing up. "Finish your coffee."

"I'm happy to start whenever you're ready."

"Good. First I show you how to make the well with the flour. This is Nonna's recipe so I will show you how to work the dough and cut the pieces for fettuccine or ravioli. Then we will use the *macchina.*"

"What a strange contraption," Prudence said. Lena was attaching a small machine to the edge of the table. Then she pulled the container of flour from the shelf and placed eggs on the board along with salt and olive oil. "First, three cups of flour like this," she said, making a hole with her fingers in the center of the mound. "Then three eggs, the salt and olive oil."

Prudence watched intently as Lena took her fork and began a light scramble, pulling the flour within the circle with each twirl of the fork until the entire egg mixture was incorporated, turning it into a ball of soft sticky dough. Then, she spread flour onto the board and began to knead until she was satisfied. "Not too wet," Lena said. "We do it together now."

Prudence stood next to her and imitated her strokes, her own well of flour filling in with a little help from Lena until she had a messy round of dough to work with. "Is this right?"

"*Questo*, like this," Lena said, ladling out another heaping spoonful of flour. "Now you knead." Lena worked quickly, her hands like a potter with clay, vigorous and gentle at the same time.

"Bene," Lena said. "*Non difficile*, no?"

"Si, not difficult," Prudence said with pride. She'd started getting an ear for words similar to English. "I can't believe I did this."

"But now, we roll and then we cut and let it dry and when Nico comes back, we cook."

"Really, that quick?"

"You will see how easy. We will cut the first sheet by hand and then we cut your dough with the *macchina*, the modern way. In Nonna's day, they used a *chitarra*, named for the strings on a guitar."

Prudence stood, fascinated. Lena rolled the small disc of dough into a large rectangular sheet. Then, taking a sharp knife, she began to cut long narrow strips. When she'd finished, she picked them up and gave them a little shake before setting them on a lightly floured platter.

"Now you roll," Lena said. "But not so thin."

Prudence did as instructed and then Lena cut the dough in thirds and only long enough to place into the stainless steel blades. Lena turned the knob just so. "First, one piece, like this."

Then she cranked a small handle and a thinner length of dough fell from the blades. "Now this." She changed the knob setting and cranked the same sheet back through the blades, and this time, strips came out looking like those cut by hand, but more precise.

"Wow, that's fantastic," Prudence said. She placed the balance of her dough onto a similar platter with pride. "I want one of these pasta machines."

"You can buy in the village. My mother-in-law still makes it by hand and I hide this when she comes," Lena said. "Now, you go, rest in the sun. It is a vacation, no?"

"I'll just help you clean up."

As soon as things were in order, Prudence headed for the hammock. She craved a nap, and her body still tingled from the previous night's lovemaking. It had been so right to come here, she thought, laying down on the heavy striped cotton swing. It was so quiet compared to the sounds of boats and squawking birds at their back door. Something twittered off-key in the distance and the air swelled with pine, closed in on her.

"There you are," Nick said, scooching in next to her.

"I must have dozed off."

"Dead to the world by the looks of it. Did you make your pasta?"

"Si, and we're going to eat it too."

"Do we have time to go back to our room?"

"What on earth for?"

"Don't play coy with me, Mrs. Pelletier." He grabbed her hand, pulling her to her feet and playfully pulled her toward the house.

"Oh Nick," she wailed. "Whatever *are* you doing?" Prudence was enjoying her role as damsel, especially since she knew what awaited her on the other side of that heavy oak door. The moment it closed, he toppled her onto the bed and began to tickle her into submission. "Oh God, no...I can't stand being tickled." She wriggled and squirmed and he stopped.

"Yes, I know, but I know what happens next too." He brought his mouth down to the soft skin of her navel and kissed her into surrender. "See, I know you want me...don't you?"

"Oh, so much." With a long sigh, she accepted him into her arms, only this time, the frantic coupling of the previous night became a sinewy expression of their feelings. Wrapped together, they rocked languidly with the sensation of the Tuscan sun reaching their souls until they reached that mutual celebration of fulfillment.

"Wow, I didn't think it could get any better," Nick said.

"I love Italy!"

"And I love you."

"How was your hike?" She'd almost forgotten he'd gone off into the hills. "Would I like it?"

"Bring your camera and sketch pad and I'll show you vistas that will make your artistic head spin."

"Let's do that later. I want to look around the village and see if I can find a pasta *macchina.*"

"Okay, right after we have some of your fettuccine, and the shops will be back open by then."

"*Alfresco,*" Lena said. She had set two places on a table under a pergola on a side terrace that had escaped their scrutiny. A bottle of water and one of white wine rested in the center. Heat from the afternoon sun rose from the stone and came down through the pergola entwined with twisted stems. The dappling of sun and shade on the tablecloth looked like a child's drawing and overhead, bees hummed lazily as they coaxed the nectar from purple and white blossoms.

"Won't you join us?" Prudence said.

"I have other work," Lena said. "*Manga,* eat, before it gets cold."

Their pasta had been bathed in a butter and sage sauce and served in a white fluted bowl hand-painted with tiny pink flowers. "This is part of her Nonna's set. I recognize the pattern from the coffee cups," Prudence said.

The fettuccine melted on the tongue. "I've never had anything like this!" Nick waved his fork at Pru, "you did this?"

"Some of it," Prudence said. "Lena's a good teacher."

"I'll say. It's delicious." He refreshed their glasses, "so, where do you want to start tomorrow?"

"There's a lot to do in a minimum of days, but according to Lena, we could drive to Greve and grab a bus to Florence. I'd love to see the galleries there, and then we could do the local churches before our week is up. There are maps and guide books in the central room, near the piano."

"Then Florence it is. And, later, when we get back from the village, let's walk off this lunch with that hike we talked about."

"Perfetto."

"You know, we might never have a need for a larger vocabulary. So far everything can be summed up with that one word."

"I know."

Chapter Six

Their afternoon flew by. They'd found the Italian version of a hardware store, and bought not only the *macchina,* but also a small porcelain-topped espresso maker. A block later, they dropped into a stand-up bar, two-deep in men lined up to call out their orders. She felt trapped in the throng and left Nick to sit outside and people-watch from one of the tiny café tables. Among the din, she could hear his voice yelling for *due caffe latte.* He had come back from that dark place too, she thought with gratitude. The words they had both wanted to say, the speeches they had been prepared to espouse about handling their difficulties, had been passed over for the sheer enjoyment of being silly and sampling new food and learning a language they would probably forget on the plane ride home.

"I want a pistachio gelato next," she said, getting up from the table. She pointed to the *gelateria* sign three doors down.

"Life is good." Nick licked the dripping cone in one hand, the other around her waist.

"Is it something in the air?"

"Maybe, but I'd like to bottle it," Nick said.

"We're going to need that hike. I'm now officially stuffed."

"It already looks good on you."

She poked his ribs and tossed her head. "Careful mister, or I'll cut off your bedroom privileges."

"Ah hah! That's a laugh. I'm surprised Lena didn't hear those moans through the heavy door."

This time she play-punched him, but not before the door of the *macelleria*—the local butcher shop—opened. The old gent tipped his hat and winked, obviously recognizing their playacting for what it was. After all, this was the land of love. Prudence blushed and patted her hair. "God, that was embarrassing."

"Don't be silly, it's Italy! They are a very expressive people." Nick winked at the old man and grinned a mischievous smile and led Prudence to their car. He was becoming comfortable with the looping roadway but still wary of the crazy Italian drivers. "We'll drop off your bundles and you can change your shoes and we'll go up that mountain."

"Not up *that* mountain?" Certainly he couldn't mean that high peak off in the distance.

"Sorry, I overstated the height of our hilltop olive grove, but it is an impressive hike."

Once back at the farmhouse, they dispensed with their packages and Prudence changed into the Keds she used when out on their boat. The light was perfect, she thought, grabbing her camera and notepad. She looked at Nick. He'd filled a small backpack with cheese, a hunk of salami, fruit and bottled water purchased in the square while she'd been checking out souvenirs. "I do believe we are going on safari?"

"Don't look to me when you get hungry," Nick said. "You'll work off what we ate earlier, believe me."

"I honestly don't think I could eat another morsel."

"We'll see."

He led the way along the path, a fairly straightforward walk until the earth gave way to wide cobbled steps. The heat of the afternoon sun radiated off the stone. At the first bend, shadows cooled the air. Brick and mortar walls closed in on them, and arches eye-browed the tall wooden doors. On a second story window, a half shutter pushed out at an angle, an eyelid just opening from a nap, the only sign of life. A few potted plants strategically placed on a stoop, or an item of clothing left out on a line strung under a window, indicated where the sunlight was most likely to glance at this hour of the day. The other shutters were closed even though siesta hour was past, and the only sound was the click of Prudence's camera. "This is fabulous!" she said. "Coming here was the perfect idea and so was coming to Italy. Thank you."

"Knew you'd like it." He cast about for a place to sit so that he could watch her take it all in. They had reached a small opening flooded with sunlight where wide rustic pavers created what looked to be a common area with a sink and tap niched into a low wall. "Wait till you see the top."

Before he could get comfortable, she had switched gears. "Let's do it," she said. "Before those clouds move in."

A few more angles, a tightening of calf muscles and suddenly the vista opened onto the Bernoli grove, spread in every direction, though much of it out of their sightline. The boundary began to their right, behind what looked to be an abandoned church.

"Get a photo of me standing in front of that giant green door," Nick said as he wandered to the right.

"The color is called *verdigris,* and I'd be happy to." She aimed her small Nikon at the bucolic scene and zoomed in on Nick's posturing. The boarded-up stone building had been the earliest villagers' original place of worship, and surely was filled with the sound of their footsteps, the critical moments in their lives, she thought, and not entirely neglected. "Someone's bothered to turn the dirt in those flowerbeds."

"There's probably a few graves up here too, and all of it tended by people who've lived here all their lives. You're just getting a taste of the history, sweetheart—wait till we get to Florence."

Prudence snapped away, her mind populated with figures— imagined marriages and baptisms and funeral masses that would have taken place up here, before the small cathedral had been constructed in Radda.

"Let's move on, there's more."

"Lead on my darling."

"How come you never talk to me that way at home?"

She gave him one of her sideways looks. "This is Italy…remember?"

"Let's look for a place with the best view."

In the near distance, she saw an interesting formation of olive trees and aimed her camera just as a cumulous cloud slid by and exposed their glittery leaves and something else.

"Were those chairs up here this morning?" Sunbeams highlighted two chairs in front of the largest of the trunks.

"I don't remember seeing them."

Getting closer, the ornately designed iron chairs rested against the gnarly trunk—'old-timers' waiting for something of interest to happen. There was a story there, she thought, approaching the tamped-down brown patches of earth beneath them. Her imagination went full-tilt. Prior occupants with years of family tales to share or even expose here in this quiet place after a hard day's work, or perhaps a Sunday walk to take in the fabulous views. "Come, sit with me," she said, patting the chair next to her. "Someone was considerate enough to give us a place to rest. I wonder if Lena knows about these."

"Perfect place for a little picnic," Nick said opening his sack.

She had already started pretending, wondering about the chairs' ownership. "Is that all you can think about—food?"

"Gotta keep this body tuned up and don't forget, this is the second time today I've made this hike."

For just a little while, they sat side by side, holding hands and drinking it all in, the aroma of salami somehow fitting in perfectly with the image in her mind. Mid-day breaks, dusting off the weekly gossip and news of relatives in a place like so many anchored to the ridge of mountains in this region. Her brain churned with future paintings.

Suddenly the sun disappeared and a light breeze moved in. "What say we head back for a nap?" Nick said.

"Just a nap?"

"Where is your mind, girl?"

He pulled her up and packed up the snacks. "We'll have these later in our room, unless you want to go back to the *taverna* tonight. I don't feel much like driving further than that."

"I like that idea—it's been a really full day, and tomorrow is going to be another one." Prudence continued photographing while they traced their steps back down the hill toward the farmhouse. There would be a lot to share with Lena during their next pasta-making session and she couldn't wait. Dropping their gear on the terrace, she and Nick flopped into the chairs to take it all in: the Brunello from Montalcino purchased earlier, the scent of pine, and the picture-book countryside that made everything possible.

"I'm not sharing the biscotti with you."

"Like I could eat another sweet…have at it."

"I wonder if you'll learn how to make these too," Nick said digging into the bag.

"Don't get your hopes up."

"Nah, wouldn't dream of it."

She sipped her wine, and he crunched the cookies, and they stared at the hills, each remembering some portion of the day. "This is going to go fast, isn't it?"

"Yes, but we can come back again, someday."

"I think I'm going to have to, it kind of gets under your skin."

He leaned over and kissed her. "I'm so happy you feel that way."

The scenery began to change, enhancing the quiet of their mutual admiration. Then the stars poked through one by one, filling in the spaces until night took the light away. The little mouse-catcher was under the table, quietly on alert but seeming to enjoy their company. "I can't keep my eyes open any longer," she said, getting to her feet.

"Me either. Let's call it a night."

Their room had been freshened and a note placed on the dresser. "Lena says coffee and zeppole will be waiting for us in the morning, to take on the bus if we want."

"Love that woman. Zeppole are a kind of fried doughnut; you'll love 'em."

Prudence groaned at the thought of any more food, but looking at his muscular body, she changed her mind about saying a word. It never seemed to hurt him, whereas before the last miscarriage, she was always watching her calories. "Terrific," she said, already wrapped in the bed sheet.

Nick rolled in next to her and somewhere between the Uffici Gallery and his description of the Duomo, she'd begun to snore—ever so slightly—an obvious sign of her exhaustion. "It's been a great day," he whispered into her hair.

The day would be one to remember and tell their friends. It had begun early—a short drive to Greve and an hour's bus ride to Florence. Beautiful, captivating *Firenze,* everything an artist or a dreamer would want. With so much to choose from and so little time, they bypassed the Uffizi with its long waiting line and opted for the Bargello Museum. Housed within walls that had once been a prison, were the works of Donatello, Michelangelo, Cellini and Brunelleschi, enough to humble any modern-day artist.

As they checked guidebooks, photographed the towers and the pink, white, and green marble façade of the Duomo, they ran into plein air artists who had laid claim to the best spots in front of the many tourist attractions. Men mostly, who composed charcoal portraits for a few lire and others, spattered with telltale oil paints, had seemed focused on major pieces to sell in galleries later on. Prudence, intrigued by the oils, was directed to Zecchi Colori on via del Studio. It was the most beautiful art supply store she had ever seen. Tiered shelves displayed every conceivable product to enhance one's own ability. Having written down the names of the colors seen on the piazza, those guaranteed to produce her own versions of the Italian countryside, she'd turned the slip over to the intriguing, soulful-eyed clerk at the store. The final tally was outrageous, but she hadn't cared, and had left the store with not only the recommended tubes of paint, but two spectacular brushes, and real Venetian glazes. In the meantime, Nick had wandered around the corner and found them an inviting, rustic trattoria.

The establishment had been filled with beautifully dressed Italians carrying on conversations in lively, heavily punctuated sentences, their hands a litany of expression. Tourists were at a minimum and quickly identified by the maps and guide books before them as they placed their orders. It was time to try the Florentine beef with zucchini blossoms as well as gnocchi topped with a gorgonzola sauce. Decadent, indulgent and perfect. By the time they had shared the food and a bottle of Chianti, Prudence had a talking jag going accompanied by all the appropriate hand waving she had absorbed as if by osmosis from nearby diners. According to Nick, he may have learned a few new words, but she was speaking in true Italian!

On their way back to the terminal, they had woven through narrow alleyways, struggled with signage, gotten lost and then miraculously found their way onto a wide cobbled street filled with the sounds of busy commerce. At one stage, a horse-drawn carriage went clip-clopping past with a homemade banner held up by a rowdy wedding party. The fanfare drew them like a magnet and shouts of 'bravo' and 'buona fortissimo', flew from their lips as everyone waved back. The city just had that effect.

Now, looking out the window of the bus, Prudence mentally ordered the day to fit the sequence of happy surprises rather than actual time. She rubbed her ankles and wiggled her toes and pictured a soak to take away the kinks.

"I won't ever eat again," she said.

"Great food, and a great day."

"Yes, and tomorrow I will be in the kitchen with Lena, and you will go with Marco, and then I'd love to do some sketching and take more photos to use when we get back to Maine. This place just stimulates every pore, don't you think?"

"I think it all looks good on you. I haven't seen you this upbeat in a very long time, even before the miscarriages."

"Maybe it's the Pill after all. Dr. Gordon said they would help balance out my hormones."

"Whatever it is, I love it," he said as he leaned back in the seat for a short nap.

She became lulled by the humming tires. The day had been filled with newness: sites, sounds, colors and food. Her senses were sated to the point of overload and she wanted to put it all in her suitcase to savor back at home. Whatever the expense, the trip had already been worth the wait, the long overdue honeymoon probably more appreciated than when they were newlyweds.

Back in their room, Prudence emptied her tote onto the bed: A green and white silk scarf for Vivien, gold hoop earrings for Kate, and a decorative hand-painted plate that could be hung on a wall, for Rita Pelletier. Nick had chosen leather bookmarks and fancy pens for his office crew and soft leather gloves for himself. She was already wearing the chunky ring and fake gold bracelet she'd bought from one of the many street vendors set up along the way to the 'old bridge'—the famous Ponte Vecchio. Once occupied by butchers and fishmongers, the little shops now sparkled with Florentine jewelry. With the last of the good light, she had taken a most memorable photograph: the mellow gold of the bridge as it appeared from the waterside with its colorful history projected onto the tiny roofed, box-like exteriors of those same stores; the stone arches filled with people-watchers, and scullers rowing languidly along the Arno River below.

"Did you have a good time yesterday?" Lena said as soon as Prudence popped through the doorway.

"Absolutely perfetto." That truly was the perfect word for everything.

"Marco will take Nico this morning if he is ready."

"He was just getting dressed, but let me run back and tell him. I know he's dying to go."

"Good, and I will fill the *termos* with the coffee and many sugars, the way he likes."

"You're spoiling him, Lena." Prudence rushed out and nearly bumped into Nick on his way in. "Marco's waiting to take you with him and Lena's made you up a thermos of coffee, and I noticed there was a small box with sweet rolls too."

"Fantastic! I'm ready. I don't think I could take another hike this morning. As my dad used to say, these dogs are barking," Nick said pointing to his feet.

Marco was standing next to the truck, waving. He held up the basket Lena had prepared for them. Nick kissed Prudence and ran off like a kid going to a ball game. They'd be gone most of the day, so as soon as she'd had her morning lesson, she'd have a go at the paperwork on those mysterious rosemary plants. But there was another burning question to ask Lena, she thought, entering the kitchen.

"Do you know anything about the two iron chairs we found in the olive grove?"

"Si," Lena said. "Did you see how the chairs come together, like old friends? Marco says it is a *segno,* a sign."

"How long have they been there?"

"Since his grandfather worked the land."

Prudence listened to a remarkable tale about the fifteen-year-olds who would sneak up there whenever they could; too young to be unsupervised, but they were in love and had made up their mind to be married as soon as they were old enough to ask permission.

"But it was too late. Someone told Ariel's papa she was in the grove holding hands with a boy and kissing. Her papa went crazy. Then Ariel's mamma died, and her papa sent her away to America, away from Marcello, to live with an uncle in New York who would be responsible for finding her a husband."

"What happened to Marcello?"

87

"It was hard on him. He was a poor boy from the next village, and he lived with much sadness. Marco's grandfather thought the boy would die from so much pain, and found him a job in the grove of a friend, but it was many kilometers away. Years later, he married the daughter of his employer, but she then died. He talked about Ariel again, but there was no money to follow her to America. And then he learned that her uncle had already made a match for her there."

"And Ariel?"

"She had no choice; she married the one chosen for her. After that, no one talked about it here, but we all knew he was much older. Her papa said nothing, but he missed her, everyone could see that. If not for Marcello, her papa would have made her stay and care for him and the house as was custom, the *normale* way of things in Italy. So you see, the old-fashioned ways made many tears for many people."

"It's so sad," Prudence said.

"Si, but it has a happy ending too. She returned to Tuscany with her son Antonio, to visit her only living brother. Antonio brought her here to the farm; she wanted to see the old grove."

"Was she strong enough to hike up the trail?"

"No, *cara*, Marco made the map for her son. They would walk the long way from her brother's house to the other side of the old church. It is longer but safer, and when they left us, Marco called Marcello. He could not believe it, and everyone knew that he still loved her. So he waited at the chairs until Ariel came with Antonio."

"This is too good to be true!"

"No, this is love. Antonio watched his mamma and the way the old man looked at her. He left them alone to visit. After a while, he went back to walk her home, but he saw how the old lovers were—still in the chairs just like his mother had said—holding hands and whispering about the future."

"Then what?"

88

"Patience, Prudenza. Marcello walked Antonio around for a while, their backs to Ariel, but she knew what Marcello was up to. He was asking her son for his mother's hand in marriage, the old-fashioned way that he had been denied years before. *Certamente,* of course, Antonio said yes, and the next day they went to visit the local priest. He is younger than Antonio—just a boy really—and the chapel in the square is all new. Young love, old love, everyone is happy and they made the date for the wedding. That was five years ago; they are eighty-nine now. But if you go to the grove on Sunday mornings, you will see Marcello and Ariel resting from the long walk, the chairs close together. They still hold hands and whisper things we cannot know; maybe the prayers they made at the mass, or maybe talk of the future. They have made their vows to each other, and that is all that matters."

"I don't think I can stand it. I'm going to cry."

"Everyone cried at the wedding—happy tears this time. The painters had finished the statues the month before, and the women who take care of the church polished the marble from Carrara and put the flowers in the big urns in front of it. Marco brought the wine from his grandfather's cellar to celebrate the marriage."

"Why didn't they use the beautiful old church in the grove?"

"It is not safe anymore—a sad story for another time."

"Wait till I tell Nick," Prudence said, watching her new mentor prepare for their lesson.

"*Ecco,*" Lena said, handing her an apron. "Enough about love, now you will make the dough for the ravioli, and I will watch. It is the same, but I will show you how we cut it for the filling. You will see, it is easy."

"If you say so." Prudence tied the apron and began to measure the required ingredients while Lena sat at the end of the table sipping her cappuccino. "When we're finished, will you let me see the stories about the rosemary?"

"Si, I put them on top of the piano so I would not forget."

The time flew and so did the flour. Prudence ended up with more on her than on the board, but she had done it correctly. Then Lena had shown her how to cut it for the cheese filling, which she had already prepared. "I made a terrible mess," Prudence said.

"Is okay, you are making the pasta!" Lena said giving Prudence a hug. Cleaning up and putting away the tools, Prudence felt at home in *la casa,* and as she worked, she thought of the small changes she would like to make in their Thatcher Lane kitchen since she had seen some decorative tiles in a store window in Greve. Just a few would do the trick, she thought, enough for a small trim near the sink, a permanent reminder of Italy.

"It is too bad that you did not see the *vendemmia*—for the harvest of the grapes. In November it is the *festa* for the olives. For this month, it is the celebration of the mushrooms and chestnuts. You will try some of my chestnut bread, no?" Lena had cut her a slice before she could respond.

What the heck, she thought, sucking in her stomach and letting it out again. "I can't wait." It was, after all, a vacation.

"Oh my God, this is amazing!" Lena's *castagnaccio* was filled with raisins that had been soaked in the dessert wine, *vin santo*, and was topped with rosemary and pine nuts. Again, the rosemary, Prudence thought, finishing up every last crumb. She couldn't wait to read up on the piney plant and then take an extended walk down the road to see how much sketching she could accomplish—as well as walk off the bread that tasted like cake.

"Angelina's research," Lena said, placing the sheets next to Prudence's plate.

The morning air was still a little too cool to lie in the hammock, so Prudence took the proffered pages to the big, cozy armchair in the corner of the great room. Angelina had provided a history of the plant indicating that, just as Lena had said, it was derived from the Latin "rosmarinus officinalis"—dew of the sea.

That was understandable, Prudence thought, since the bush was native to the seaside regions of the Mediterranean. The girl was thorough and had copied information that took the plant back thousands of years when it was believed to grow in the gardens of the righteous and protect from evil spirits. It was used in both Greek and Roman remedies and thought to preserve health and beauty. She would definitely need to plant bigger pots, she thought, running her hand over her face. There was a quote from Saint Thomas More about his garden walls and how the plant was sacred to remembrance. Angelina had provided notes taken from works of Shakespeare where both Juliet and Ophelia were also honored with rosemary for remembrance, but it was a particular phrase attributed to an English poet that Angelina had highlighted...'but rosemary will with you go'...that made her tear up. Her emotions had remained very close to the surface even with the addition of the Pill. She wiped her cheek, but a few tears had already fallen onto the page where facts met folklore. Supposedly, one's true love would appear in a dream if rosemary was placed beneath the pillow. Was it a rosemary sprig or a kiss that woke Sleeping Beauty from her long sleep? Angelina was definitely a romantic, Prudence thought, wishing she could have met her during this visit. With so much to ponder, she was ready to walk and breathe in, everything she imagined from those sheets of paper.

Placing the sheets where Lena would find them, she dashed back for her gear and a sweater. It was a fickle time of year even here in Tuscany. Maybe they could come back one day during the harvest or even in the summer when sunflowers and poppies were in bloom. This place had touched her soul, she thought, as she sauntered down the tree-lined road. And wherever they were in the future, the scent of rosemary would not only trigger thoughts of Italy, but the place by the sea that she called home.

Dust rose from her footsteps and a hare poked its head from a clump of brush. She had just put her bag next to a half-hidden log. A hazy mountain range awaited her attention, but the little critter had other ideas. He was flirting with her, darting back and peeking out again with a long ear cocked and his nose twitching. A small blue pickup truck growled toward them and the hare shot away in fear. The strange Piaggio was a three-wheeled Ape—pronounced ah-pay according to Marco when he'd offered another word for their new vocabulary. A smudged, jowly face leaned out from the efficient cab and the man touched his brown cap in greeting. The grassy aroma of new oil hit her nostrils and she wondered if the truck was from the Bernoli press. But before she could ask, the truck rumbled past, taking the scent with it. Vibrant herbs, truffles, wood smoke, grapes on the vine and olive trees—Tuscany in the fall—an intoxicating mixture. If only she could paint the different smells, she thought, as she began to draw the back end of the funny vehicle set against the blue mountain in the distance.

The day had never really warmed like the previous ones, and had passed without further traffic and only birds chirping in the distance. She sketched, took more photos and began a mental compilation of work—paintings for Donny Bales. Excitement flooded in. He ran a trendy new gallery in Portland that brought in a lot of the tourists, and local residents with large wall spaces so she wouldn't necessarily be confined to small pieces. The days had flown. Here it was Saturday and they only had till Monday to cram in everything they wanted to do. Between her day in the out-of-doors and Nick's tour with Marco, she wondered if they would even pay attention to the highly touted food at the *Ristorante Piccolo* in Greve that evening. Tomorrow would be nearly as hectic. As much as Prudence had wanted to chance a sighting of Ariel and Marcello in the grove, she and Nick would be heading south to Montepulciano to tour the small churches and whatever else they could find, and they were committed to meeting Marco's mamma, Nilda, before departing. Packing up her supplies for the day, Prudence could only imagine what the dynamics would be like between Lena and her mother-in-law.

Marco's truck was already in the driveway and as she neared the house, she heard voices coming from the great-room. The smell of wood smoke meant a fire had been lit in the kitchen where he and Lena would have their evening meal. Nick's laughter was like a warm hug, she thought, walking into the room.

"Ah, Prudenza," Marco called. "Join us for a little vino."

He obviously hadn't received the message Prudence had hoped to convey regarding her name.

Nick had made himself at home around Marco's wines and poured her a glass of Chianti from the sideboard bottles. "How was your day?"

"The tortoise and the hare," she laughed. "Saw one of those wonderful Piaggios and a giant rabbit at the same time and then I think I did more daydreaming than sketching—it was lovely," she said. "How about you?"

"Well, let's just say I'm glad I never had to run those stone presses and am happy for Marco's men that they have all this modern equipment now. The whole operation is impressive but in truth, I'm not sure I like the taste straight from the vat like that."

"Your palate is not used to such a taste," Marco said.

"It was thick, a funny green and tasted like vegetables—no offense Marco—but at least I tried it."

"I'm surprised you did, since you barely tolerate the kind of oil we buy at home, and I doctor that up with lemon juice and mustard in order to put it on your salads."

"Well, then you know what I mean."

"I take Nico to see the old *conca* that my grandfather used for storing the oil. The European government has forbidden the use of the terra cotta and now we must use the stainless steel containers and equipment, but it is good for the tourists to look into the past when you go into our cellars," said Marco.

"We brought you a tiny bottle so you can taste too, Pru…it's in the kitchen with Lena," Nick said.

"Thank you kind sirs," Prudence said.

Walking into the kitchen was like another hug. There sat Lena back-dropped by the inviting hearth where Luigi lounged. The wood smell mingled with the customary herbs and a *zuppa di fagioli,* bean soup, simmering on the stove. Lena looked up from a large desk calendar open to November. "We have two men from New York City for the olive *festa* next month and they ask to make the *cavatelli.* "

"Is that hard?"

"Just more work, *cara,* and I will like teaching the men. It is good they do this, no?"

"Si, but I won't expect the same from Nick. He's very happy to use the barbeque grill and that's about it."

"What time will you leave for Montepulciano tomorrow?"

"When does Nilda arrive?"

"*A mezzogiorno in punto.* " Lena said. "Exactly at noon."

"Okay then." Prudence reached in her bag for the dog-eared page of her pocket dictionary. "We will leave at *dodici e un quarto.* "

Lena clapped her hands. "Perfetto!"

"What's all this noise?" Nick said. "Are you having your own party?"

"I just told Lena we're heading out at 12:15 tomorrow. Speaking of heading out, I'd really like a short rest before we go into Greve."

Nick winked. "I'll join you."

"What do you recommend we have for dinner tonight?" Prudence said. "The *ristorante* is listed with three stars in the guide book."

"To try the truffle oil, you must eat the *insalada* with Parmigiana and for the mushrooms, eat the *risotto con funghi.* Maybe you eat the rabbit stew?" Lena said.

"Yikes, not after staring down that sweet hare this afternoon, not for me thank you very much!"

"I guess that means you don't want rabbit stew," Nick said.

Lena was laughing. "Ciao," she said waving them away.

"I got a little carried away, right?" Prudence said.

"That's okay, they understand," Nick said, ushering her out. "Ciao, Marco."

"Eat, walk, sleep, eat some more, sleep more, how will we ever get back to work?"

"I haven't a clue. I hate the thought of leaving all this but my brain has already been formulating paintings based on everything I've seen. At least I have photos and some rough sketches to back it all up."

"Just as long as I don't lose you to that studio the minute we step off the plane."

"Nick...we've had this conversation before. Please don't make this about ignoring you again. I'm comfortable about waiting a while before trying to get pregnant again, so that we can focus more on 'us', but even with my leaving the store to others, I can't be at your beck and call at home every day either."

"That's not what I meant and you know it."

"Then let's put it to rest, we only have a few days of living this life before Mainers start heralding in Halloween. Then we'll be decorating and planning for Thanksgiving and before we know it, it will be Christmas and there are only so many hours in a day. I told you about Donny Bales' new gallery, so you know I'll have a deadline. Since I'm feeling stronger, I don't intend to let myself go to that dark side either. I know my priorities."

"You're right, I'm just jealous of our time together. This trip has given me my girl back and I do respect your work ethic, believe me. I guess I just liked coming first."

"You are first in my heart," she said. "But don't you get it, if I can't have children, my work might be my only legacy."

He stared at her open-mouthed; he hadn't thought of that at all.

Nick's breath sputtered out in small snorts and she lay there rehashing his words. Why would he bring all that up again? She had made insecurity her middle name for many years, but he'd never gone that route, always on top of his game and confident. Tuscany and its environs had brought her back to life, made her feel whole, and here he was spouting nonsense. This better not become a habit, she thought, or she'd start sleeping at the studio just to make a point. Taking a stand was akin to wearing a shield of armor against feelings of inadequacy, but he hadn't gotten any of it.

Sleep had finally come, but at a price. Against her will, Prudence's mood stayed through dinner and into dessert—a rich, *tiramisu*, layered in liquor and sponge—and more wine than she needed. By the end of the evening, a pall hung over the table, heavy and silent with unspoken words. "Are you cross with me?"

"I thought you were being cross, not me."

"Let's both stop right now or we'll spoil this whole event. I choose to focus on Nilda and the thought of Lena's feisty mother-in-law should ease your good nature back into place. How 'bout it?"

"Okay sport, since we're playing a new game..."

"This isn't a game, Nick, it's us and we're important."

He finished his wine, paid the bill, and escorted her gently to the car. Once in the confines of the small rental, he leaned over and put his chin to the top of her head. "I'm sorry."

"Forgiven," she said.

No words were spoken for the duration of the drive except for pointing out a road sign or two and they let themselves into their room just as quietly. There was nothing more to say, she thought, but there remained a sliver of anger, the type that could fester if left untended. They undressed in silence and slid into the bed, side by side until their hands found each other under the cover. They touched, squeezed lightly, and murmured goodnight. "I love you," she said into the air.

"I love you too."

As had become habit, Prudence was up and out first, leaving Nick to his morning ablutions while she had coffee with their hostess. Lena was canny and immediately picked up on the change in Prudence's personality. "Che bella, what is wrong?"

"Nothing, why?"

"You have the expression like Luigi, no sparkle in your eyes and a frown on your forehead."

"Why are men so complicated, Lena? We were having such a good time and with one sentence, he spoiled everything."

"Not everything, cara, just one thing and it will change this morning. You will see, when he comes in for coffee, it will be gone. They are not complicated. Just boys in big pants."

"Who's getting new pants?" Nick asked entering the kitchen.

"No one, dear, Lena is mending Marco's." Such subterfuge, Prudence thought, but Lena had been right, he looked exactly like he had the morning before. Maybe the key was to wait these moments out before reacting. She had become deft at reactionary responses. "We'll wait to meet Nilda and then be on our way," she said to prove she was fine, too.

"I need lots of coffee if I'm going to tackle the highway again."

"I'll navigate."

Suddenly, there was a commotion in the other room.

"It is mamma," Lena said.

Prudence thought there had been an imperceptible straightening of shoulders as Lena ran her hands over her dress. There might as well have been fanfare for the way Signora Bernoli was ushered into the kitchen. Marco held a box—freshly made linguini—in front of him as if he were carrying a crown for royalty. The old woman had an aquiline nose that appeared pinched against an invisible odor. She wore black from head to toe and clasped her hands in front of her at the waist as if to avoid

97

contact with her surroundings. The only smile was Lena's. Marco appeared strained, but his wife knew how to handle Nilda.

"Mamma, these are our guests, Prudenza and Nico, from America!"

"Ah, *Americano!* She tilted her head at Nick, ignoring Prudence. *"Bell'uomo!"*

"Mamma is saying your husband is very handsome."

Nick's face blazed red. "Well, thank her for both of us," Prudence said. She was beginning to understand the reason the male ego was so strong here.

La signora turned to Lena, *"Tre minuti."*

"Si, mamma." Lena gave Prudence an eye roll. "She's making sure I know the pasta takes only three minutes to cook, as if I haven't done this my whole life."

"Please tell your mother it was lovely to meet her, Marco," Prudence said. It was time to make their exit. Lena's stress level was showing. Marco said something to his mother and she in turn, beamed at Nick. Her gaze lowered to meet Prudence's face, "e troppo magra."

"Mamma!"

"Scusa, Prudenza, but mamma speaks this way to all the young women, even her granddaughters," Marco said. "She is just saying you are a little thin."

Nick stifled a laugh and Pru pinched his hand. "My sentiments exactly," he said to Marco.

"I'm standing right here," Prudence said feeling like the third wheel. "Isn't it time we left, Nick?"

Lena walked them to the doorway, "Don't mind her, she likes to be the center of attention."

"We will talk in the morning, Lena." Prudence was beginning to believe that Rita Pelletier had a foreign clone. "Ciao," she said and hugged Lena goodbye.

"Ciao, and watch for the drivers."

Chapter Seven

Uphill, downhill, all around the square. Montepulciano was not for the meek in spirit or limb. It boasted many things. Among them: a battle for its allegiance won by Siena in 1260, its grand facades of the church of Saint Agostino and the Oratorio della Misericordia, and its two highly touted wines—Vino Nobile di Montepulciano and Rosso di Montepulciano.

Prudence read from their guidebook, "The main square is named Piazza Vittorio Emanuele, but everyone calls it Piazza Grande."

"Are you up for climbing that tower?" said Nick.

She checked the page for the hours the Town Hall Tower would remain open.

"Before we do that, I'd really like to see the famous painting of Santa Maria Assunta inside the Duomo."

Nick was beginning to lose interest. The list went on and on, and while he enjoyed the architecture of the medieval village, he had difficulty getting into the religious works of art and had begun to tune out the long names and pertinent dates Prudence was feeding him minute by minute. "Maybe we should stop and have a glass of their famous vino first."

"If we do that, you'll never get me up there," she said, pointing to the fortification with a smallish platform for viewing the countryside.

"It's not a very impressive building for a cathedral," Nick said as she led him toward the church.

"It was never really finished. The book says that they ran out of money, so it wasn't sheathed in marble as anticipated. They're stuck with the brick. But apparently, it's what's on the inside that makes it special—the interior architecture plus the rich painting by Sienese artist, Taddeo di Bartolo.

"Oh Nick!" The doors opened onto three long aisles. Another young couple and a single woman, all studying similar guidebooks, walked around them in silence. Many hands borne of different centuries had placed their mark, not only on this building, but on the entire ancient Etruscan city. Tourists were left to question every scroll and curlicue, fountain and wall, inscription and stone tablet, even the unexpected 'Punch' sculpture—of Punch and Judy fame—that clanged the hours on the clock tower.

Nick was walking down one of the side aisles, but Prudence tugged him toward the center. "Look at that!" A huge gold-hued triptych glorified the space, a painting that told the story of the assumption of the Virgin surrounded with smaller figures of saints. The detailing and use of colors were remarkable. She prattled on until she realized Nick had moved into one of the pews taking the guidebook with him.

"I'm sorry, but I'm getting hungry. I thought I'd find us a restaurant while you're looking around."

"It's unbelievable," she said turning away from him. "The old masters had techniques I will never learn and it only makes me want to try harder."

"They're all beginning to look alike," he said. "What do you say we hike that tower and then I'll take you to this *fattoria* just outside the walls?" Nick tapped the page. "It used to be a monastery, and we can eat and drink there instead of that pricey little tourist place in the square?"

There wouldn't be a lot more enthusiasm; she had pushed his limit of concentration on topics of light and color, and she knew better than to force the issue. "Okay, sweetheart, we can take that tower like the troupers we are and then you can wine and dine me."

At the entrance, they paid their fee, and Nick went in ahead of her. He needed this, she thought, bracing her palms against the walls, trying to widen the air shaft with her will. Her husband sought challenges, always had—whether racing boats or

100

jumping into the icy Maine water in January for a good cause or a simple hike up a tower to see an imagined kingdom. It seemed she had become his latest challenge, the realization that he would also be losing something when she left the bookstore for a new endeavor, one that could change their routines in a big way. This trip had served many purposes, the least of which was to open her eyes to Nick's insecurity within the confines of an artistic world. It wasn't that he wanted her tied with an apron and to the stove, but she would forego the general nine to five routine for those hours that might continue into the night if the spirit and ideas moved her. It was that drive that had so recently confounded him, an intangible stirring in her soul that pulled her out of bed at night to sketch an idea that had come in a dream. This is what he struggled with, she thought, a concept as alienating as understanding the techniques of Italian artists.

"Look at this!" Nick's words broke into her thoughts before she had time to dwell. They had reached the platform.

From this vantage point, a hush fell across Tuscany. The light, diluted of color, was stingy where it blurred the edge of the mountains as they disappeared into the sky. Tiled roofs created dimension, and far-away lakes mirrored the pale sheen from above. Trees stood dark and straight, lined in a row like soldiers, or clumped together as protection for the nearby farms. The verdant fields and striated rows of vegetation appeared to have been laid out with mathematical precision, squared off and angled, as if Da Vinci had had a hand from his place in the heavens.

"Oh Nick, this makes me want to cry it's so beautiful."

"Stand at the rail so I can take your picture."

She could not look down. "There's another small village on a hill," she said, shielding her eyes with her free hand. "Can you take the photos for me?"

"Are you okay?"

"It's the height…it's gorgeous up here, but it makes me a little dizzy.

101

"I'll get a shot from each angle and you can decide what you like," he said, snapping four or five in succession.

"I think I'm ready for that wine now."

"Thought you'd never ask."

Nick led the way down and she kept her hands on the comfort of solid walls as she had before.

"Did you check the time? Don't forget, these places close for a couple of hours between lunch and dinner."

"I screwed up," Nick said. "It's nearly three and they won't reopen until seven."

"Let's just grab a table over there." Relaxing under umbrellas, fellow tourists—backpacks at their feet—were sampling the local wine as they perused their maps and guidebooks.

"When in Rome," Nick said.

"Cute."

"Well, I'm trying to be adaptable."

"I think if we stayed longer, we'd be able to adjust our routines, but it looks like we'd better grab some of the famous Pecorino cheese and maybe a bottle of Chianti for later. Frankly, if I have a big bowl of Tuscan bean soup and crusty bread right now, I'll be all set."

"You win. I'll just have the extra-large bowl."

Fortunately, other patrons were lingering over their meals, making it easier for Prudence and Nick to fit in a quick order of soup and bread. Afterward, they picked up some cheese and wine to take back to Casa Bernoli.

"Another great day," Nick said, getting behind the wheel of the rental.

"Absolutely," Prudence said. "It's flown by and there's only one more place I'd like to see before we leave tomorrow."

"What's that?"

"The church of San Nicolo."

"Well, that makes perfect sense. After all, I am rather saintly."

"*Right!*"

"Isn't that the church in the brochure?" Nick said. Take a look at the map and see if it's an easy route from the farm."

"It is, and we can do that as soon as we get back and uncork this lovely wine. It's our last night to speak to the moon from our private terrace."

"You have become the ultimate romantic." Nick said.

"It's going to be strange hearing the surf again, isn't it?"

"Probably...for about a minute." Nick said.

"Well, you have to admit, this has been nearly perfect."

"Nearly?"

"Until Nilda decided to dis me."

"She got under your skin, didn't she?"

"Sort of. Truthfully, I think she reminded me of my own mother. Maybe that's why I sympathize with Lena," Prudence said.

"I've watched the way you two communicate; you've gotten close."

"We've promised to stay in touch, and I hope we do. She's very special. It's going to be hard to say goodbye."

"Their car is gone. I bet they're at Aldo's," Prudence said. "Lena mentioned having dinner over there this week. I'll leave a note in the kitchen about our change in plans so we won't miss seeing Marco in the morning."

While Prudence went into the main house, Nick took the wine and cheeses to the small table in front of their room. The cat had been waiting for their return and wound herself around Nick's leg, emitting a loud purr. "Gonna miss you too." He knelt to pick her up.

"Caught you!"

"She loves me; what can I say?"

"You feed her, that's why."

"We set for tomorrow?"

"Yes. I wrote that we'd have an early coffee and head for Radda immediately after. She'll be disappointed, but she'll understand."

"According to the map, we have about a four-hour drive from Radda to the airport. Allowing for car return and check-in, we're going to be cutting it close."

"What do you think?"

"I'm game if you are," Nick said. "We only have to throw a few things in the suitcase, grab some coffee and say our goodbyes. Of course, we'll have to take into consideration women shedding tears, but we can handle it."

"We?"

"Me and Marco."

"Pour me some of that wine—please."

"Yes dear, and by the way, it's excellent."

"So is this Pecorino," Prudence said. She broke down and picked off a tiny piece for the cat. "Did we ever learn what her name is?"

"Marco calls her Clara."

"Well, she's their cat, but I would call her Mimi."

"What kind of a name is Mimi for a mouse catcher?"

"A pretty name for a sweet kitty," Prudence said stroking the cat's ears.

Night closed in, holding them rapt in the mystery of shadowy hills and trees. "Goodbye landscape, goodbye cat, goodbye Italian lifestyle…"

"That extra glass of vino got to you, didn't it?"

Prudence got up and kissed Nick full on the lips. "Well, I guess it did."

Nick grabbed their glasses while the cat remained unconcerned under the table, cleaning her face with a fluffy paw. "Clara, you keep an eye out for intruders," he said following Pru to their room in anticipation.

Prudence, curled up like a child with her hand tucked under one cheek—that's just the way Nick wanted to remember their trip, he thought, as he watched his wife in peaceful sleep. He slipped from the room to clear off the terrace table, his bare feet padding with caution. The old fixture hinged to the outside wall afforded little light. Its glow encircled where the cat had been, but not enough to cut through the coal black night. Nick had just gathered everything when headlights in the distance halved the darkness, catching him in their glare. The Bernolis returning home, he thought, aware of his nakedness. Pru stirred as he re-entered the room, but did not wake. He slid beneath the cover and whispered, "We'll come back again, I promise."

Chapter Eight

It had been a tearful farewell. Marco kept patting Nick on the back, perhaps the son-in-law he would have liked to have, and Lena hugged Prudence and simultaneously put more food into a sack for them to eat along the way. Committing to a return visit had made it easier on both women, but still Prudence cried most of the way to Radda. Time was the enemy that morning, and since cars were not allowed within the center of the small city, they had only managed a peek into the Church of San Nicolo and a quick photo-op of the exterior with their limited time. It was not a remarkable building, having been partly bombed during World War II, but it had brought on the need for Prudence to bow her head for a brief, silent prayer. The gesture was not lost on Nick. And even after they had boarded the plane and gone through all the inflight instructions, he had been reluctant to ask what Pru had prayed for, hoping not to disturb the aura that had grown around them. He knew the emptiness she still faced back home in the small room that was to have been a nursery.

Much to Nick's amazement, Pru had fallen asleep in-flight, only awakening as the dinging and pinging and commands spat from the loudspeakers. "We're in New York, honey."

"I was dreaming that I was painting with gold leaf and it was sticking to everything but where it was supposed to."

"Should we have the Newcombs for dinner this week so that you can show off your new talents?"

"Maybe not this week, but soon. Let me get myself sorted out and have a look through the photos first before I work on our social calendar. I promised Kate I would share Lena's recipes, but first I need to get my head around what I'm going to do for the Bales' gallery if I'm going to have Donny's support."

Nick kept his thoughts to himself as he collected their things from the overhead bin. It bothered him more that it bothered him at all, that she could switch gears so rapidly. "We need to run for our connecting flight. If you like, we could stay over in Portland, maybe have breakfast in bed like we used to."

"Why not, it's probably the last chance we'll have for a while to be so pampered."

"Then pampered it is," he said. They made their way through customs and the throngs of people heading for the myriad gates, arriving at theirs with only minutes to spare.

The flight into Portland had been turbulent, the hotel not quite up to their memories, and their exhaustion apparent late Tuesday morning when they pulled into Thatcher Lane. "Coming home to this house is the only thing that makes leaving Tuscany bearable," Prudence said.

"I see its appeal, but I still think we'd be better off with a newer one."

Learn not to react, she thought, catching a whiff of the sea and instantly remembering the aromatic herb. "I'm going to Olsen's Greenhouse this week and buy us a large rosemary plant. I think I can keep it going through the winter if I put it in the sunny corner with the orchids." She unlocked the door, dropped her suitcase and rushed to the kitchen.

"Look, Kate hasn't managed to kill your plants," Nick said from behind.

"I won't tell her you said that."

Prudence looked at the suitcases, but all she could think of was an outline for the new series she had in the back of her mind all during the flight. Tired as she was, she was pumped, and high on artistic adrenaline. Nick had given her an exquisite holiday, provided the basis for new ideas and loved her with more fervor than she could remember experiencing. What happened next was all on her. Relationships never became less fragile, she thought, they just created new cracks to fall through if one weren't paying attention. Again, it was all about balance.

Kate had left a note: Food in the fridge, quiche ready for the oven, plants watered. Will call tomorrow as I know you'll be tired. Love, Kate.

"What a great friend," Prudence said.

"I'm going to toss my laundry in the hamper and then I thought I'd run by the office and see how they fared."

"Don't forget your gifts; they're in the carry-on bag. I'll catch up with Vivien and Kate tomorrow and give them theirs."

"Need anything while I'm out?"

"Grab a paper so we can see who did what to whom while we were away."

"Which reminds me, I'd better check on Lloyd too."

After Nick left, Prudence changed into a more comfortable outfit, throwing an old zip-up sweater over a turtleneck tee. The house was chilly, so she prepped the fireplace for his return. The sky was clear but the sun lacked the feel of an Indian summer. Who knew what the rest of October would hold. With the change in season, her daylight hours in the studio were even more precious. There was an intimacy innate within coastal villages, she thought, taking in the familiar surroundings. And like the others, Oyster Cove would soon go dark without divulging secrets behind its closed doors.

There was no way she was going to unpack, she thought, not while she could still move. She would crash after she checked her art supplies to make sure she had everything in stock that she would need. Grabbing her jacket, Prudence headed for the old reliable 'Beetle', knowing full well it would start right up, as always. The urge to see her studio was greater than the urge to mull. The little engine that could, chugged awake like a tired lawn mower, but like the house, she refused to part with it. There had been potential buyers, many over the years, who had stuck notes on the windshield or in her mailbox and even inquiring with Zack, the mechanic at the gas station, who had worked on it from the beginning. The little white 'Bug' had required a lot of TLC back then, and if she ever relented, he'd be the person she would sell to, his lust for the late 70s model always apparent. Not for a long while, though, she thought, lovingly patting the dash as she drove away.

The water glinted like shards of glass. Cleaned by nature, the weathered driftwood, docks and floats and shiny boat hulls had returned to postcard perfect. She parked and getting out of the car, the smell of diesel struck her. The elixir of the harbor, she thought, as she walked the rest of the way to her studio.

Once inside, the faint smell of stale paint blended with that of seaweed drying in low tide beneath the deck. Her footsteps echoed against the board floor as she opened the window. On the new shelf, ready to catch the light breeze, were her silent companions, those early painters of Maine who resided within the collected volumes: Henri, Bellows, Hopper, Wyeth and Kent. She now understood the impact of her first trip to Monhegan and how it had influenced their work. Many had taken up residence in cabins like this one on that magical island. Long ago those artists established a reputation that still lured painters to its high cliffs and cathedral woods.

Mentally measuring canvases, new ideas floated in off the sea, and as she breathed deeply of the organic fragrance, something happened—an imagined seascape. Taking a 9 x 12 canvas and a #4 bristle brush, she began to sketch by rote with thinned Raw Umber oil paint. Conjuring the incoming waves and their sound as they tumbled pell-mell to kiss the rocks and then tug the heart as they retreated, she began to scumble in the necessary shadows, along the wave line where the presumed light would fall. An hour flew by and her brush moved in synchronicity with her brain until she had enough formulated to leave it for another day. It was an exercise that had always propelled her out of stagnancy and created the momentum for new work. Each artist had their favorite routines and this was hers. Even if left unfinished, the movement had been enough to shake out the cobwebs. The pre-trip doldrums had been vanquished.

Nick returned to an empty house. Maybe she had gone to Kate's after all, he thought, until he noticed her shorthand indicating she was at the studio. Pulling a beer from the fridge, he began to pace. Should he drop in on her to show that he was interested? No—because he wanted to talk about what he'd heard at the office, not more art legends. Instead, he changed jackets and mixed a jug of Clorox and water with an attached spray nozzle and went out the front door to clean the mold that had built up in the previous month. It always helped to be physical when he wanted to quell his frustration. He was still there, having worked his way around the side when Prudence pulled up.

"And I didn't even have to ask," she said, getting out of the car.

"I figured it would get ahead of me if I didn't. How are things at the waterfront?"

"Lovely. I think Jake has a new stern man, but I wasn't close enough to see who it was. The Paulsens waved from their rowboat; they'll be leaving soon too. I don't think they had a very good season because of all the rain. None of the schooners went out much last month. The harbor is already less populated than when we left, but the ghosts and goblins are out—lots of pumpkins too. Would you mind getting us a big pumpkin for the front step? I'm not in the mood to do much more, but I hate to seem anti-social."

"Sure, but you're not going to believe this. Dickie had to handcuff a couple of 'leaf peepers' last week. They were filching tee shirts from Clausen's, and then one took a swing at him with her shopping bag when he tried to confront them!"

"No!"

"I bet he won't turn his back on any old lady ever again. Oh, and I told him we'd have them over for dinner one of these days soon to sample your fabulous pasta."

"Nick, please, I'm more than happy to share my new prowess in the kitchen, but you're getting ahead of me. I promise I'll give Debbie a call and set something up with them, maybe when we have the Newcomb's over, but probably later in the month, okay?"

"Just trying to spread the joy."

"Speaking of joy, wait till you taste Kate's quiche." Prudence said.

"Does it have curry in it? I really don't like curry."

"For your information, she got pretty tired of it too after a year in India."

"Just wondering."

Prudence went into the house to put the quiche in the oven. "It'll be fine, you'll see." She poured a glass of red wine.

Nick followed, "We should get a case of the Montepulciano, so we'll have it for the holidays."

"That's the spirit. Now, while you're finishing up outside, I think I'll unpack while dinner heats up."

"You were right, her quiche was terrific," Nick said. "Are you as tired as I am?"

"Uh huh." Prudence picked up the dishes and put them in the dishwasher. "Is eight too early to go to bed?"

"Not tonight, it isn't." He turned off the light and grabbed her hand. "We can finish up in the morning."

"I see you're not *too* tired," Prudence said as they undressed.

"What can I say?"

"Feels funny not to roll to the middle."

"But it's nice to be back in our own bed again," Nick said, pulling her to him.

"You're here! I've missed you." Kate greeted Prudence at the door and pulled her inside as though she had been gone for a month.

"I brought you a little gift from the Ponte Vecchio; it had your name all over it."

"Earrings...oh they're gorgeous! Kate said. She opened the gift box and removed the studs she'd been wearing, and threaded the new hoops into her pierced earlobes. Then she turned her head back and forth in front of the mirror. "They're the perfect size, thank you."

"You're welcome. I thought they'd suit you, and I can't thank you enough for taking care of things while we were gone."

"You do the same for me, silly. And you may have to soon enough. The powers that be are already lining something up for Michael, but I'm getting ahead of myself. *You* look wonderful."

"And you were right, it brought me back to life. I had no idea it would be so beautiful and that eating would be so enjoyable again. But I can't say enough about Lena Bernoli. She had me believing I might have a little Italian in my blood—isn't that a hoot? But all kidding aside, I really believe we were meant to know each other; she called it *simpatico.*"

"That's a nice compliment. Funny, it's the way I thought of you and Julie when we first met."

"Me too. I promise we'll have that pasta-making lesson and even a dinner party as soon as I get organized. We brought back the cutest pasta machine and I haven't even unpacked it yet. I'm too anxious to start painting to try and make dough."

"I understand; it's an overload thing."

"Sensory overload...that's it. I couldn't think of the term. We went everywhere and saw everything we had time for, but I have to say, I sensed a change in Nick as soon as we opened our front door. He was so relaxed having me all to himself, and one night even mentioned trying for a baby again. Not right this moment, but in the near future."

"Oh that is good news."

"Yes and no...Now that the opportunity has shown up, I'd like to get my feet wet in the Portland art scene before taking on the role of full-time mother. I know what I'm like, and I'd want to be hands on with a baby instead of dropping it off at daycare. Our girl Julie has mentioned more than once in her letters, how quickly Addie has changed from day to day, and we've tried too hard to get pregnant for me to miss anything."

"You don't suppose you're just avoiding the possibility of loss again."

"Maybe, I don't really know. But I do know that I have to work at what I love."

You're probably right, not that I would know, but I'm sure Julie has learned enough for both of us."

"That she has; gosh I miss her." Prudence followed Kate into her bedroom.

"Me too," Kate said. She put her precious diamond studs in the jewelry box tucked into a drawer. "So what's next on your agenda?"

Prudence sat on the edge of the bed while Kate changed her hairstyle to show off the new hoops. While in Italy she had seen a woman who was the spitting image of Julie, wearing identical ones, and the yearning for the friendship that began on St. Thomas had reasserted itself. "I got a pair just like those for Julie," Prudence said. "After this, I'm off to see Vivien."

"I miss Julie too," said Kate. "She'll be back, don't worry."

"I know, I guess I'm just feeling a little melancholy for that first summer in Oyster Cove. I'll snap out of it, and I'm anxious to bring Vivien her gift."

"It's only been a week, but we have lots to catch up on," Kate said.

"I'm not rushing off, but I do want to find out what's happening at the bookstore, and then I want to lay out all my ideas for that one-woman show while it's still fresh in my mind."

"My friend, the artist. I can say I knew her when."

"Hah, don't go getting ahead of me. First things first."

Prudence whizzed through the minutia of the flight and the lengthy drive, and with descriptive details brought Kate to the Bernoli's doorstep. "It was the most romantic place I've ever seen. And you were absolutely right about everything."

"I'm so glad. I was worried about you."

"Don't be, I'll be okay." Prudence couldn't bear nitpicking her husband's concerns; she'd said enough for today. He was sure to come around once he saw how much it meant to her.

"Oh God, look at the time. I really have to run, Kate, or I won't have time to catch Vivien."

"We'll talk soon," Kate said as she opened the door for Prudence. "I still have to tell you the rest of the town gossip. Ciao, for now, and grazie for the beautiful gift."

Prudence took one look at the interior of North Sky Books and was shocked by the transformation in such a short time. The shelves had been moved around and her favorite color had been covered over with a pale green paint. A little institutional, she thought, as she made her way through the maze in front of Vivien's desk.

"Are you in there?" Prudence said.

"You're back," Vivien said from behind the chaos. "We've been in the middle of housecleaning so don't trip over anything, please."

Prudence digested the look, "Are you remodeling?"

"Not really, just moving things around so we can paint and give it a fresh look for the holidays. I thought it made sense since we've had it like this for six years."

What was there to say, Prudence thought, that the color is crap? It would be silly to tell Vivien her feelings were hurt because she hadn't been consulted or even warned. Prudence had stepped away, and Vivien had taken charge, as expected. "I wanted to bring your gift by before I got busy."

"The box is too small for an Italian," Vivien mocked.

"Little guy," Prudence said.

"Very funny...oh, this is beautiful." Vivien wrapped the scarf twice around her neck, leaving room to slip one end through the loop so that it would fall to the front with style.

"It suits you," Prudence said.

"I love it!"

"Is there anything I can do to help; you look like you've got your hands full."

"Not really, not unless you just want to hang for a while and tell me all about your trip."

"I can, for a little while anyway."

By the time Prudence had regaled Vivien with all the places and nuances of her newly discovered country, it was time to think about dinner. As she got up to leave, she took a closer look at the wall. Naturally, she thought, green in any shade—Vivien's signature color.

"I'm so glad you came by," said Vivien, "and I hope you don't mind that we replaced the terra cotta paint."

"Not really," she lied. "Green suits you, but after being in Italy, I'd probably start all over and paint in ochres and blues. Maybe I'll do that to my studio walls; you never know."

Time had gotten away from her. It was nearly five and she hadn't done everything she had planned. Loud strains of Vivaldi's Four Seasons filled the Thatcher Lane kitchen as Prudence directed the legendary orchestra with her spatula. She hadn't made it to the studio, but that hadn't stopped her brain from walking through the oneiric visions as the smell of meatloaf in the oven permeated the air.

"You looked like you were in a trance," Nick yelled into the room.

Only then did she hear the cries of gulls wheeling just beyond their window. "Just daydreaming about a show," she said, turning down the volume.

"Smells good in here."

"Meatloaf and mashed potatoes."

"Perfetto!"

"We haven't said that once since we came home; thank you for reminding me," she said, kissing him tenderly.

They would be okay, she thought, if they could just keep finding that balance. She would prove to him that the hours were worth it, that she had something to offer, and if not, at least she would have tried. "Let's eat in front of the fire tonight?"

"Fine with me. That fireplace is one of the things I actually love about this house."

Prudence didn't respond; at least he really liked that, and no amount of talking would change his mind about an aging building that would continually need work. But she was in too good a mood to say anything at all. Instead, she pulled out the trays and cutlery and poured him a drink. She could hear him humming as he fiddled with the logs, getting them stacked just right for a proper blaze. He always added more to whatever she had put in place—it was a 'guy thing' he'd often said. Pulling the meatloaf from the oven, she thought of all the times she had heard that phrase and until she had married Nick, she never really understood. As she watched his frame through the doorway to the living room, she realized how manly the task really was and how it suited him. She carried in the trays; it was going to be a really nice evening.

Chapter Nine

As the calendar rolled toward 2006, the days grew shorter and Prudence's studio—plunged into seasonal darkness—glowed from within. The stretch between Halloween and Christmas would pass with the usual blur of color: pumpkins, marigolds, and faded lawns playing host to numerous straw people clothed in red and green checkered shirts. Historically, with the first dusting of snow, Oyster Cove glittered from rooftops to door yards where conifers imitated their indoor counterparts. Through it all, the bookstore window would reflect each holiday as portrayed by Vivien's talents and now aided by Ursula's deft hand. Tantalizing aromas filled household kitchens and invitations were exchanged: dinner parties, cocktail parties and potluck suppers. The Pelletier's were once again circling each other with care.

"Want me to get a tree while I'm out on Route 1 today?" Nick said.

"Sure, but not as big as the one last year, okay?"

"Fine. Are we going to do anything for Christmas?"

Whatever tranquility protected their peace after their arrival back home, had dissipated into thin air as Prudence threw herself into her work, once again shortcutting her meals and exercise habits, all the things Dr. Gordon would chastise her for. "Please don't be that way," Prudence said. "I'm trying my best, and I will, I promise, have our friends over for a meal very soon."

"Seems like you've been saying that for weeks. It's embarrassing."

"Why should it be, everyone knows I'm working."

"Because we said we would, that's why."

"You're being unreasonable. You've known my schedule for weeks now."

"And that makes it okay?"

"I didn't say that."

Now you've done it, Prudence thought, as the slammed door reverberated throughout the house. She had feared this would happen. Having pushed his patience, she had worked day and night as she readied for her very first gallery show, scheduled for the sixth of January. Then, she had hired Tony Moss to sit for her in the mornings, primarily unclothed. The idea of working with a model had tapped into a new energy source, and while she had been in her element, trying new colors and glazing compounds, Nick had been building his case just as he'd done before they had gone to Italy. Why he couldn't understand was beyond her, but she loved him too much to ruin their holiday. Taking the wall calendar down, she began to jot a few dates to present to their friends. Then she picked up the phone.

Nick had cooled off as soon as he smelled the fresh cut pines stacked against the shed at the tree farm. Even in forty degrees, the scent reminded him of the flourishing herbs in Tuscany and that memory helped to ease his jealousy. It was foolish he knew, to be angry with Prudence for doing what she was meant to do. In truth, his venting had more to do with his mother than with his wife. Unbeknownst to Pru, his mother had been calling his office instead of the house. Every word Rita Pelletier flung across the miles was meant to remind him of his familial duty. As a result, he had been secretly sending her money; her debts had gotten out of control since his father's death, and she had somehow run through the insurance money. Prudence would kill him if she knew he was expected in Denver to figuratively extricate her from the potential clutches of the IRS. Talk about a rock and a hard place, he thought, mentally juggling his business calendar. Christmas was right around the corner, and Pru's show right after that.

Nick tied the medium-size fir to the top of his jeep, the upside-down cone shape a reminder of Christmases past, the scent of balsam temporarily spiriting away the worry. At that moment, he wanted Pru in his arms. In that vein, he stopped at the market and picked up a poinsettia plant and a California red for dinner. He had to tell her, he thought, but not tonight.

Prudence untied her paint-smeared apron and hung it from the edge of the easel. She had used her time wisely, and Tony had just proven that he was a good model. Today was mostly about matching skin tone and defining male musculature on a slim body before the real work began. He was well-built but not in the way of someone who worked out constantly. More of a cyclist's body, she had noted when they first met and confirmed again when he'd undressed today.

"We're almost done here," she said.

"I'm in no hurry."

"No, but I am." While Tony was easy on the eyes, she hadn't told Nick that he was also a flirt. Innocent enough, but still, not something her husband would understand. "There, all set."

"You sure I can't buy you a coffee or maybe a drink?"

"Thanks, but I need to get home."

"Maybe some other time then, when you're in the mood," Tony said, getting into his jeans.

She knew exactly what that look meant, but it was hard to find a model in a small village like this, especially a man with Tony's appeal. Prudence was taking a chance, she knew, but ideas flowed freely as she pictured the canvases she hoped would entice Donny into a second show: Tony, clothed in a white dress shirt for a night out; Tony wearing western boots and a towel draped strategically; Tony, with his back to her, cowboy hat in hand, offering an over-the-shoulder look which would speak volumes and a stance to accentuate the lines and angles of his body from head to toe. That trip to Florence had been the impetus for such bravado in her own work. This wouldn't be like the statue in front of the Uffici, but if she pulled it off, it would make people smile.

Set off to the other side of the studio, the Italian series—larger canvases than originally planned, leaning against the wall—was ready to be framed. The scenes filled that area: undulating hills, partial ruins and her favorite grove where the chairs had been discovered, and all accomplished with the foreign-bought paints best to interpret the landscape. And skies created by her own evolution of color choices, to create the cornflower blue—all remembered visions. The smallest piece was the one featuring the departing, dusty *Ape*, and the driver waving the telltale backward hand signal. She had titled it 'Ciao'.

After Tony left, Prudence sat in the rocker in front of the stove watching the last of the sparks die out while she changed from her work shoes into her boots. It had been a truly productive day. Nick would be pleased that she would be at home to decorate a tree and surprised when she told him about the extended invitations—the Bronsons and the Newcombs for a dinner party this coming Sunday, the week before Christmas. Kate was going to come over during that afternoon to watch her prepare the pasta dough and take notes. That would take the pressure off while Prudence cleaned up, since Kate would insist on helping and no one set a prettier table than Kate.

Nick had the tree in its stand when Prudence arrived home. He'd changed into his navy blue fleece—half of their wardrobes consisted of varying shades and weights of L.L. Bean's finest—and flannel pajama bottoms that he never slept in. The fire was blazing and two wineglasses rested on a corner table.

"It's perfect," she said. "And what a nice bottle."

"An old favorite, and my way of saying sorry."

"Me too. I'm finished with the series, for the most part anyway, so I can relax a little. And, I've invited our friends over for Sunday dinner."

"Fantastic!"

"Now, if you'll pour me a glass of that wine, I'll run up and get the lights from the hall closet," she said, pulling off her boots. "Hope you don't mind burgers for dinner; I didn't have time to plan anything else."

"Burgers and fine wine…a total American classic."

Peristalsis knotted his gut—the booked flight and Pru's expected reaction—forcing him to bolt for the downstairs bathroom. He made it back to the living room just in time.

"Why so glum?" Prudence walked in, dressed a little like her husband but in different colors.

"Just thinking about work." Nick was certain LIAR was written across his forehead.

"Do we have to send Christmas cards this year?"

"I don't know, do we?"

"Maybe I'll do up a holiday letter instead since I'm so behind. It takes too long to write individual messages. Would you mind?"

"No, that works for me."

Pru handed him the box and picked up her glass. "Here you go. I'll get the burgers ready while you get started on the lights."

Nick plugged them in, which revealed three or four dead spots on the strip. He sipped his wine as he searched the box for extra bulbs. As he replaced the bad ones, he contemplated the mess he'd gotten himself into. The homey aroma of grilled burgers came from the kitchen, the stovetop cast iron griddle having replaced the need to shovel snow to get to the barbecue unit on the deck even though he loved to grill outside.

"Let's eat by the fire," Nick hollered. He never could resist this fireplace.

"Fine, but come and get the ornaments from the high shelf in the cupboard, please." Prudence watched as he set the three small boxes down on the counter, part of his face in shadow. Something was bothering him, she thought, that had nothing to do with her.

"Are you okay?"

"Sure, why?" Nick said.

"I don't know, just a feeling I guess."

Should he or shouldn't he? He turned one of his famous smiles on her and hoped he could pull it off, "Just thinking about your Christmas present."

"Nothing too expensive," she said. "We spent a bundle in Italy."

"Not to worry."

"You say that, but I do, especially now that my funds are on a limited payout."

While they'd been in Italy, Nick had bought her a simple gold ring inlaid with her birthstone. But imagining the coming debacle over his mother, he had special-ordered a small collection of Italian cookbooks before he'd left the office, just to appease his guilt. "Can we eat now?"

"Changing the subject won't help. We promised one gift only and within reason, remember?"

"Okay, okay, but you won't hold it against me if I got two, right?"

"You're hopeless, you know."

The fire crackled and the alcohol did little to soothe away his rough edges. As he ate, his stomach churned with all the unsaid truths; it was killing him. "All we need is that final touch on the top of the tree."

"It does look good, doesn't it?" They sat there bathed in the mixture of burning cedar wood and scented candles. She removed their trays and returned with coffee, taking in the way the miniature white tree lights resembled the fireflies of her youth.

"All of this makes me think of Hannah and the hard life she led while making memories in this room. I wonder how she and

Tim would have brought in the New Year. We're really very lucky."

"I know." He smoothed the hair away from her eyes. "My mother wants me to come back to Denver right after Christmas," he blurted.

"What!"

"Hang on. Let me explain before you go all wild-eyed."

"This better be good."

Nick started slowly. But even though he made a good case for the pleading phone calls and how bereft his mother had sounded, he could not bring himself to tell Pru about the loaned money. Mostly, because it wasn't really a loan; he'd never get it back. "So you see, she's in trouble, and I'm all she has now. I can't turn my back on her, can I?"

"You're asking the wrong person, sweetheart. But you go ahead, fly out there the day after Christmas. Just remember, if you don't make it back in time for my show, you'd better plan to stay there a lot longer."

Nick's stomach churned again with unsaid words. Pru's face in that moment would haunt him for a long time. "Can't you try and understand, please."

"Isn't there any other way you can *try* and solve her problems without leaving?"

"Don't you think I'd like that? Since Dad died she hasn't been the same."

"You underestimate her, Nick. She's savvy and she's tough. You just can't see it because she has you wrapped around her arthritic fingers."

"That's just plain mean and you know it."

"We'll see." Prudence's temper was reaching a crescendo. The gall of that woman, she thought, not just rotten timing, but so very Rita. She got up from the couch.

"Pru, wait. I don't want to spend the next two weeks fighting. We can still have a great Christmas, and I'll be back from Denver before you know it."

"Fuck Denver," she yelled from the stairwell.

Now he'd done it. Ruined a perfectly good evening, blew any chance of staying in her good graces until he had to leave; he would be a pariah by this Sunday's dinner party. He stayed put in front of the fire until sleep clawed at his eyes and the flames had burned completely out. Pru wasn't in their bed and he knew better than to seek her out in the guest room. When she was really pissed, she never tossed him out of their room, preferring instead to leave him totally alone to ponder his misdeeds. To his credit, he thought, this grandstanding had only happened on two other occasions during their five-year marriage. It still hurt, and more to the point, he deserved it. Nothing would have been accomplished had he waited longer, but he might have salvaged some pride if he had told her when the calls first began.

Breakfast and his wife's presence, were both absent when Nick walked into the kitchen the next morning. He filled the reservoir on the coffee maker, dumped in the requisite scoops of French roast, and then confirmed that her anorak, woolen scarf and boots were missing from their spot in the alcove. She's at the studio, he thought, feeling worse than he had the night before. He had hardly slept, tossing over the ways in which he might be able to help Rita and remain in Maine. The family lawyer had been called upon, but because he was about to retire, said he wasn't up to the challenge, though he and Charlie Pelletier had been golfing buddies and Nick had tried a play for sympathy. Rita's situation required more finesse and time than the attorney could muster. It was going to be a very long day, Nick thought, perhaps the longest ever.

Prudence threw her brushes, flung the books from their shelves and stomped her feet—her anger peaking just as Tony stuck his head in the door. "Hey, what's all this?"

"None of your business."

"Ouch, that hurt. Want coffee?"

"Oh, all right," she said, suddenly embarrassed by her display of emotion. "What are you doing here so early?"

"Can't really say, but I'm glad I am. You could use some help." He began picking up the clutter she had so strategically thrown. "Glad this isn't paint."

"I'm crazy mad, but I'm not stupid."

"Let's go get some coffee and you can tell me all about it."

"Fine."

Prudence trudged along beside him, her wool tam tugged over her ears and her mood as dark as early morning seawater. Poor guy didn't know what he'd gotten himself into, she thought, as they rounded the corner to the General Store. She stopped in her tracks, a moment's hesitation as she thought of the gossip about to be promulgated by this one act. A handsome, younger man—a stranger—and a fairly well known married woman, out walking in the dreary cold at this hour of the morning. All she needed now was the appearance of Lloyd Tucker and her day would be complete.

Chairs scraped the pine boards and heads turned. Coffee cups clanked and voices rose as if to emphasize that no one was paying attention when she and Tony walked through the door and approached the counter.

"Two coffees, please," Tony said.

"I'll grab us a table." Prudence headed toward the only table for two out of earshot of the counter. The girl at the register was taking her time, leaning into Tony as she pointed out the fresh sweet rolls and cinnamon-sprinkled doughnuts specially made by the owner each Christmas season. Prudence prickled at the sound of a familiar voice.

"Mornin' Prudence." Lloyd had sidled up next to her chair.

"Hey Lloyd."

"Gettin' an early start, I see."

"Yep, that's me, a workaholic."

"Here's your coffee," Tony said.

Lloyd's head whipped around. "Well, hello there young fella—thought you were Nick."

Prudence left the pained smile on her face and introduced Tony. "My assistant," she said, knowing Lloyd would not know the difference.

"Well, you two have a nice day." Lloyd tipped his hat and walked over to the counter.

"Be prepared. We are grist for the gossip mill today."

"You're too sensitive. What does it matter?"

"You're right, but today is not the day to be testing whether or not it matters."

"Anything you'd like to share?"

"No, but thanks for asking. Are you still working on your thesis by the way?"

"Yeh, but with the holidays and extra hours bartending, its slow going."

"I barely finished the gallery work in time myself," Prudence said. "It's hard to be split in so many directions."

"Speaking of, do you really need me this morning? Seems like maybe you might need a day off, and I could use the time to get my car registered."

"I'm just going to futz around there for a while, thanks, but you do what you need to. I'll give you a call when I'm ready." The day was shot, she thought, and productivity would be replaced by a mixture of anger and worry.

Nick hesitated at the door of Pru's studio. "Okay if I come in?"

"Beware of artists throwing paint," Prudence said. Her initial anger had barely softened. "Are you here to tell me something else about my mother-in-law?"

"Easy girl. I just wanted to apologize and try and explain."

"What's to explain? You're walking out just when I need your support. And frankly, I don't give a damn about Rita right now."

"That's harsh and you don't really mean it."

"Don't I?" Prudence had lost her filters the day she had faced her own demons in this very same space months before. "Don't test me Nick. Your mother is playing you—she always has. Charlie saw it, rest his soul, but he was the buffer."

"That is not fair and you know it. She was very concerned about you when you miscarried."

"Right. How blind you are."

"Enough. This is ridiculous. What if she were ill or dying?"

"Then I might be more inclined toward understanding."

"I can't fight anymore. I've booked my flight and I'm returning on the fifth of January. That should give me enough time."

"Do what you have to do." Prudence turned her back and pretended to be tidying her supplies. Even she wondered at her stubbornness. He wouldn't go if it weren't important, would he? Was she making too much out of her one-woman event? It might open to a lackluster crowd, or no crowd at all. "I know you'll do your best to get back on time."

"I will." Nick walked up behind her and wrapped her in his arms. "Thanks for cutting me some slack here. See you back home later."

Tears fell as soon as he had closed the door. This room had become the repository for so many emotions. If walls could talk, these would weep for all that she had shared. Her paintings appeared less joyful than they had the day before, but she would find her way again. Of that she was certain.

Chapter Ten

Thatcher Lane, like all of Oyster Cove, lived and breathed by the seasons, and it wasn't only the aging fishermen who awoke in the cold morning hours with aching joints. Even relative youngsters like Nick and Prudence suffered from repetitive strains, particularly hauling and stacking wood. As the temperature dropped, it took longer and longer for the pint-sized demon in the corner of the studio to crank out suitable warmth; Prudence was never warm enough. Officially, winter arrived just before the red-suited hero made his journey from the North Pole. Hardening ice rinks and pumping furnaces attested to the changes, and residents of the northeast battened down the proverbial hatches against the storms that would come. Children prayed for snow, lots of it.

The long-awaited dinner party had been a near-disaster; the pasta machine clogged up with Prudence's first attempt at using it. In a state of utter despair, she had enlisted Kate to procure store-bought linguini in hopes of salvaging that part of the meal. Saint Lorenzo, the patron saint of food, had also been employed. According to Lena's folklore, he was called upon for everything from sauces to *semi-freddo*. "Thank goodness for him tonight," Prudence said. They had all gathered at the door, each a little wobbly from so many toasts to the patron saint and anything else they could think of.

"Good thing I don't have to work tomorrow," Dickie said. "I'm not used to fine wines." Debbie poked him, "Maybe you should get used to it. I wouldn't mind your sharing the beer cooler with one or two of those bottles."

"Okay you two, no fighting," Kate said.

"Right," said Michael. "Let's see…we've sorted out the weather, invoked a saint and eaten some damn good Italian food. Did we miss anything?"

"Well, I suppose we could have prolonged your protracted views on local politics, but no, I think we've covered the waterfront," Nick said.

Moans erupted in unison. "Okay, I know, corny as hell...too much vino."

"Thanks for coming," Prudence said. "Sorry it wasn't sooner, but it really was a fun night."

"Our place next time," Kate said, luring the group outside. "Our girl here is beat."

"'Night all." Nick closed the door. "Well that went well."

"It was great, but I really am tired."

"It's been a tough week, I know, and again, I'm sorry about everything."

"Let's drop it for now. Our friends had a good time and now I just want to go to bed."

Christmas Eve brought the truce Nick had longed for. With the successful party under her belt, Prudence had softened her tone and for that he was grateful. With her series intact, she had relaxed her stance and if the weather gods had any conscience, Nick would be home in time to celebrate her success.

"Do you like your ring?" Nick held her hand as the opal picked up the firelight.

"I really do, and the books too, even though they were overkill. I mean, the whole set?"

"It was the least I could do after what happened with my mother."

Prudence handed him a box and kissed him full on the lips. She had to get past her anger. "Hope it fits."

"It's wonderful—the perfect color and really, really soft," Nick said.

"Cashmere—very Italian. You can show it off in Denver and the tan will look great with your sport jacket when you accompany me to my opening."

"Seems like you really planned ahead. I won't let you down, promise."

Snuggled under Hannah's heirloom throw in front of the fire, it was easy for Prudence to believe him.

Christmas morning brought its own gift—ominous clouds portending a coming storm. Nick brought their coffee into the bedroom. "Merry Christmas." He placed the mug on the nightstand next to her side of the bed.

"And Merry Christmas to you. What a nice surprise."

"What would you like to do today?"

"I dunno, maybe just have a quiet day in together."

"That's fine by me. Want me to make breakfast?"

"Would you?"

"I'll yell when it's ready."

Steam from the coffee drifted lazily over the small stack of books she hadn't had a chance to read. The bookstore had been the outgrowth of her childhood love of literature and the escapism it provided. But it was Christmas, and the bad days of her mother's reign were behind her, mentally deposited into the sea beneath her studio floor. She blew on the hot coffee and reached for the top book. Little red bumps were evident all along the inside of her arm. Nerves, she thought, as always getting the best of her. Nick, rattling around in the kitchen, a harkening back to their first year together when he always made Sunday breakfast. He built up his business and she hers and their evenings had been full of enthusiastic conversation about the direction in which their future would go. He had received accolades for contributions to the community of Oyster Cove with his fund-raising projects and she had been honored by the Chamber of Commerce for book events centered on the area of Stonycroft. They had begun to have it all, or so they thought.

Now, after two miscarriages, the sale of Prudence's business and Nick scrambling to keep up with the ever-changing real estate market on the coast of Maine, it seemed as if they had lost an essential element of their cohesive bond. No wonder her skin was breaking out, she thought, jumping out of bed to join her husband. All she had to do was keep it together for another day—not show her hostility and enjoy their quiet time without even bothering to dress. She could make something from the new Italian cookbooks; he'd like that. But a kernel of doubt had already found its way into her psyche, and deep down inside, she knew that Nick's going to Denver was all wrong. She just couldn't identify why.

Red blotches had blossomed on her neck and forehead and her midriff. Waking to the thought of her husband flying in this weather, had undone her. There had been such strong winds this season.

"You're not going to help me pack this time?"

"I'm afraid I might slip in a nasty note for Rita to find when she helps you unpack. And don't tell me, she doesn't try, because I won't believe you."

"Pru, please, that old diatribe is ridiculous. I thought we had called a truce?"

The jibes and barbs she had stoically taken from her mother-in-law had been unkind, but her husband was nothing like his mother. "I can't stay mad when you look at me like that now can I?"

"I hope not," Nick said. He had rolled a ski sweater his mother had given him, into the bottom of his case and was trying to fold the long sleeve shirts without success. "I'll call you when I arrive and every night thereafter, promise."

She caved when he held his fingers up in a Boy Scout pledge. Rushing in to give him a kiss, she accidently bumped her forehead to his nose, which then began to bleed. "Oh God, what have I done?"

"Medic!" Nick hollered as Pru found him a cloth to stanch the trickle of blood. "How do I explain this to your mother-in-law?"

"Tell her I have a violent streak, then I know she won't pick on me the next time I see her."

"I have a feeling that reunion is a long time off sweetheart. Now will you finish my packing?"

Prudence stood in the doorway watching Nick's Jeep disappear from view as the wind buffeted her with its winter fury. Pulling her robe tighter, her thoughts went to another time six years earlier when she had stood exactly like this as Nick rushed off to be with his dying sister. A one-time girlfriend, Diana had been waiting to console him back then. And watching him leave, Prudence fully believed that everything bad that had ever happened between her and Nick, had to do with his trips to Denver.

Prudence awoke to the sound of wet snow pelting the windows. This was not a good sign, she thought, scrunching further under the big winter quilt. Four days until Nick's return. Her paintings had been framed and delivered, but her skin still itched with the uncertainty of it all. With Nick gone, she had resorted to smelly tinctures and Calamine lotion liberally smeared, but nothing seemed to help. Nerves, at least that's what she hoped it was. Kate, knowing Prudence's propensity for fretting, talked her off the edge of disaster most days, and joined her for wine in the Thatcher Lane kitchen on others.

The bitter cold first days of January had gripped Oyster Cove—ledges iced blue in the waning sun and frost-patterned windowpanes. Prudence's hopes soared in anticipation of Nick's return. And then she got the call. Denver was now snowed in. Roads had been closed off by small avalanches and digging out of his mother's home would take time, Nick had stated with characteristic familiarity of his surroundings. Prudence had been too upset to say anything. She blamed Rita and then she blamed Nick and then churlishly mugged for the hall mirror, berating her own expectations.

"Foiled again." She tweaked an imaginary mustache as she watched her tears flow with abandon. At least he wasn't in the air, she thought, realizing how selfish she must have sounded. Kate and Michael had offered to drive her to Portland; they too wanted to be there for her grand opening. She wouldn't really be alone.

On the day of the show, Prudence donned the outfit most likely to offer comfort: a calf-length wool skirt, white blouse and short boiled wool jacket. Of course, everything had to be stuffed into a down quilt coat, rendering her a caricature image of the mighty Michelin man. Portland streets had been cleared of the recent snow, but the bricks were slick and dirty from the plows and the air was frigid. Entering the gallery, Prudence was shaking, both from cold and a case of nerves. They hung their coats behind the entry wall where Donny had placed a rolling rack for the event. He spotted them and rushed over with a small tray of flutes filled with golden bubbles. Prudence released the breath she had been holding behind a canned smile; he seemed pleased with the turnout. She had always admired what he had done to the interior of this old building. It was high-ceilinged with light neutral walls, and he had installed track lighting better than any other gallery in town. Beams from different directions now entered her paintings and invited the viewer to follow. At the far end and centered, was the twenty-four by thirty-six inch still life, the largest one she had ever painted. Prudence had used numerous photos, which had been taken of Lena's table settings both under the pergola and in her kitchen, to accomplish the desired effect. Prudence had created the image around the hand-painted china gifted by Lena's Nonna, but she had used one of her own bowls for the studio set-up while she recreated the one in the photograph. The painting exaggerated the nesting lemons, limes, oranges and pomegranates, and she had taken great care to imitate the Italian-made tureen with its delicate, curlicue handles and base.

"Oh!" Prudence sighed with relief.

"Everything is beautiful," Kate said.

"You are extremely talented," Michael added.

"Take a breath, Prudence," Donny said. "I'm really pleased with the way it all looks and you should be too."

"I'm more than that." Prudence leaned in and kissed Donny's cheek. "You've done a fabulous job of hanging. I never thought my work could look so grand."

"It's obvious those women think it does." Donny casually nodded toward a far wall.

If only she could hear what they were saying, Prudence thought, as she watched the foursome he was referencing. Three were dressed in black slacks and sweaters, high-heeled black boots and wearing chunky turquoise jewelry. The fourth wore a long denim skirt, chambray shirt, a fitted vest, and low-heeled suede boots. She might have just arrived from Taos and a gallery showing her own paintings of the southwest. Prudence's pride grew; they were here to see her work, the way she had always dreamed. It didn't matter if they bought anything; those women and all the other guests were taking the time to witness what she had accomplished and that meant the world. As she stood mesmerized by the scene before her, the room continued to fill and voices grew louder. Corks were popped and fresh glasses appeared on the refreshment table. Donny had thought of everything and Prudence's heart swelled in gratitude.

"I'm just sorry Nick couldn't be here," she said.

Before she could work herself up again, Donny took her elbow and steered her toward the interested parties. No longer standing shoulder to shoulder, the foursome noted earlier had stepped apart and back a few paces to take in the full impact. "We have potential buyers here, Prudence, so put your game face on and schmooze for a while, okay?"

"Thanks, Donny, you don't know how much this all means to me."

"I think I do, really."

"At least four paintings sold," Prudence said from the backseat.

"And one of those was your centerpiece…that has to feel good," Kate said.

"It does, but you know, I got pretty attached to that one. One day, I'll have to paint a smaller version for the house…to remind me of Lena."

"And, don't forget you'll get a lot of good press out of it too," Michael said.

"The guy from the Herald was really nice, wasn't he? And, I think since Donny jacked his prices up, I might have made a small profit."

"What a nice way to start the New Year," Kate said. "Nick will be very proud of you."

"I know he will, and I'm glad you took so many pictures for me. I'll drag him down there when he gets back; the show will be up for the entire month."

"I doubt you'll have to drag him, Prudence. He raves about your work more than you realize," Michael said.

"Thanks guys, I really feel loved tonight."

"You are loved, you silly twit," Kate said.

Music poured from the radio and smoke pumped furiously into the frigid air. Nick had been gone for fifteen days, a long time for them to be apart, and she had worn her worry under the salves she used to heal her skin, which had cleared up right after her show. By that afternoon—January eleventh—she had outlined a schedule that would work with her model, and had come into the studio early to feed the stove so he'd be comfortable disrobing. She'd had all she could do not to submit to his advances during Nick's absence. Tony had quickly picked up on her loneliness and doubt as if he'd had special radar for just such things. Maybe that's how affairs got started, she thought, trying for a sketch, but all she saw were doodles. She hadn't heard the scuffing sound coming from outside. The door burst open and Nick filled the doorway. Tony, with only a towel for cover, stepped out of the tiny bathroom.

"Hey Nick, how's it going?"

"You're finally home!" Prudence jumped into Nick's open arms before he could say anything. She took the cold off his body into hers and on her lips. "I'm so mad at you."

"You are?" He kissed her and as he opened his eyes, he noticed that Tony had made himself comfortable on the stool near her easel.

"Sort of."

He kissed her again.

"Hardly."

"Good, now we're getting somewhere. "

Prudence threw on her jacket, and steered Nick back outside, hoping to distract him from what he'd seen. "Tony, give me a minute, please."

"He doesn't need to know our business," Prudence said beyond the doorway.

"For the record, I really, really tried to get home on time. But at least I accomplished what I set out to do, *and* Mother was very sorry she dragged me away. I told her all about your work and then she scolded me for coming." What he didn't tell her was that his mother had also invited his old girlfriend, Diana, for dinner on the night of his arrival.

"If you say so."

"Prudence."

"All right."

And it was—for a while.

January's bitter cold had blanketed Oyster Cove like hoarfrost on a pond, but even as the days crept toward February, the sun had remained steadfast. It was this dichotomy that puzzled those from away who questioned the sanity of anyone choosing to stay for what they believed would be wall to wall gray. By

November, RVs—with barbecues and bikes strapped on— joined the long parade departing the anticipated winter, creating a snaking train of vehicles heading south along Route 1.

January was also a time for ice fishing and since Nick's return, he and Dickie Bronson spent a couple of Sundays out on Fuller Pond just outside the village. When the roads were good, Prudence had taken advantage of her time alone to visit other galleries. Since her debut show, there had been more interest from one in Stonycroft as well as two Down East galleries, though they wouldn't open their doors again until June. Donny Bales was already talking up a new opening, this time featuring the nudes. Nick had been duly impressed by the first, but she could tell from his responses, not quite standing on his head with joy over the second.

Nick had viewed the new paintings in varying stages of completion and by the end of February had done his best to be supportive, offering a small suggestion here or there for as long as he could stand looking at the handsome model transformed on canvas. At least they were creatively composed in order to suggest rather than see what he had no desire to look at—what Pru looked at every day—Tony, in stages of undress. Her hours away from the house had again begun to gnaw at him, especially since the model was with her quite a bit of that time. She had been clear when explaining to Nick that she was trying to put together a series that would depict different aspects of the harbor based upon the seasons, but not calendar shots like one of the neighboring fire stations had been selling. Although she still used items of clothing or props for effect, she also handled the traditional poses with a drape or the angle of his body insinuating what the viewer might see if the model were to turn just so and acknowledge her. In the end what bothered him was that she had managed to bring the canvases to life without any reference to the harbor, which made him even more jealous.

To fill in the empty hours while Pru stayed at her studio, he had begun to spend more time away from the house. He coached basketball and joined the meets taking place around the state, arriving home most nights too late and too tired to give a damn. And if he wasn't at the school or at a town meeting or handling some small crisis in the office, he bristled with the fact that she was spending that time with Tony. Wracked by guilt every time he thought of Diana, he silently accused Pru of behaving the same way with her single model.

Prudence had penned many of her sentiments about her studio work and even included the newspaper review from the Portland show in her last correspondence with Julie, which had elicited squeals of delight during a rare long distance call. Julie had already sent photos of Addie in front of their Christmas tree or with her on Cooper's lap, both now attached by magnet to the side of the refrigerator. And there had been continuing correspondence with Lena. Letters from Italy had come to life with the descriptions of their holiday preparations and especially the epic family gathering that unfolded in the quiet village. The Bernoli daughters had been home, boyfriends in tow, and lots of cousins, aunts and uncles on hand for Christmas dinner. From her Thatcher Lane kitchen, Prudence mentally bridged the gap beyond the ledge and across the sea to Lena's, picturing Nilda dispatching her views on the boyfriends while she orchestrated the making of her famous cannoli. Prudence smiled. Meeting Nilda had been like stepping into Oz, the diminutive woman in black with the long nose, stretching any ideals she may have had of her own grandmothers, the ones she hardly knew. Hannah had become the keeper of family history and everything Prudence wanted to know, had been documented and left for her in the Thatcher Lane attic.

As Prudence had promised herself, a rosemary plant—talked to and loved—flourished in its special clay pot on a bamboo stand near the dormant orchids. The scent of Tuscany she had come to love, blunted only a little now by indoor heat and cooking odors. Most of the week had been below zero, too cold to work in the studio, and the last snowfall, hard-packed and crusty, saddled the ledges. Waves pounded, leaving frozen tentacles on the rocks, but the radiant sun lacked the heat to defrost them. There hadn't been enough heat anywhere to thaw Nick's chilled responses to the hours Prudence spent with Tony Moss.

"You staying in today?" Nick said, entering the kitchen.

"At least until it gets a little warmer. I need to get the finishing touches on the portraits." Nick hadn't actually accused her of any wrongdoing, but the implication was there. "You could stop by and see how much has been accomplished."

"No thanks; he's not my type."

"That's a bit childish."

Nick had difficulty looking at the paintings, that's all there was to it. "Whatever," he said.

She understood his jealousy because when he hadn't come back for her show, she had come awfully close. Tony would have been a distraction—his words—to the empty hours during that bleak waiting period. To this day, she thanked the voice in her head that stopped her from doing the unthinkable. But she didn't want to pick a fight with Nick.

"I got a nice letter from Lena; want to read it?"

"Later, I have an appointment in Stonycroft," Nick said.

"Have a good day," she said to his back. There was too much to do to feed into his mood. Donny had promised he would come to Oyster Cove and select the ones he wanted rather than having her cart them all down to Portland. He had decided spring would be best for a new show anyway and spring in Maine, would be a while coming. It had been well documented as well as personally experienced, that major nor'easters could consume the state in April.

Prudence sniffed the stationery, Lena's latest letter bore a trace of her marinara sauce if that was even possible, or it was just Prudence's longing to return to Italy. The thermometer rose slowly, and by eleven it was high enough to open the studio. When she finished perfecting the portraits, she would paint from memory: the winding paths behind the farm, flowers from Lena's garden, anything to transport her to that other land.

The tiny cabin was still freezing, even though the thermometer had gone up five degrees. But then what had she expected. There was no way she would be able to work like this. How depressing, she thought, knowing she should have come in earlier and lit the fire. Cabin fever was the name for winter's discontent, and for Prudence, her cabin had always been the cure for such a thing. Apparently, not today. The thrum of diesels had moved further out in colder waters and the snowbirds had flocked back to their roosts months ago. Normally, that was when Prudence was happiest, a time when she could contemplate the world around her and solidify her place in it. But she had a restlessness that wouldn't go away, a feeling she was unable to define, which Julie would label as prescient thoughts. Perhaps it was only the winter blahs, she thought, remembering her oldest friend's admonitions about such things.

"How about we go out for dinner tonight?" Nick had walked in on Prudence curled up in the favored nook, staring out the window, melancholy written all over her face.

"Okay, but not the Dory. The roads are clean, can we run into Stonycroft?"

"Sure. What are you in the mood for?"

"Italian."

"We have that here, are you sure?"

"Mine never tastes as good as a real chef; I need more lessons."

"Speaking of, what'd Lena have to say?"

"Mostly trivia—Aldo got a new truck, Marco is underfoot, she misses us."

"We'll go again someday."

"I know, but that day seems a long way away."

"You do need a night out."

The small, busy restaurant tucked away on a side street in Stonycroft had been the perfect antidote to Prudence's mood, the aromatic room redolent of another place. It was on the menu, but there wasn't a lobster in sight. A powerful mainstay of the Maine coast, it was a crustacean that she had subsisted on for her first year in Oyster Cove, and was often displayed live in large tanks, but not here.

"I feel like a time-traveler."

"What do you mean?" Nick said.

"Well—and you know how much I love Maine—I crave being there, with them, the Bernolis, the Italians, all of it, like I'd been there before."

"I don't see how."

"Me either."

"Well, you look better than you did a little while ago."

"I feel better." Prudence put her fork down on her empty plate and smiled. "This is just what I needed, and you can't tell me that your *zuppa di peschi* didn't bring back good memories."

"It really was good, but expensive."

"Maybe, but I think it was worth it."

"It was, just to see you smiling."

"I smile."

"Mm, not so much lately," Nick said. "Are you okay?"

"It's just winter. It seems really long this year and I guess that's because I'm not schlepping to the bookstore every day, talking with customers and venting with Vivien. I miss it, I have to admit."

144

"Maybe Vivien could use your company too. Why not spend a few hours there instead of moping around the house."

"I'm not moping."

"Whatever you call it. When you're not painting, you're bored. It's obvious, and I could always use a little help at the office."

"That won't work; you're too bossy."

"Hah, listen to you. That time right after we got married, you made an appearance and rearranged my desk, told my sales people they didn't look professional enough because of the way they were dressed, *and* you listed all the restaurants handy to Route 1 so we wouldn't lose valuable hours hunting for one between appointments."

"I did not! You make me sound like a shrew."

"Well, let's just say, you've mellowed, okay?"

Mellowed was right. She had become downright soppy by his accounting. But the evening out brought them back to center and that night they made love the way that had in Italy. Kate had been right when she had told Prudence that couples had to keep working at being together. Obviously, she had never learned any of the right lessons from observing her own parents. But now she had learned that it wasn't enough just to be in the same house, or performing similar tasks. It was all about sharing feelings, both good and bad. And don't forget humor, Kate had stressed.

"Wonder what it's like in the Cayman's," Prudence said.

"Michael gets the plum assignments, right?"

"And Kate reaps the benefits." Prudence thought of her friend basking on the sun-stretched strand of Seven Mile beach. Michael had been assigned to the banking industry's Caribbean hub for a whole year and Prudence and Nick had been invited to visit. "Do you think we could go?"

"Maybe. Funds have been a little tight, but we'll see."

Prudence didn't like to push. She wasn't bringing in the same money anymore, and the house was once again a topic to be avoided. The furnace had been acting up and Nick had been throwing out hints regarding some listings he favored. In their absence, Prudence checked in on the Newcomb's house, and each time Nick would remind her that it was a far better investment than the Thatcher Lane house because it was only ten years old and probably more sound than theirs. She had never bought into that theory, saying that houses like theirs had proven their worth by their very longevity; they were obviously sound.

Taking Nick's suggestion to heart, Prudence had offered her services at the store. Vivien had been thrilled and given her carte blanche regarding her hours. What was most important about those hours was the way in which they turned back the clock, peeled away the layers of change until they reached the core of their friendship. With laughter and even a few tears, they unwrapped the story of their journey as young businesswomen grasping a need for their beloved bookstore, and running with the idea without regret. The retelling included silly olfactory highlights caused by the foods they had once shared, and began to share again as they worked: garlic-scented golden cheese 'coins', which had been served at their opening party; Beth Jenkins' lobster casserole, which had been derived from the original version produced by the late Aurora Durn—a rich, complicated recipe harkening back to the 1940s. Some things never changed, they agreed, but sadly some had. They had lost their Thatcher Lane role models to age, and Beth and her unflappable husband Herman had moved to Houlton to be near an ailing relative, where he would continue his laboring over old houses just as he had Hannah's.

For Prudence, that time spent at the store had a curative affect, but she also followed the days on the calendar as if faithfully reading a bible, as she looked forward to new beginnings provided by the Bales Gallery. Not to be sloughed aside either was the date when the boat would be put in the water again. She and Nick made a point to shake out the sails on the *Mystic* as soon as the weather was right. For all other outdoor sport, Dickie, who was also a Maine Guide, had always been Nick's go-to guy. They fly-fished in spring and had at one time done a little cross-country skiing when their schedules allowed. When not traveling, Kate was the person enlisted for gallery hopping or shopping. Vivien demurred, preferring she said, to curl up in front of a fire with her cats and read a good book. They certainly had access to them all at North Sky, so who could blame her.

Even with the extreme cold and her distaste for it, Dr. Gordon claimed that she was healthier than she'd been in a long while, though beginning to be on the thin side again. During her last checkup he had indicated it might be a good time to get off the Pill; prolonged usage might be harmful. As he was talking, she had imagined ever-so-tiny booties springing to life on knitting needles in Lena's hands. But was it the right time, she wondered, now that she had made her commitments?

Chapter Eleven

By mid-winter, a stack of postcards were propped up on the 'pie-crust' tilt-top table—the antique mahogany piece, which Herman had once fixed, and still trembled whenever someone walked by. But now, instead of flowers, it was adorned with picturesque reminders of the Newcombs' whereabouts, a colorful note to the brown drab of plowed snow heaped outside. Nick and Prudence had fallen into their respective routines with the inclusion of 'date night', her idea for quelling any possibility of a disconnect occurring as it had in the past. March, the tease, she thought, as she spread salt on the front walkway. Because of the roads, she had been forced to stay close to home, her now twice-weekly visits to the bookstore curtailed by black ice and high winds that threw the little Beetle around like a toy. Maybe it was the perfect time for a thorough house cleaning, a cleansing of the soul Hannah would say. Just changing a body's energy could sometimes propel new ideas to flow, perhaps another series buried deep that would find its way onto canvas. It was worth a try, she thought, as she decided where to begin.

The time slipped by as she filled a small box with gently used hats, gloves and scarves—mostly gifts they hadn't cared for—from the downstairs hall closet. Prudence had saved all the cartons from the attic when moving in, intuiting their usefulness in the future. A larger box, taped and labeled, contained frames that were of no use to her as they were either too ornate or were meant for glass, as well as an old coffee maker and blender stored there for convenience. Both boxes were ready for Nick to haul to the car when he returned. Before heading to the second floor, she spun the dial on Hannah's old radio, and raised the volume to high so she would be able to hear it as she worked up there.

Standing in front of their clothes closet, thinned now of her giveaways, Prudence ran her hand over Nick's side of the rod, pushing his jackets apart. Did she dare dispose of the old ones; they still fit him, but not as attractively as she once thought. Laying each one out on the bedspread, as if they would speak to her, she picked over the old favorites: the navy wool (for yacht club events whenever his office sponsored a race), a tweed he loved to wear when he went back and forth to Denver (the one with leather patches on the elbows), and a tan one that was still presentable. Last, there was a bomber jacket that she had never liked. Picking up the navy, she held it to the light searching for moth holes and signs of frayed fibers on the pocket insignia. Deeming it satisfactory, she hung it back up. Then she held up the tweed and a scent of cologne wafted off the shoulder. It was not entirely familiar or perhaps it had just gone stale since his last flight. She ran her hands over the material noticing the fraying cuffs and the inside of the collar. This really had been worn to death, she thought, remembering those times she had met him at the airport before they had married. No wonder men's jackets had leather patches. It was the only part of the jacket that was still presentable. With working so many hours, she had obviously overlooked a lot.

She would have to break it to him over dinner. "Honey, don't be mad, but I'm tossing your favorite jacket," she rehearsed. "We'll buy you a new one, won't that be nice?" Laughing aloud, she checked the pockets. Nick had a habit of squirreling coins. But instead of quarters, she found an envelope. It had been folded into thirds and tucked in an inside breast pocket. It had Rita's return address. What's the old biddy up to now, she thought, opening the envelope? A hint of cologne reached her nose, but the envelope was empty. Odd that he had bothered to save it, she thought, and then tossed it into the wastebasket.

Prudence did not want to concentrate on Rita, it never ended well when she did. Tires crunched across the poorly cleared path as Nick pulled in behind her VW. Putting on a good face, or so she thought, she tromped down the stairs. It was always tricky where Rita was concerned.

"You're home early."

"I need some papers from my old canvas briefcase, the one that I used for a while after Italy."

"It's in the hall closet where you left it."

"I see you've been busy," Nick said, stepping over the boxes.

"My new project—empty out everything we no longer need, wear, or want. Spring cleaning come early."

Nick held the case to his chest as he unzipped it. "Found it."

He kissed her quickly on the lips, forgetting to put the case back on the shelf as he made for the door. "Are you okay? You have that look."

"What look?"

"You know, when you're mad at me, but you won't tell me why. Did I do something wrong?"

"I don't know, did you?"

"You're talking in riddles again. I've got to go—maybe you'll tell me later."

"Maybe."

Prudence was being obtuse and it was intentional, because it was difficult to communicate feelings that had to do with intuition, which never made sense to Nick. He had left the closet door open, and hadn't taken the box. Damn! The old L.L. Bean briefcase tilted against the doorjamb. Why did men have to be so messy—cupboard doors left open, dresser drawers half shut, shoes and socks by the chair? The list would go on if she allowed her mind to go there. Reaching for the case, it fell over from the unbalanced weight; Nick must have been using it as a filing cabinet. What a mess, she thought, seeing the way the heap of papers defied the old zipper. Changing her mind about putting it away, she brought the case to the table, opened it flat, and pulled out the contents, thinking all the while that she would be doing him a favor. Organizational as she was, she began to sort by form—letter versus listing, bills opposite pink phone slips, all things by size at first.

Once stacked, she shifted her attention to the larger papers, the sales contracts that were outdated and then letters from interested parties out of state who followed the local newspaper listings. Mixed in between were a few letters from Nick's mother. He never mentioned that Rita had been writing him at the office, but maybe that was how the empty envelope had come about. But then, did she really care if her mother-in-law didn't like her well enough to include her? Why not, she thought, going in for a closer look. The usual drivel headlined the letter dated last fall, after their return from Italy. Then her eyes caught the name Diana. Nick's old girlfriend was coming back to Denver, Rita wrote. Going through a bad time, Mrs. Pelletier's words—as far as Prudence was concerned—beseeched her son to care.

Well, she can just go to hell, Prudence thought, reading quickly to ensure there was nothing more to make her blood boil. If she confronted Nick, he would be angry that she had been reading his mail and maybe even mad that she had bothered with *his stuff*. Prudence decided to disrupt the order she had created and shuffled the papers back to a semblance of what they had looked like, not that he'd notice considering the jumble. A check fell from the pack, a canceled one from the Pelletier Realty checkbook, made out to Rita. It was for fifteen hundred dollars. Nick had never said anything about giving his mother so much money, funds they couldn't really afford to give. What else had he been keeping from her? Prudence had that déjà vu of a tidy world crumbling as it had the year before they married. She sank into the corner nook, her breathing erratic. Nausea threatened and she put her head down on her knees.

"You okay?" Nick walked into a dark kitchen. Pru was huddled in the corner staring out the window at wind-swirled waves. The room was cold; she hadn't even turned the heat up.

"How much did you loan her?"

"Who, what are you talking about?

"How much money have you given to your mother?"

"Let me explain."

"How much, Nick?"

"Altogether —about four grand."

"Oh Nick." Prudence hated this feeling—he really didn't *have* to tell her what he did with earned funds, but somehow it still felt disloyal. If nothing else, they had always been so open with each other about that topic.

"I know, I should have told you. But I also know she won't be able to pay it back and that's what bothered me the most. But damn, Pru, she's my mother!"

"I don't think I know you anymore." This was the exit line, she thought, the reason—like in the movies.

"What other lies of omission, Nick?"

"Nothing, why would you ask?"

She couldn't hold her tongue. "Anything I should know about Diana?"

"Have you been going through my mail?"

"That's all you worry about, whether I've been snooping. I thought I was doing you a favor, trying to sort that mess you left in the closet. You and your mother have done the rest."

"Don't be crazy. Mother's always been lousy with money and after dad died, she ran through the insurance money and got into debt with creditors and that's why I went. I told you that already. Believe me, she doesn't have your business acumen."

"I don't think that makes me feel any better toward any of you."

"I know I should have told you everything from the beginning. But let's be honest, if I had mentioned Diana at all, you would have gone ballistic. And, if I told you my mother needed money, you would have done the same. How could I win?"

"Now it's all my fault you didn't tell me?"

"I didn't say that, but at least try and understand how trapped I felt."

"Trapped!" Spittle flew from her mouth as she screamed the word. He had no idea what that meant to her right now, especially since Dr. Gordon had frightened her into getting off the Pill with his admonition regarding long-term health. "Lies of omission are just as serious as an outright lie. You've really done it this time."

"What do you mean?"

"You'll see." Prudence couldn't bring herself to articulate what had been going through her mind for hours. "I don't feel well, I'm going to bed."

"Hang on, you can't just run away. I need to know what you meant."

What did she mean? "You wouldn't understand, Nick, leave it alone."

"How can I?"

"I don't know what to believe right now, and I'm afraid I'll say or do something I'll regret, so just let it go." She left the room.

Nick was quiet; he knew they would be sleeping apart tonight and nothing he said would alter that. How had his world tipped upside down so quickly? If he was going to keep a secret, he should have been smarter about it. Too late now, he thought, pulling a beer from the fridge. He went into the front room, lit a fire and turned on the TV.

Days passed; the chill inside the house as bad as that outside. Nick had no clue how he would turn this situation around. He had shown Prudence the bank statements, vowing not to write more checks behind her back. She was right, there really wasn't enough extra to be supporting Rita's bad habits. He'd finally put his foot down and found another way to resolve her problem. It

154

would mean selling their family home, but in the end, it would leave his mother far better off and after all, she didn't need a big house all by herself. At first there had been an outcry with Rita stating it was there for his future, but being the salesman that he was, as well as the dutiful son, she soon came around. He had called upon a realtor out west that he'd known since college, to handle the showings and any transactions. And Nick was to be kept in the loop. Prudence still hadn't said much about his efforts.

"I'm not quite sure how I feel." Prudence and Vivien were in the keeping room of Vivien's idyllic Cape-style farmhouse. A fire blazed in the giant hearth and Vivien's Siamese cats were curled together in front of the window watching birds feeding beyond their reach. Every so often, one of them would swat at the glass with an expression that was both comical and sad.

"You really don't believe there was anything more to it," Vivien said.

"It's all I think about. I've never forgotten how much we went through before he proposed. He and Diana have a past, a dangling participle to my latent thoughts and many of my nightmares. You must remember, because all I did was cry on your shoulder. Then thanks to your worldly wisdom, I said and did the right things and he came home to Maine, but I'll never really know what happened between them. Since it was before we were married, I don't even have a right to know. But now Rita has put it on my doorstep, and I'm not sure how to handle this."

"Why do you think he's changed?"

"Because he's been so secretive. He never mentioned that she was out there after Christmas, let alone that he'd seen her. I believed the trip was all about helping his mother out, but now I feel like such a fool."

"Oh, Prudence, the man is crazy about you. Don't you think you might be blowing this out of proportion?"

"Maybe so, but he knows what a sensitive subject Diana is, and yet he kept it all to himself."

"Perhaps that's just because he knew how you'd react and because he's a guy. They don't always know how to communicate, you know, at least not to me. True, I thought Nick was different, but he still puts his pants on the same way."

"You have just reminded me of what Lena said to me—they're just boys in big pants."

"I think I'd like to steal that one if you don't mind."

"Be my guest. I'm sure Lena would be pleased."

"How about a martini? It must be cocktail hour somewhere and I think you could use one. I've missed our time together. Ursula is a dear woman, but we don't have the kind of ease that you and I have. I wouldn't dream of talking the way I do when I'm with you. I'm not saying you made me swear, but I could always let my hair down in front of you."

"Why thank you, Miss Vivien," Prudence said.

"Why does that make me feel like the hooker in Pretty Woman?"

"If the boots fit?"

Vivien tossed one of the sofa pillows at Pru's head. "I'll have you know, these are designer boots from the fancy store at the mall. They cost a bundle."

"They really are gorgeous, and I would love a drink, but I think a martini would put me over the edge. How about a glass of wine instead?"

"Coming right up."

Hours later, Prudence pulled up to a darkened house. It was nearly seven-thirty and Nick's car was parked, but there was no sign of life. She opened the front door and walked toward the kitchen. From the corner of her eye, she saw a glimmer of light coming from the top of the stairs. For some reason, she didn't announce her presence, but listened to his laughter coming from their bedroom. He was obviously on the phone and hadn't heard her come in. Hair rose on the back of her neck, like a cat hearing an intruder. The worst part, she was positive the voice on the other end would be Diana's. Prudence did something she had never done before. With the lightest grip of only two fingers, she picked up the downstairs extension. Being right was not going to make her feel better, she thought, just as a breathy voice said goodnight and the line went dead. Then she heard footsteps.

"I didn't hear you drive up," Nick said.

"I thought you were asleep since the house was dark."

"No. Just checking on my mother."

What could she say? That she was eavesdropping?

"How's Vivien?"

"Good. How's Rita?"

"Fine, she just needed a little reassuring, that's all. Nothing to worry about."

Like she would, Prudence thought, remaining in her coat. "Have you eaten?"

"Yeah, I did take out from the diner...chowder and biscuits. There's some left if you want it."

"No thanks, I think I'll read for a while."

"I'm going back up then.

Prudence's mind flew in every direction imaginable. She was good at building mole hills from nothing, but damn it something was not right. Did he want to go back to Denver? Was he bored with their marriage after all? It was just all too much.

She let herself out of the house as quietly as she had come in and drove to her studio, the one place she felt safe. She curled up on the daybed for warmth, thought about calling Tony for attention and spite, and waited for the tears to come. It must have been more than an hour when the door burst open.

"Are you trying to scare me to death?"

157

"Go away."

"I called Vivien's and then anyone else I could think of and drove around like a crazy person because I thought you were hurt or in a ditch. Why are you here; its freezing."

"I said go away."

"I'm not going anywhere until you tell me what's wrong."

"Don't play the innocent; you know perfectly well what's wrong. I walked in on you talking to *her*—from our bedroom phone no less." Prudence couldn't help herself, it was as though by using that phone, he had contaminated their private space.

"Oh for God sake, Pru, were you eavesdropping on me? I only said it was Rita because you wouldn't understand. You know that Diana's an old friend, and I already told you about her divorce. She called to vent because I'm the only one of the Denver crowd who knew him best."

"Call it what you like, but she hasn't been on the radar for years and suddenly she's everywhere I turn."

"You're being unreasonable."

"Am I now?"

"You know you are and it doesn't look good on you."

"So now you don't like the way I look?

"I can't win; there's nothing I can say that will stop the way you're feeling right now. What do you want me to do, tell me?"

Prudence didn't dare answer. It could be the ruination of their marriage if she spoke the words that were piling up inside her brain, ready to spill off her tongue like venom. Was he denying any wrongdoing because there had been none, or was he saying words she wanted to hear to save himself? Infidelity of any kind would be a difficult pill to swallow. She didn't know where to turn for the truth.

"Well?"

"Go back home, I'll be there in a little while."

"Fine!"

The door slammed. Prudence stood and shook herself out. The rocker beckoned and she pulled the box of Kleenex from the shelf and dried her face. There weren't many directions she could take on an unmarked road. When talking with Vivien, she had opened a door to an improbability that had just become more real than anything she actually expected. She had so wanted to be wrong, and yet. What if he were telling the truth? She stood a very good chance of taking it too far and crucifying him unnecessarily. Her head ached with all the questions pounding against her skull. "Go home." The words lashed out at the silent room and she took their advice.

Letting herself into the house a second time that night, she walked directly to the kitchen and poured a glass of water, grabbed an aspirin from the cupboard, turned out the light he'd left on, and headed for the guestroom. She would not be able to face her husband right now, and she knew he would be brooding behind their bedroom door.

A week went by and the Pelletiers moved within different timetables, anything to avoid a confrontation. To do that, they had to listen for steps on the stairs, doors closing carefully, water running in the pipes, all the ways in which they identified the other's whereabouts within the creaky old building. With Kate away, and no one to lean on daily, Prudence had been stocking books with Vivien so that she could have private time before or after Ursula's hours.

"How's Nick coping?" Vivien asked.

"I'm not sure; I hardly ever see him."

"You can't go on like this."

"It has taken on a life of its own. Even if I wanted to talk to him, I don't know how anymore, and I really think he believes he's in the right."

"I'm not sure there is a right or wrong to this, Prudence. You have five great years invested and even if he's made a mistake, can't you guys talk about it?"

"I tried writing him a note because I didn't trust my words but I feel so small, like they've been laughing at me behind my back."

"Just promise me you won't do anything rash right now."

"You mean like run off to Italy."

"You wouldn't!"

Prudence didn't know what she'd do; she had never felt this way about her husband. It was like she was all hormonal again. And she missed Lena as if the woman had been her long lost mother and not just a loving friend. "Maybe."

"I don't like the sound of that at all. Do you want to bunk at my house for a few days, maybe make him come to his senses?"

"I think I have a better idea. You know me, I need real proof or I'll never sleep the night through again."

The next morning, after Nick had left for work, Prudence went into their room, put on fresh jeans, a heavy sweater, wool socks and fleece slippers, a sturdy work outfit suitable for the cause. Looking in the mirror, her dark circles and pale skin hinted at illness. She pinched her cheeks and tried not to think of anything but getting the job done. She had never gone in search of evidence like an agent in a spy thriller, but this morning, she would be a sleuth. Sending up a silent prayer, she wished to be wrong. The tiny voice in her head—the one she had always believed—told her otherwise.

Starting at the top, the attic was dust-laden—no sign of fingerprints or anything out of place. All of which would have been obvious since only she knew where everything had been stored and in what manner as it had been Hannah's storage room. Prudence moved on to the master bedroom where she emptied and restacked each drawer with care hoping to make it look like she really had been tidying and not snooping, but there was nothing unusual there. The bathroom was next. It was a room without a lot of storage space and again, she came up empty-handed. The same in the guestroom, checked earlier, and was about to go downstairs when she thought of the nursery. He wouldn't dare, she thought, imagining the room as it was to have been. She held her breath and opened the door. It looked the same. Unopened paint cans, color swatches and a box containing a crib blanket received before bad things happened. Opening the closet door, she was startled by the colorful mobile on the shelf. She had forgotten. It had been purchased first simply because they couldn't resist the little flying fish in yellow and blue colors. And the stencils that Nick wanted to apply to the walls. Choking up, she brought the box to the floor where she could unwrap them and spread them out. The alphabet in two sizes with matching numbers ready to display the baby's name, the one not yet chosen. Emotions kept at bay began to surface, but refusing to give in, she wrapped the stencils and placed the box, along with her dreams, back where she'd found it.

Passing the hall mirror, Prudence saw that she'd left their bedroom closet door wide open and how unsightly it looked in reflection—a gaping dark hole in the otherwise pretty room. That's when she had an epiphany. Why hadn't she thought of that earlier? Nick's black suitcase had been propped on end in the darkest corner of the closet, and she had ignored it. She went back and pulled it out and began going through the side flaps and pockets that were so useful for long flights. And, after his last trip, he had unpacked it himself. In an outside pocket—deep and especially handy for extra shoes—she spotted a corner of white card stock. With pincer-like fingers, she slid it out and held it as if it might sting.

I miss you Nick, more than I can say. My life is a mess, my marriage a shambles and I need to see you. Rita said she would ask you to come and I'm praying you will. Please, please come. With love, Diana.

Gut-punched, she held her stomach and steadied herself on the bed. How she had wanted to be wrong. But then, maybe she was overreacting, she thought, the note wasn't all that incriminating, was it. Diana was asking for help, so what? But why all the subterfuge? Because he still loves her? God, don't let that be true. Prudence slipped the note back and called Vivien, the one person she could tell, and asked her to meet her at the corner café near the bookstore so that Ursula wouldn't be involved.

"Do you think it really means anything, or is he just playing the role of her protector for some strange reason?"

"You tell me?"

"It doesn't seem like him, but then I'm not married to him. Are you going to accuse him outright?"

"What else can I do? If I keep quiet and he continues to lie, what does that get me? If I tell him what I found, then he can deny or explain or whatever. What choice do I have?"

"This is pretty circumstantial if you ask me."

"I don't know what else to do, Vivien…help."

"How about something like…make him a really nice dinner, pour some wine and just talk. Don't be confrontational, just let him feel safe and see what happens."

"That's it?"

"I don't know what else to say. Before the trip to Italy, you had suffered a lot of loss and going away did you both a world of good. Maybe, just maybe, he's just reverting to that man who felt alone, and Diana—through his mother—tapped into it and is using it to get to him. She sounds like the type who would do that."

"You have no idea how much I'm hoping you're right about this. I know I reacted like a wild woman, not only was it unattractive, but it immediately put him on the defensive. If I'm honest, it's all pretty textbook. I suppose I could make one of his favorites from that new cookbook, maybe get some fresh sage on the way home, and see where it all takes me. Maybe I just really needed to vent; as always you came to the rescue. If this works, I'll buy you a special bottle of your favorite wine."

"No need, just trust that Nick loves you."

Prudence had to admit that it was a real one-eighty, to be shopping for a romantic dinner when just hours earlier she wanted to throw the damn pasta machine at her husband. But she also knew that one of her prime problems was reacting before thinking. If she hadn't talked with Vivien, she might be on a plane headed to the Caribbean by now, trying to find the Newcombs.

Nick smelled the sage before he'd walked all the way through to the kitchen. Candles were lit and Prudence was dressed in a buttery soft sweater and dark slacks she had worn in Italy. He tread with caution, "What's all this?"

"To tell you the truth, I'm not sure, but I think this meal is necessary. I'm tired of feeling so hardened every time we talk."

"All I can say is, thank you." He didn't try and kiss her for that might be pushing his luck right now. "Can I help?"

"How about putting on some music, one of Ella's albums?"

Nick was stunned. He knew he was in big trouble and had been practicing his speech for days. Pru wasn't going to berate him for the money, but she would tear him a new one if she knew how often he and Diana had talked, or that they had seen each other the entire time he'd been at his mother's house. How could he tell his wife that his old girlfriend made him feel better just with the way she purred his name and laughed at his corny jokes? It was all so cliché and he'd been such a fool.

Between the music and the candles, Prudence relaxed. Dinner was almost ready and she had poured their wine and taken a glass out to him. "Cin, Cin," she said.

"How did we get off track, Pru?"

"I'm not sure, but my instinct tells me it has a lot to do with my need for approval. I know I put in a lot of hours and I also know that bothers you, even though I'm not sure why and you don't tell me. I can't promise that the hours will change much, at least for a while, but I don't deserve to be lied to either."

"I know, and I'm sorry."

"Is there anything between you and Diana, Nick? I have to know."

She'd gone straight for the jugular. "No." Call it preservation, salvation or plain stupidity, but he suddenly placed himself in a noose and unless they changed this subject, he would hang before nightfall. "Let's have some dinner," he said, kissing her with a great deal of tenderness.

They sat side by side on the small banquette, their limbs touched together suggesting intimacy. They talked about the Bernolis, the Portland Gallery, his latest clients and stayed away from everything else. As dinner was ending, she picked up on his desire but said nothing. Any misstep right now would be disastrous. Vivien had been right, Prudence thought, as once again she had taken a good friend's advice. It hadn't been difficult at all. Nick had been straightforward and there wasn't any need to browbeat him. He had just been acting like a good friend and taking into consideration the way her mother-in-law had always behaved, it was obvious why he had been silent. Sipping her wine, Prudence ran her fingers through the back of his hair. This was tantamount to signaling her needs and even that surprised her.

"What a great night." Nick rolled over and embraced Prudence who was just stirring. "I'm glad the siege is over."

"You really are something else," she said. "But I'm glad too. No more keeping things back, okay?"

"Okay." Anxiety ran through his veins. He had lied, she had swallowed the lie, and he would choke on the lie, and all he could think of was keeping her mind off Denver until he figured out a way to resolve his own stupidity. "Want to catch that new play in Portland next Sunday?"

"Ooh, the one I saw in the Sunday paper about the actor who plays multiple parts. I'd love to. I thought I was going to have to force Vivien to go with me."

"I'll get tickets and then take you out for dinner in the Old Port after."

"Wow, last night's dinner and entertainment was better than I thought."

Nick would grieve this moment when he said goodbye to the good man she thought he was, but he had no choice. "Just my way of saying I understand why you were mad and there are no hard feelings."

What an odd thing for him to say, she thought, but stopped herself from nitpicking a mere sentence. He wasn't always articulate after just waking up. Instead, she said, "Clean slate," and rolled out of bed.

Chapter Twelve

In like a lion and still roaring, Prudence thought, examining the ground under her feet. Spring had officially arrived, but someone had forgotten to tell the locals. Plow attachments continued to dominate the scene and drums of sand, near empty, had been laid on their side at various town facilities to accommodate those who needed extra. For the Pelletiers, it was life as usual, or more to the point, without strife. Nick had gone out of his way to treat her with kindness, but solicitude still filled the empty spaces between questions and answers. As a result, Prudence's nervous system was as out of whack as possible, and her sleep patterns had gone awry. She was edgy and moody and consumed with self-doubt.

"These are terrific, but I can see on your face you don't believe me." Donny Bales paced the small distance of Prudence's studio, examining each carefully. "Your guy Tony is a splendid model."

Prudence wasn't quite sure if he meant the poses or the specimen, but at least he liked the paintings. "I'm glad you like them. I have to admit, I was a little worried."

"Every artist I've ever had dealings with is a *little worried*, Prudence. In truth, you are all scared to death. Rejection never comes easy, not even to know-it-alls like me."

He had never been so frank before, and it did help put her at ease. When she first walked into his gallery, before introducing herself, she had heard him yelling at someone over the phone. When she realized the person on the line was an artist, she turned around and left the gallery without speaking to Donny. It wasn't until she had taken a long walk, rationalized the possible scenarios for his behavior, that she returned to ask for gallery representation. She would never have thick skin, but she had at last learned to trust the patrons who had begun to buy her work. "Do you know which ones you want, Donny?"

"All but this one," he said, pointing to the one with the cowboy hat. "That's just not working for me. I wish you had used something else for that great pose. Would you consider doing another?"

"I should have gone with my gut and had him holding it instead of putting it on his head. Unfortunately, Tony's not available right now, so I'm not quite sure how I'd change it. Let me think on it for a while and get back to you."

"Fine, no immediacy. I'll hang these as soon as Portland shows signs of spring migration. We're going to want to attract a different crowd for these guys."

Prudence liked the way he pluralized Tony's image, which was something she had done when creating the multiple doppelgangers. "Did you bring your van?"

"Yes, it's parked in a no-parking spot so I could be close to your door. If you'll just give me a hand with these, I'll take them to their new home."

Prudence grabbed her jacket and she and Donny wrapped each painting in large plastic coverings. "Have you got some cardboard or something to slide between them?"

"I do and a couple of old quilts as well. I saved everything from my mother's estate and have found use for even things like old blankets. Artists can count on me to keep their work safe."

Each time she had an opportunity to listen to Donny at length, she was always impressed by the rather gallant way he spoke, about everything. He was always impeccably dressed, natty one might say, with colorful breast pocket handkerchief and gold signet pinky ring. He had been wearing a royal blue jacket, striped tie and gray slacks when she first met him and his shoes had been highly polished. Minute details of a man who was brought up in a household with the fine oriental carpets now underfoot in his Gallery, or simply one who went for an image that would make a difference to those A-list patrons beginning to find the art scene in an up and coming city. Either way, she had grown fond of him, she thought, handing over his smart, camelhair coat. "I'd love to get one of these for Nick someday."

"Let me know when you're ready and I can get you a good discount."

Even with a discount, she could tell it was out of her price range. "I will."

Donny waved from the cab of the van, and Prudence did a little happy dance as she walked back to her studio. Then she looked at the painting left behind. How on earth would she make it better? She bent closer and was suddenly dizzy. Kneeling on one knee, she remembered that she had forgotten to eat. An old habit she thought she had overcome. Must be a power bar here somewhere, she thought, as she toppled a couple of tins kept for oddments that found their way into a working studio. Sure enough, there was a half-eaten nut butter bar, heaped with enough sugar to send a healthy person into a diabetic coma, but she scarfed it down anyway. Relief came quickly and since she still had her coat on, she walked over to the General Store for some soup. And, of course, there was Lloyd.

"Hey Prudence, how ya doin'?"

"Just fine, and you?"

"Can't complain; nobody'd listen anyway, right?"

"Well, I don't know about that, but..."

"It's true, my brother was just tellin' me about his wife's mother's operation and said she'd been complainin' to the doctor bout that bump for ages. He didn't listen either."

"Well, yeah, I see what you mean." Prudence knew where the conversation was headed and not wanting to wait for the soup to be dished up, moved to the pre-made section, grabbed a wrapped sandwich and handed over the exact amount of money and rushed past Lloyd. "See you."

"Sure thing," Lloyd said as she whizzed by.

Tony eyed her from across the room, tilted against the studio wall, the painted expression saying what she never allowed him to say in person. With her eyes glued, she finished her sandwich, and with the final bite, realized why seeing Lloyd bothered her so. It was something he had inferred when Nick was away, a phrase he'd used while Tony was coming and going from the studio. 'While the cat's away', that was it. Don't go there, she thought, even if it was the other way around. She had done everything in her power to get past the awful outcome of his last trip, and until seeing Lloyd, she'd been doing a pretty good job of it.

"How'd it go with Donny today?" Nick said.

Prudence was in the hall, changing out of her boots when he walked in. "Really good. He took all of them but one."

"Terrific, looks like you're on your way to fame."

"I doubt that, but it's nice to be sought."

"I wouldn't know about that—I just lost the land deal I had cooking."

"What happened?"

"He couldn't come up with the money after all; his bank pulled out."

"Come on, you've weathered this stuff before," she said, trying for cheery.

"Friggin' business," he said as he brushed past her. "What time's dinner?"

"I hadn't gotten there yet; it's early."

He rummaged the fridge for something to assuage his hunger, but also appease his guilt. The damn checkbook still reflected the loaned monies, the six not four thousand he'd given to Rita. It was the worst time of year to have done that since it was the slowest time for sales. Not that he could tell Pru any of this. The only person he trusted enough to let his hair down with, was Dickie. Poor guy had been dumbfounded. Nick thought that might have been more about the fact that Nick had had that much money to spare than whether or not Nick told his wife. But at least, Dickie let him vent and was able to keep a secret. Thank goodness, Pru's friendship with Dickie's wife Debbie was that of comfortable acquaintances who only got together because of their husbands, otherwise he would really be screwed.

"I'm going for a walk, Pru, shake out this nasty mood," Nick said, heading out the back door.

She got a large container of broth out of the fridge and emptied it into a pot on the stove. As she retrieved all the ingredients, she kept an eye on him through the window. He was kicking at the snowy ledge like a kid might. He'd only gone a few yards, when he stopped and raised his fist to the air. It appeared that he wasn't just talking to himself, and if there had been more of it back there, he would have made snowballs to throw at his audience, he was that mad.

Prudence stuck her head out, "Want some company?" she yelled.

"Nah, I'm coming in…too cold to hang around."

Well, so much for trying, she thought, closing the door against the cold draft. But he didn't come right back in. Instead, he stomped around some more and walked a little further away and turned, repeating the paces two or three times. The man was possessed by something, she realized, and he definitely wanted to be alone.

"Soup for dinner." Prudence held up a bowl as Nick pushed through the kitchen door.

"Just what I need."

"Anything you want to talk about?" She had been meticulous in keeping them on track ever since their big fallout.

"Not much to say." The lies came too easy.

"Fine, but promise me you'll share if you need to."

Nick reddened. Here we go again, he thought, with nowhere to hide. "I'll be fine, you'll see. Soup smells good."

"Chicken with leeks, carrots, and tomatoes for good measure."

"Cure for the soul, isn't that what Hannah told you?"

"You remembered?" It had been years since she first told Nick about things in Hannah's letters; it was touching to know he had listened. "She'd be close to a hundred by now, but I still wish she were here. Maybe that's why I bonded with Lena; she seemed to possess the same kind of compassion and wisdom. There were so many times when I've wanted to reach out to that mother figure."

"I didn't mean to make you cry," Nick said, ashamed that he was probably the cause for her need to reach out on many occasions. "So tell me more about what Donny had to say."

"Just that he wants one of the paintings changed and I don't have a clue how I'm going to do that. Unless you would sit for me, or stand in this case."

"Oh no, you aren't going to wrangle me into posing for hours. Besides, I have a business to run."

"Just teasing, but I do need to find a solution."

"What if you removed the hat altogether and maybe use tuxedo suspenders for your prop. You know, hang them over his shoulder like he was getting ready for the symphony. After all, the gallery is in Portland. And you already have one with him in a dress shirt."

She grappled him in a bear hug, "You are a genius. But I don't have suspenders."

"I do. If you recall, I used to go to the ballet in Denver, before we were married. I'll dig them out for you."

"Oh yes, and I remember who you used to go with." Her teasing tone fell flat. Diana had once again entered the room. "Anyway, that was a long time ago, and I would love to borrow your suspenders…that sounded strange, didn't it?"

"In a nice way."

Staring at the Goethe quote on his office wall, Nick understood this brewing storm wouldn't build the character that the deceased German writer inferred. It wouldn't be preceded by high winds and weather forecasts because, as Nick suspected, it had just come by way of the mailman who was already climbing the steps of the insurance company next door. He had dumped Nick's packet of mail as though the contents might be harmful to his health instead of Nick's, and fled in his unlaced Bean boots, ready to unleash bills and notices to the unsuspecting neighborhood recipients. It was the beginning of Mud Season, the fifth season in the lexicon of a Maine calendar, a time known for its slick brown sludge, and slippery slopes. A time for disaster to strike, Nick thought, as his hand closed around the ecru envelope from Diana. How had he let this happen? A couple of nights with her and she believed they would get back together. What in God's name had he done?

He closed the door to his office, and removed the scented paper from the envelope. The perfume obliterated the written words, the same fragrance that clung to the two letters stashed away because he had enjoyed reading that in her eyes, he was wonderful. When he'd gone to Denver it seemed that if Pru wasn't spending hours with Tony, her nose was stuck in a book, and he had justified his behavior based on *what*? How could he have been jealous of the things that made her who she was? How stupid could a guy be? Sweat marched from his hairline and down his jaw. He put his head in his hands; he was so screwed.

Marrying Pru had been the best thing he had ever done. If he was totally honest, he had squandered any hope he had of regaining her trust the moment he had allowed Diana back into his thoughts. He should have put his foot down with his mother, and made it perfectly clear to Diana that he was happily married. But, no, he had to play the hero to her divorce woes. He had allowed her customary flattery to turn his head, and rationalized everything by using the image of Tony Moss sitting semi-naked in Pru's studio. What a fool he had been. Prudence needed him far more than Diana ever could in ways Diana would never understand. All she really cared about was snagging her prey.

And thanks to his ego, Diana had once again made Nick fair game. No more, he thought, the letters had to stop.

Prudence sat on the padded stool, staring at Tony's image. Then she went back to her sketchpad and drew his head without the hat. It had been a week, and Nick still hadn't produced the suspenders, and bugging him when he was busy wouldn't accomplish anything. Struggling, she sketched thin lines, hoping to simulate where the straps should fall over Tony's shoulder. The effort was frustrating without the real thing, and she made up her mind to look for them herself as soon as she got home, which by the waning sunlight, wouldn't be long now. As far as she was concerned, April this far north was only an imposter swindling the hopes of those salivating for spring, and she already hungered for the coming summer.

The car path on Thatcher Lane was grooved and the Bug's tires made a slurping sound as the treads hit the soft muddy sluice. Entering the house through the kitchen, she immediately shed her boots, switched on the radio, and opened the fridge. Its harsh light accused her of neglect. The space looked to have been ransacked with only a half-empty container of cream holding its own with a stoppered bottle of white wine, both stark reminders of how long it had been since she had shopped. The freezer was not much better, but a package of pork chops would do for tonight's dinner. Scribbling out a quick shopping list for tomorrow, she surveyed the cupboard. On the shelf, her dry, flavorless rice cakes stood sentry-like next to Nick's Cheerios— open as though he'd eaten out of the box. The only other contents, a new jar of Dijon mustard and a plump pound bag of all-purpose flour—items she could use to make a roux for a cream sauce. Going back for the frozen peas, she checked her watch. There had been a 'lightbulb' moment on the way home—

a place for something like suspenders to be tucked away—a hole in the wall, literally. Old houses were notorious for their lack of closets and this house was no exception. At some point, a wise carpenter had built a cupboard into the wall between the second floor landing and the attic, and without Herman, she would never have noticed it. When she had first hired him for repairs to the ailing house, he had complimented the earlier workmanship, and tossed in a bit of local history as well. The wooden door matched the wainscoting in the stairwell making the entire cupboard easy to miss.

Passing her reflection in the hallway mirror, Prudence swiped at the sketching charcoal smudged across her cheek, and removing the purple knit cap, fluffed her flattened hair. There would be time to grab a quick shower and fresh clothes when she finished up here. The voice of Bette Midler singing "Wings" floated behind her, paying homage to the last of a peach and mauve sunset falling across the landing from the window in her bedroom. Switching on the hall's overhead light, and making herself comfortable on the steps leading to the attic, she twisted the miniature knob on the curious aperture. It emitted a feeble squeak followed by a strenuous complaint as the door—in need of lubricant—was eased to one side, exposing stacks of shoeboxes filled with Nick's salvaged objects: boat pennants, hardware, and the odd tool found in old houses—and, maybe, if she was lucky, his old suspenders.

As the boxes piled up next to her feet, darkness pulled the shade on the second floor and the overhead light cast a gaudy glow on the interior of the wall cubby. So far, the containers held pretty much what she had expected, and even a bonus—two rolls of twine that may or may not have anything to do with boating. He really was a string saver! One more box and then she would quit, with or without the suspenders, she thought, as her stomach growled. Nick would be home soon anyway, and then he could resume the hunt while she cooked. Kneeling, she reached way in to the darkest part, begging spiders and mites to stay put in their corners. This last box was identical to the others except the lid was branded with a logo from a high-end store in Denver. Satisfaction filled her, and they would laugh over her fear of spiders. She lifted the lid, sneezed at the displaced dust, and stared at Nick's black suspenders. They were in the tissue paper where new shoes had been, and cradled like nesting birds, ebony straps, imagined against a starched snowy shirt. They denoted elegance, a time of grand performances shared without her in Denver, a time before they had married. Maybe he would take her to the opera one day, she thought, bringing them to the mirror. Laying them over her shoulder, she fiddled with their clips, adjusting for what she believed would be the right angle for Tony's size and how they would look in the painting. Sniffing, she detected a light fragrance, not the expected odor of stale cardboard.

With the treat of finding them, Prudence forgot her hunger, and went back to the box. Underneath the first layer of paper— but wrinkled from carelessness—were a black bow-tie and matching cummerbund, along with a similar set made up in a rich plaid. She refolded the silky material, and as she put them back in their nesting place, her fingers brushed something stiff-edged. Lifting the layers from the box, she put everything down next to her.

Suspicion and dread collided and her heart began to race. She had unearthed two envelopes, unsealed and begging to be searched. Reluctantly, because she could already smell the fragrance, she pulled out the notepaper. Prudence's mind rewound the day months ago when she had found Diana's note hidden in Nick's suitcase. With a few choice words and even a clever sexual innuendo, it was clear as Prudence scanned the lines that Diana intended to replace her. Diana had the gall to say that she had never gotten over him and how good they were together. Prudence's stomach did a little flip and bile reached her throat. Why would he have saved such incriminating words? And why had there been anything to write about?

Like a sleepwalker, she returned the other boxes back to their hidey hole, but stayed put on the stairs, the open letters splayed before her. Grief was something she understood when someone died, but this time it had arrived in the form of betrayal by way of the postal service. And at that moment she wasn't certain she would ever again be without it.

Nick entered the house through the kitchen door, and wiped his feet vigorously on the washable doormat. Hannah's Bakelite radio blasted his eardrums. Maybe he would buy Pru a Bose for her birthday, he thought, turning it down. The house, without the radio blaring, was eerily quiet.

"Pru, you up there?" With his long legs, he took the steps two at a time thinking she'd gone to the attic, but found her sitting trance-like on the stairs in front of the attic door instead. Then he spotted the Denver logo of the lid that had been tossed aside, and the sheets of writing paper on her lap. "What the hell, Pru?"

She heard his voice as though it had come through a tunnel and shaking her head, "I read them, but would you like to tell me WHY?"

He could not have conjured a worse scenario. Running his hands through his hair, he walked over and sat down next to her. "Will you listen and not scream at me if I try to explain how it happened?"

"*What* happened should come before how."

"Don't make this any harder than it is, please, Pru."

This was one of those seminal moments, she thought, that can change a life forever. A quiet settled over her, visions of the upcoming social commitments and how she would go forward— by not saying a word because the situation was too absurd for those who knew them to digest? Keep moving, one foot in front of the other, and no one will notice the deficiency in your steps, the halting staccato of your movements—the changes in your breathing?

"Pru?"

"What should I do?"

"Don't overreact, please."

"Overreact, are you crazy?" She jumped up and took a swing at him and when he ducked, she fell forward.

He reached for her.

"Let me go," she screamed.

"Stop fighting me!"

"I hate you!"

When he relaxed his grip, she stood near the wall to their room, and short of a fire in which to throw them, she tore the papers in shreds and threw them in the air, watching as if she were in a movie, as they rained down around him. He paled and she stared, her stomach threatening to fail her again. "What were you thinking?"

"She needed me, Pru. It's as simple as that."

"I need you too."

He couldn't think straight. "Sometimes I'm not so sure."

"So now what do we do? I'm not sure I can even be in the same house with you. And right now, I think I'm going to be sick," she said running for the bathroom. When she came out, Nick was standing at the bedroom door.

"Are you all right?"

"I don't know if I'll ever be right again." She pushed him away and shut the door in his face. Not very many days ago they had made love, their pattern consistent since Italy, and she had been safe. Looking around the bedroom, she had the urge to throw something, but the furniture was too large. Instead, she threw her beloved books against the wall and dumped his clothes on the floor of the closet, physically expelling the pain, which was lodged far deeper than her stomach acid.

He was still sitting there when she came out of the room. He looked broken, and she had the urge to reach out and comfort *him.* Love didn't go away in a heartbeat, she thought, watching the tears flowing from his eyes. Yet what could she do? Was there a manual or guidebook that would make the exposed liaison with Diana go away.

"Leave me alone for a while Nick; I can't talk about it just yet."

"If you're sure."

"Just let me be for a while."

Prudence stayed awake most of the night, Diana's words of endearment going round and round in her head. She had heard him rustling around the guestroom, and nearly laughed at the absurdity of the situation. They had exchanged places as if it were required depending on the hierarchy of the grievance. Even if this were the very first time in their marriage and only for a short period of time while he was in Denver, she had tried to find something to own about what had happened. How else was she to get through this? The shock had finally given way to tears, and as dawn broke, she was reminded of Hannah's rigorous determination not to be a victim of her own tragedy. If Prudence pushed, her choices were slim: a legal separation leading to a divorce, which was what she assumed Diana desired. Or do something completely for herself. The idea of finding Kate in the Cayman's had crossed her mind first, but then, seeing one of her art magazines on the floor, the notion of going to Italy to paint took shape. It was exhausting to formulate ways in which her mind jumped ahead, predicting this or that when all she really wanted was to lie very still and pretend it had been a very bad dream. Of course it wasn't, and now it was up to her to make choices, which would by their very nature, have major consequences. The situation, if not handled well, could become a sadness that would cling for a long time, and she was reminded of Julie and the wisdom she had brought to their friendship all those years ago on St. Thomas. But what if she were somehow responsible, she thought, reminded of Tony's approaches and the subsequent glow she'd felt while Nick was away. What if she had presented the wrong message to her husband? But now what of her choices: let him wallow in his guilt or let his affair break her spirit.

She had never wanted Kate's counsel as much as this very moment. Vivien still believed Nick incapable of destroying their marriage. Downstairs, Nick ground coffee beans, and beyond the window lobster boats churned up the water—the soundtrack of life as it had been before the reveal. Everything from here on in would be framed as before or after the discovered letters. With her hair still damp from the torrent of tears, she lay in their marriage bed and listened, and rehashed the last months and the joy they had taken in each other.

"Would you like coffee?" Nick said, entering the room. "What can I do to make it up to you...just tell me."

"I don't know myself; how can I tell you?"

She watched his back, his slumped shoulders as he left. And she watched the clock, waiting for the right time to place that long distance call. Downstairs, the kitchen door banged against the jamb. Nick had probably taken his coffee out to the ledge. They both used the spot as a place to think or rail about whatever needed sorting. While he was out of the house, she went into the kitchen and got herself a cup of the strong coffee he preferred, adding milk and two sugars since she hadn't eaten the night before. He was far enough away from the house that he wouldn't see her watching him through the window. Was it her imagination, or had he gotten older overnight? Her chest tightened; how she loved him. She went back upstairs; it was time to place that call to Kate.

Staring at the gulls staring at him, Nick assumed they too could see how he had failed his wife. They bobbed on the waves, moving with the current, expecting more than he had to offer. He kept walking, and they followed with their beady eyes on the mug in his hand. Diana was trouble, had always been that way, but why had he been so weak? It was not a word he'd ever associated with his demeanor, nor was cheater. If Pru ever forgave him, he'd damn well make sure whatever had come over him, never happened again. But would she forgive him? If the roles were reversed, would he?

Prudence studied the words she had composed for an email to Lena, having completed a lengthy conversation with her closest friend. The crux of which was that Kate thought it best that Prudence take an extended trip to Italy—to paint, to sort herself out, to do whatever it would take to make things right. And especially, to avoid becoming the subject of village gossip by way of Lloyd Tucker. Why bother with a short stint in the Caribbean, Kate had said, where Prudence would feel idle and bothered by the constant presence of Michael. After all, she couldn't very well get rid of her husband for two weeks, or even two days for that matter. The condo was too small and he refused to be a beachcomber. The advice had been a consensus of opinions, but only if Lena would have her. Prudence did not intend to be a burden, would even do their desk work if the Bernolis wanted a little time off. They had someone who came in to clean the rooms, but she would do anything required, and would use the time in Tuscany wisely. Look what the first trip had produced.

She dialed the bookstore with shaky fingers and quickly hung up. Vivien had to be told in person, after which Prudence could send the email from the office computer. The smell of burned toast reached the second floor; Nick not paying attention. Her stomach turned at the thought of food, but she craved a shower. By the time she came out, Nick had been in their bedroom and grabbed fresh clothes. If she didn't get away, this would be what they had to look forward to—living like strangers, at least that was as far as she could get in her newly imagined world. Kate had asked her about sending Nick away, but that would only mean to someplace else in Oyster Cove where Prudence would still have to face him, and everyone else. On one hand, she felt protective of them both, wanted to conceal the infidelity completely from prying eyes as Kate had suggested. On the other, she wanted to call each and every person in their address book and flood the wires with her personal pain. Had she been the type of wife who talked about marital issues, the latter option may have been enough to keep her from running away. But she wasn't, and so she would leave and, if possible, work it out in the privacy of a foreign land.

Nick was reminded of the tigers he'd seen as a child, pacing their cages as if seeking something unseen by others. He was in his back office, walking and cracking his knuckles, a habit cured by his father during that same youthful period. Nervous energy Charlie had called it, but it had grated on everyone's nerves. And now, it grated on his, but it was the only thing he could do without screaming at the top of his lungs what a schmuck he'd been. If only his dad were alive, maybe he could figure out what had made Nick jeopardize so much for a one-night stand, or three nights if he were entirely honest. Diana had other ideas. Prudence was going to do something drastic; he could feel it. He could take anything but her leaving him.

Vivien stopped what she was doing, and moved away from the stack of new novels about to be placed in the bookstore window. "Something bad has happened, I can tell by your face."

"I need to use the computer to email Lena, then I'll tell you everything," Prudence said.

She went into the small office and logged on to their server and copied out her thoughts for Lena without the use of extraneous words. Now all that was left was the waiting. In the back of her mind, Prudence hoped something would happen to change the trajectory she had devised. This was such a huge leap of faith, and it could also backfire.

"It all hit the fan last night. I was right, he's been cheating. I found Diana's letters," Prudence said, rejoining Vivien out front.

"I wanted to be right; that he'd never do that!" Vivien said.

"You like to be right about everything, and this time I wanted that too."

"What did she say?"

Prudence rushed through the words that started it all. No one likes to think of their spouse in another's bed, but she also knew Vivien would be hurt by Nick's betrayal. She loved him too.

"What happened next?"

"I'm embarrassed to say I took a swing at him. It frightened me and shocked him. I've never swung at anyone in my life."

"I might have clocked him given the chance, but I'm glad you stuck up for yourself," Vivien said. "And Italy still beckons, even with all the problems it presents?"

"It's so strange, but with what feels like the bottom dropping out from under me, the flying part doesn't seem all that scary anymore. It's like I don't have anything to lose."

Except she really did. Without further demeaning her husband, Prudence begged a ride to the airport when the time was right and left Vivien to mull Nick's fate.

A note with Prudence's name leaned against a vase on the kitchen table. The small bouquet threatened to undo her stoicism. Instead, she reached for the phone and called Donny Bales.

"I'll finish that last piece before I go," she said, reiterating the made-up plan. "The workshop is a once-in-a-lifetime opportunity, and I knew you would want me to participate."

"It's a terrific opportunity, Prudence, I only wish I were going along. I love Italy, and I know you'll produce some wonderful paintings when you return," Donny said.

She hung up and turned her attention back to Nick's small missive. It stated that he loved her, and expected to be given a second chance. *Expected* was not the word she would have used if the situation were reversed, but they were both walking new ground these days, and that ground was shaky at best. She couldn't help but think that he'd been trying to get caught. None of it made sense.

Nick went into work each morning and arrived home at the same time every night, always hopeful that there had been a breakthrough and his wife would see his pain and embrace him. How he missed her. He had spent innumerable hours trying to reason out what had turned his head away from his marriage, even for such a brief time, and had come up wanting. Tonight, like so many, he walked into the dark kitchen to the sound of crying.

"Oh God, Pru, when will this stop? I can't bear to see you in so much pain."

"I can't seem to stop," she said. "I'm so hurt I don't know where to turn. Do you think I want to fly all the way to Italy...by myself no less...just to punish you?"

"I don't know what to think."

"Remember when we met and I told you about the man on St. Thomas who walked out on me the morning of our wedding?"

"Yes."

"I never ever wanted to feel that way again. And you made me a promise that you wouldn't ever hurt me like that."

"I know, and now I can't undo what I've done and I'm so, so sorry."

"I think you are, but I don't know how to forgive you just yet. That's why I need this trip. If there's any hope of us returning to what we had, I have to learn to trust you all over again. And right now, going away from you is all I can come up with."

"I know this is trite, but I never would have let that thing with her go on; you have to believe me."

"But it did happen…the whole time you were there."

He didn't know how to respond. There was no point in arguing over the numbers; one or three or all the days mattered little now. "I love you too much to lose you Pru, so I'll do anything you want; just promise me you'll keep an open mind. I might have been stupid, but I need you."

"I'll try; that's all I can do."

Chapter Thirteen

Each day had been more difficult than the one before. The hurt so obvious they never voiced it, but went about their routines in separate bubbles of pain as the days slid from the calendar and the season spoke of change. The first days of May—freshened by rain and abundantly green: fern, moss, asparagus and viridian, inspiring shades on a spring palette. Light breezes blew through Oyster Cove scenting the air with sea and pine, and apple green tips looking like freshly daubed nail polish, waved from distant branches. The earth rendered up buried cones, moldy leaves, and an embroidered promise of summer. Prudence spent her days alone in her studio with only Tony's portrait for company. Lena had finally responded with a lengthy letter, her command of English indicative of the years of welcoming tourists from America. In her wisdom—perhaps a gift of an ancient culture—she had somehow read between the lines of Prudence's request. They would be happy to include her at Casa Bernoli, and would put her to work. She would stay in Angelina's room; their daughter, they had just learned, would not be home for a visit during the summer.

Nick had been working longer hours to make up for the funds he had given Rita. But it was also to avoid confrontation or simply because he hadn't been able to combat Pru's determination to leave home, especially without an exact return date. After challenging her on every level, he'd given up, stormed off, and kept quiet ever since. His anger showed more in the abruptness of his movements and careless heed to his appearance, and she noted, he too had lost weight. As her departure date loomed closer, her resolve threatened to deteriorate. She would leave on the 17th, soon after Donny retrieved the final painting, content in his belief she was going away to paint more of the beautiful landscapes. Fall and future shows seemed a lifetime away.

Hoping for a follow-up letter from Italy, she pushed her foot to the pedal and drove into the small path next to the house just as the mail truck was pulling away. There were bills but no correspondence. As she flipped through the useless junk mail, she rushed to answer the insistent ring emanating through the open window. The voice at the other end was discharged like an angry rifle shot.

"Nicholas told me I'm supposed to apologize," Rita said. "But you're the one running off to Italy."

"This isn't helping, Rita. It's between me and Nick and I don't want to argue with you."

"Well perhaps you should think twice about leaving him."

"If you're insinuating that it opens the door for Diana, then I suggest you say that to him and not me."

"I don't like your tone young lady," Rita said.

She had hung up before Prudence could say more. As expected, not ten minutes later, Nick called. "This feud has to stop, Pru."

"I didn't start it."

"I already told her she's not allowed to speak for me…isn't that enough?"

"What's enough, Nick, is that Rita is out of bounds and I'm not going to tolerate it. You deal with her."

Nick stared at the receiver, waiting for it to crackle and burn. Pru was right, of course, but he had always left the emotional stuff that involved Rita to his father. The old boy had a way of taming her attitude about everything: politics, family, grocery prices, the whole lot. Nick did not have the constitution for dealing with petty quarrels, and now Rita had alienated Pru to the point where it was difficult for her to sort out the difference between mother and son. He kicked at the desk chair causing the hard back of it to spin and bump the edge of his desk and overturn a cup of scalding coffee. "Shit." It was like September all over again—his head filled with doubt and his lack of understanding of women still consuming too much time. Maybe because his father had been so good at hiding his discontent, Nick never learned the right lessons, or maybe he was just plain stupid. Though he never once told Pru, he personally knew others in Oyster Cove who cheated, not that this knowledge would help his case, he thought, dropping his head into his hands? Maybe he'd just go for a beer with Dickie, who was no stranger to confrontation of any kind.

Lifting his head to the sudden knock, "Hi Lloyd, what's up?"

"Sorry to barge in," Lloyd said, sticking his head around the door.

"Just wanted to know if I'm supposed to pull that stuff for Prudence's studio out of storage; it's that time of year."

"So it is. But let's leave that for a while."

"Everything okay? You look like you could use some sleep."

"Fine...just a little under the weather."

"Then you take care. I've got the cottages handled—water's turned on and everything's ready for summer," Lloyd said before stepping out of the office. "Oh, one more thing...her studio door could use a coat of paint."

"Fine. Ask her if she wants a different color, and then go ahead and take care of it."

After Lloyd walked away, Nick picked up the phone and dialed Dickie.

"I don't know where to start." Nick pulled on his beer, set the bottle down on the long Dory bar and looked Dickie in the eye. "Have you ever cheated on Debbie?"

"Hell no. Wanted to once, but only because I was pissed at her. She was yammering on about all the things I wasn't doing around the house and how our relationship was going downhill—we'd been married sixteen years—and I just lost it. One night I told her I had to be on patrol, but instead I went over to a bar in Stonycroft. Anyway, long story short, nothing really happened, but I've regretted it anyway, especially since I hold my breath every time we go out and I spot a woman who looks familiar. It's no way to live, believe me."

"We've only been married for five, and now that Pru knows, I don't know what to do."

"Anything she wants brother or you will be toast."

"I just wish I knew why I did it in the first place."

"Check that thing in your pants," Dickie said, "And don't roll your eyes at me, you're one of us—the abused male not getting enough attention or some stupid thing. That's what Deb says when we argue, but now I know how to handle it. I make jokes and then do the dishes like she asks," Dickie said. "What's this Diana like?"

"Beautiful, educated, wealthy…once her divorce goes through, but frail too. Maybe that's the wrong word, but she relies on me, or at least while I was out there."

"You really are thick. I don't read a lot of books, but she played you. Man, you really surprise me. I always thought you were smarter than that."

"Me too."

"Now that's out of the way, what's next?"

"Pru's going away for a while, but I'm afraid she won't come back."

"All I can say is you better make sure she does. Divorce is really messy and expensive these days."

"That's the last thing I want, but not because of the money. Hell, I'd give her anything to keep her here."

"Let me buy you another beer," Dickie said. "You're going to need it."

Prudence inventoried her supplies readying them for UPS to fly them off to Italy: a dozen small painting panels, two palette knives, three brushes, tubes of the primary colors, apron, sketch pad and colored pencils. A journal had been added at the last minute along with two books on relationship behavior. If nothing else, she might find the words needed to understand and therefore, make the right decisions. Staring at the book covers, Hannah's letters came to mind; the woman had been through it all. Prudence straightened her spine and taped the box. Anything forgotten or required once she was in Italy, could be purchased at the supply store in Florence.

Donny had picked up the last painting, which had turned out to be his favorite. Though he'd had no idea of the ordeal behind the found suspenders, he had been intrigued by their use and ended up buying that painting for himself. And it would still be displayed with the others on opening night of the exhibit. If there were inaccuracies in the shape of Tony's head without the previously painted hat, Donny never mentioned it.

Whenever Nick was home, door slamming was expected, the noise emphasizing his discontent, while the tickets to Italy lay silent on her nightstand. She had packed and unpacked more than once, each time weighing her options for laundry and weather. Vivien was set to drive her to the airport, and Marco, staying with Angelina in Milan the night before, would meet Prudence at the airport on the morning of her arrival. This time, the possibility of her luggage getting lost would be greater since she would have to change planes to save money. With an advance on her bookstore income, some of her savings and Donny's unexpected purchase, the extra money would make her less beholden and suddenly, she tasted the irony of freedom.

On the 17th, Prudence hauled her luggage down the stairs, her heart thudding in time with each bump of a wheel against tread. A note had been left on the kitchen counter, along with a square red box.

Keep my heart with you at all times—learn to trust me again, please. Love, Nick.

Inside the satin nest lay a tiny gold heart-shaped pin, simple and elegant. She tucked it in her purse and allowed the tears to fall on the paper before turning it over for Nick to find.

The pin is beautiful, thank you. Give me time. Lena will send an email when I arrive at Casa Bernoli. I can't promise when, but I will write. P.

A horn honked and a moment later, the clang of the ancestral doorbell, the crank style replaced by a knocker, but still used by friends who just couldn't help themselves. "You okay?" Vivien said entering the kitchen.

"I will be once I'm on that plane. Nick left me this." Prudence plucked the pin out of her purse and put it in Vivien's hand.

"Ooh, pretty. He's got balls, I'll give him that."

"Vivien!"

"Well, what should I say?"

"Nothing, let's just go."

"You can always change your mind."

"No, this is the right thing to do."

With the seatback slanted, Prudence closed her eyes and pushed away the fear that always came with a plane's upward trajectory. Was it right, she thought, running away like this? She had told her two dearest friends it was. Lena would see how thin she had become and would immediately take her to task. Food didn't appeal, especially the greasy stuff she smelled at the kiosk in the airport terminal. The engines thrummed, and Prudence's body gave way to sleep and dreams of Italian vistas. She walked through cornflowers and poppies and held a tiny hand—a weepy-eyed mutt trailing behind. When at last she was jostled awake, the appearance of a flight attendant by her side prevented her from falling from the clock tower. "Are you all right?"

"Just a bad dream. I don't like flying."

"We're about an hour out; try and stay calm," the attendant said.

Prudence retrieved her book, which had fallen on the floor. It was historical fiction and guaranteed (by Vivien) to prevent her from crying during the flight. For some reason, Prudence had been attracted to Nicholas Sparks' books recently, which only seemed to exacerbate her present situation, leaving her spent and anxious. Would her story become a tragic novel only to be shunned by readers as being too self-absorbed or pig-headed because she chose herself over Nick—at least for the moment? As she flipped the pages, it hardly mattered what anyone thought; she was alone and unhappy and had just had a dream that included a child's plump, delicate hand. Lena was going to have to walk her through that one, or maybe Nilda. Prudence shuddered at the thought.

Marco flagged her down at baggage claim, embracing her like some long-lost relative. "*Bentornato,* Prudenza, *bentornato.*"

"Grazie, Marco, it is good to be back."

"Lena is making the pasta just for you; you will see, *delicioso!*"

"I can't wait to see her. How is Angelina?"

"*Bene*, grazie, but she works too hard. Her mama would like her to be home in Tuscany, but she is an independent woman. And now, you will have her room."

"I'm so grateful, and to you for picking me up."

"*Non e niente.* How is Nico?"

"Fine."

"Fine?"

"We're taking a break for a while. I'll tell you and Lena all about it later. There's my bags," Prudence said, happy to change the subject.

"Your box arrived at la casa," Marco said.

"My painting supplies…I plan to work while I'm here. And, help you out too, whatever I can do."

"Lena will see to that. It is her office and I stay out of the way."

Marco led her to the car and piled the luggage in back. *"Domire un po,"* he said getting behind the wheel. "I will wake you when we reach the village."

"Grazie, Marco, I didn't sleep well on the plane."

"Benvenuto!" Lena practically hauled Prudence through the opened car door. *"Dai, dai,* Marco will bring the bags."

"I've missed you." Prudence began to cry as Lena took her in her arms.

"You are so thin!"

"I knew you would say that; I can't eat."

"Nonsense! You will eat my gnocchi with the butter sauce and the sweet fennel roasted and all the things I have made for the dinner. It is a perfect day for al fresco!"

Prudence took a step back, wiped her tears and sniffed. The air was redolent of wisteria and jasmine wafting from the pergola around the side entrance. "Oh I've missed this Lena."

"It is good, no?"

"Definitely good."

"Come, you rest, unpack and we will talk. Marco will go with Aldo for a while."

"Please tell me I'm not a bother."

"No bother, and you will like Angelina's room. There are many books and the *albero di limoni* you will help me water," Lena said, indicating the height of the little tree with her hand at her hip. "I made the promise and sometimes I forget."

194

"I'm happy to do whatever I can; you and Marco are kind to let me stay a while."

"*Silenzio*. We are happy you are here."

Prudence believed her. Their daughter's room was small, but well laid out. Prudence would be in her element. The bookcase was its main feature. Angelina's lemon tree stood in a clay pot resting on a stand with wheels. It had been placed in the corner where sun burst through the gauze curtains, and where it could be wheeled through the side doorway and left to bask against the building's radiated warmth. That would be Prudence's job—to make sure it got enough water and sunlight to keep the young plant going. She opened her purse and removed the pin and placed it on top of the dresser. Then she took off her shoes and lay on the bed and immediately fell asleep.

Prudence woke to the hum of a mower in the distance, though even that could have been in her dream. Someone was knocking.

"Si?"

"*Ora di pronzo,*" Lena said.

"I'll be right there." The nap had not left her rested and lunch would be her dinner since she would not stay awake for the traditional European dinnertime. Not that she was hungry, but it was unwise to refrain, especially in front of Lena. She slipped on a simple shirt and capri pants and a pair of flats and joined the Bernoli's on their terrace under the pergola. Was it only last September, she thought, as the bees twirled and looped lazily above their heads.

"Ah, Prudenza," Marco said, pouring her a glass of wine.

"I almost forgot how lovely this spot is," she said.

"Mangia!" Lena had moved in behind Prudence's chair and was placing a bowl of gnocchi on the table, directly in front of her. "You will eat now," Lena said with authority.

"My appetite isn't the same as it was last fall, but I'll do my best," Prudence said. "But this tastes just as good as I remember." Taking a forkful led to a complete serving. Then she dunked a piece of crusty bread into a circle of olive oil sprinkled with pepper and licked her fingers. Food hadn't tasted this good in weeks.

"You see," said Lena, "This will make you strong again."

"I will go to Aldo's now," Marco said. "You and Lena talk."

"My husband is a wise man," Lena said, topping off her wine glass. "Now *cara*, tell me what is happening."

Where to start, she thought, rearranging her body in the wooden chair. "When we left Italy last September many of our problems had been resolved, the ones to do with my failed pregnancies and work schedules, et cetera. I wrote you about my big art show, but I didn't tell you that Nick wasn't there."

"*Perche no?*"

"Because he was called back to Colorado where his mother lives."

"His mamma was ill?"

Prudence couldn't help but smile at the notion of Rita's illness—a malady for which there was no pill. Lena listened, her face devoid of judgment, as Prudence filled her in on the whole sordid chapter that had been culled from months of unhappiness. When she was finished, spent and in need of a hug, Lena reached over and patted her hand with palms that were made smooth by years of contact with the olive oil from their press.

"What does Nico say?"

"That he loves me and is sorry for everything."

"And?"

"I don't believe him."

"So you will stay in Italy until you do or until he comes for you?"

"I guess."

"Then we must make you strong. But first, let me tell a story about husbands, the one I tell to my daughters. Our men, they are fragile creatures. They need love, food and attention…like the *alberello* in Angelina's room, only more. Without even one

196

of those things, their eyes reach for sunlight wherever they can find it. Sometimes they find the attention with a new woman, and sometimes the food is disagreeable and they look for another cook. And, sometimes they can only feel love if the light shines totally on them and their full bellies."

Prudence gawped at Lena. She had never heard anything remotely like this. When it all came together in her head, she doubled over with laughter. "Where did you learn such a thing?"

"From my mamma. Papa went with another woman—once. When mamma found out, she threatened to cut off an important piece of him. Papa knew she meant it, and never strayed again. You Americans call it a mid-life crisis. Mamma and Nonna called it *normale*."

"I don't want that kind of normal." Prudence refrained from asking if Marco had ever cheated; she really didn't want to know. To be here in Italy with this warmhearted couple was all she had thought about. To learn otherwise, might destroy the singular note she had played all the way here.

"No, but you can help him see what he is destroying—the goodness you are in his life."

"Oh, Lena, I don't know. I'm so tired I can't think straight."

"You will sleep and eat my food and when you are stronger, we will cook together again and you will paint something beautiful for me."

Lena walked her back to the guestroom and turned down the pretty lace coverlet. She picked up the photo of her daughters and blew them a kiss, and then kissed Prudence on both cheeks. "*Sogni di oro.*"

"Same to you Lena, and thank you."

When the door clicked shut, Prudence picked up the gold heart and slid it under her pillow in hopes of a better dream. If she had been looking for an immediate answer, Lena had given her the type to confuse rather than clarify. Maybe it was more about opportunity than an exact science.

She woke to the sound of water. Marco was outside cleaning off the stone terrace. She had slept through the night and most of the next day, but her body ached as though she had run a marathon. Maybe it was due to coming off the Pill, she thought, looking at her puffy face in the mirror. She expected changes; if only she could shake her depression. Dressing in shorts and a tee and a pair of sandals, she went through the side door and into the sunshine.

"Can I do that for you Marco?"

"Ah, Prudenza, you are awake. Would you like to water the plants for me so I can help Lena?"

"Si, that would make me feel useful."

Marco handed her the hose and she filled the large watering can halfway to make it easier to lift. The scent of rosemary once again carried her off to another place, a place where dreams could come true. Tonight she would place a sprig under her pillow instead of the pin.

When she finished, she dropped into the familiar hammock and immediately fell asleep.

"Pru, wake up." Lena stood at her side holding a tray of cheese and olives.

"What time is it?"

"What you call cocktail hour," Lena said. "To keep your strength."

"It seems familiar…eat, sleep, eat some more…like last fall."

"*Di preciso.*"

"I see you are still feeding me new words too, and I love it."

"One day you will speak fluent Italian."

"I don't know about that, but with your help I might be able to get by on my own."

"You won't be on your own, *cara*, Nico will be with you."

"How can you be so certain when I'm not?"

"Experience."

Chapter Fourteen

May in Tuscany was quickly brushed aside by June's breathy heat. It swept through the open windows of Casa Bernoli and placed a wreath of fragrance around the stone building, much of which filtered through the open windows in Prudence's room. Each night she placed a new sprig of rosemary under her pillow and each morning she awoke from a dreamless sleep. Time was less complicated and the adjustment to being there, a near natural transition. Maybe it was a feeling of belonging or, not being judged, but she adapted quicker than expected, especially since she was assigned tasks allowing her to feel useful. She greeted tourists, helped with the B & B's considerable mail and in the afternoons, tried out new recipes in the big kitchen while everyone else was out. Writing in a journal became a different type of therapy, and she jotted those sentences with alacrity. Sundays at the Bernoli's were a time reserved for Nilda, and whenever she could, Prudence went to the grove to look for the elderly couple in Lena's story. With her sketch book in hand, she meandered the trail, taking the steps thoughtfully, looking for photographable moments. Unlike the first hike with Nick, the windows in the apartments leading to the grove, were open in the early morning hours, the aroma of strong coffee wafting out and a foreign chatter spilling through the lacey curtains—even the fragrant smell of simmering sauce being prepared for Sunday dinner. She had seen Ariel and Marcello only once, leaning in close as they walked ever so slowly from the grove, but they were too far away to see their faces. She sketched their retreat; she needed the reminder for posterity, a link to a timeless love. Then while the family spent lengthy hours under the pergola, she returned to the kitchen and pounded the pasta out by hand to rid herself of unwanted emotions. As time went on, the journal entries changed too.

June 18 - Letter from Nick. Sense his frustration, but not getting what he's talking about. Something to do with his father and being afraid of fatherhood. Garble; he's probably been drinking.

June 20 – Too busy to write yesterday – plumber on the premises to fix backed up line somewhere within the walls. Marco said the lines were crumbling—kind of scary to think about.

June 21 – Going to market with Aldo today. He's taking me in the three-wheel Ape they use for the grove, a red one. Says he'll let me drive if I like. Wow!

June 25 – Been laying low, bad stomach, light fever. Lena wants to take me to the doctor, but I don't feel comfortable about that. It's probably just a bug.

June 30 – A new visitor to the farm today—a youngster really, but with an air of nobility. He's standing on the terrace wall like he's waiting for an invitation from our resident mouse catcher. Perhaps he's come from one of the larger villas I've spotted on the way to town with Marco. When he caught me watching, he jumped the wall in a hurry, his large green eyes skeptical of what he's discovered here, but I think, because he looks like their cat, Clara, that he'll be back.

July 1 – Sure enough. There he is taking in my easel and the painting I left to dry. It's the one I'm doing for Lena, and Marco of course, but the one I knew Lena would like best. The painted flowers must look real because our fluffy visitor just stuck his nose in to sniff and oh no, he has paint on the end of his nose. Now I have to go out.

July 3 – No more word on Nick. Received an email from Vivien—he's gone to Denver – left her a message to get to me—he's tackling his issues and will then come to Italy. What issues and I don't want him here, not yet anyway. So confusing. I miss him, but I don't. I love it here, but I miss the sea. I'm tired, but I want to paint. And thanks to Clara, the haughty tom has been installed as part of our household. Looks like Clara had been doing more than catching mice, and whoever she took up with had a very royal manner.

On the twenty-sixth of July, Prudence gave Lena the finished painting.

"*Bellissimi fiore,*" Lena said. "I will put this in the great room near the piano."

"I'm so glad you like it."

"But of course I like it, and I love you," Lena said embracing her.

Tears, so many these days. She was loved and she was lonely too. "I wish I knew what to do," Prudence said.

"You will call him."

"I can't...he doesn't love me enough."

"You are acting like a child. He will fix his mistake if you give him a chance."

Prudence continued to create, using the August guests as subjects for charcoal drawings—even the cats had been included. All the while, Lena's words and her belief in the bonds of matrimony remained installed in her mind as she went about her chores. Each time she thought of Marcello and Ariel and what they had gone through to be together, she felt ashamed for blowing off her marriage vows in such a casual manner, even if Nick had been the one to break them. She could tell from his mail, though, that he was eaten up with guilt. It was then that her journal entries developed a less accusatory tone. Because of Lena's intervention, Nick had been emailing more frequently too. They were short and to the point, each one written late in the evenings when Prudence presumed he'd gotten up the courage—with a little liquid help—to say the difficult words. The last, which she had printed out and taken to her room, told her things she would never have guessed.

While you've been gone, I've done a lot of soul searching. I also discovered a lot about my parents while I was in Denver. But, bear with me, it's still hard to explain. I think I've been cheating on myself too. The idea of fatherhood frightened me more than I realized, and a lot of that comes from what I'd never been told. Charlie withheld the things I should have known—the fact that he left my mother for a short time before I was born. When I moved east to be with you, she felt like I was running out on her too, and that's why she's been so hard on you. She really wanted me to marry Diana and stay in Denver; she needed that feeling of control. And I was struck dumb by the fact that Diana still wanted me—badly. It had nothing to do with you. Now I can almost hear you huffing, but it was all about an ego trip down memory lane. Dickie says we men are hardwired to cheat (though he claims he never has), but I don't believe that. I wanted to know what it was I hadn't finished before I met you, if you can understand that. Rita called it unrequited love, and maybe it was to a certain extent. No matter what it was, I'm sorrier than I've ever been in my life—we had it all, and I blew it. Please come home.

Imagine Rita sounding so sensible, Prudence thought as she excavated the phrases searching for that one golden nugget with which to bank on. Prudence hadn't been the only one with a troubled childhood, and Charlie hadn't been the perfect husband and father she had imagined. And now that she had questioned her own reasons for wanting children, Nick's words held more weight. Maybe they were both flawed by their pasts, and just maybe they could use that to become decent parents when the time was right. Unrequited love. A topic not covered in the books she had brought. Was it really possible that a man of Nick's intelligence would have felt the need to take that route— have an affair for the purpose of filling some empty gap from years before? Think hard, she mused, a woman out of the past letting him know in no uncertain terms that he was 'unforgettable'. Heady stuff. Top that with an approval rating by his domineering mother. Freud would have a field day! Vivien would never believe the thoughts swirling in Prudence's brain; the books were at the moment, useless. Men were not good at communicating not only their feelings, but their insecurities, but with all that out in the open, what was next?

Maybe it was time to reconsider her hard stance. She dressed for her day in Raada. Marco had a meeting and would drop her off to do her shopping; her waistline was expanding from all the good food foisted on her by Lena.

"What do you hear from Nico?"

"He wants me to come home."

"That is good, no?"

"I guess." Each day brought a different reasoning; her feelings were all over the place.

"Prudenza, he is your husband."

"I know that Marco!" She snapped. "I'm sorry. I don't know what gets into me some days."

"Maybe it is the heat. You will shop and be happy while I am making the business with the bank, and before we leave the village, I will buy you a big gelato!"

"You're a prince Marco, but I think I'm putting on enough weight."

"It is good—you will need it."

"What do you mean, I'll need it?"

"Did you not think you might be with child?"

"Why would I think that?"

"Lena hinted, so I thought…oh, I put my shoe in it, right? Isn't that what the Americans say?"

"Close enough, but I can't be pregnant—I just can't."

"You are scared just like Nico."

"I don't want to bring a baby into a bad situation. And until Nick and I sort things out, this would be a disaster."

"No baby is a disaster, Prudenza."

"You know what I mean."

"We will talk about it with Lena. I am getting myself into trouble."

Prudence walked the streets in a daze. Could she be? After Dr. Gordon's warning, she had stopped using the Pill, and her body had reverted to doing its own thing without regularity. And with her life in turmoil, getting pregnant had been the farthest thing from her mind. But according to Marco, Lena had seen a change in her figure. Prudence's hand flew to her waist; there was a thickening for sure. Crying had become as natural as turning on the tap, but she had attributed the ready tears to her situation with Nick. Her mind wandered back to those nights of lovemaking, before everything had hit the fan, and she realized that of late, her breasts had been extra tender. If she'd even given it a second thought, it would have portended the arrival of her period—not that she could possibly be pregnant. All those years and months of wishing and it could be happening now with her marriage in crisis? Impossible. She tried to remember the last cycle, but she could barely remember the days of the week. In Italy, she had become another person, swathed in motherly love, and stargazing her worries away. Lena was right, she had been acting like a child. And if Lena was right about this, she and Nick were going to need some serious discussions and soon. As she looked around for the clothing store, she realized how intimidating it would be seeing a doctor in a foreign land without Lena's help. And this was not the dark ages, but she had been on a pill to prevent pregnancy. How would Lena react? Would her modern daughters have discussed such things? Prudence was still a stranger to the Catholic mores of both the Bernoli family and the villagers. Suddenly, there was no joy in the idea that she might be pregnant—not without her husband by her side. It was supposed to be the happiest time of her life.

She nearly missed the small clothing shop. So unlike American stores, there was no bold lettering to grab her attention. A narrow window to the right of the doorway displayed a two-piece outfit set against a yard of silken fabric, but nothing else. Timidly, she walked inside. It too was small, and instead of racks of clothing, items were shelved behind a counter and on a table in the center of the room. A very handsome woman wearing long gold earrings, a well-fitting navy dress, and leather shoes that had to have been handmade in Italy, was dusting off the counter. Prudence could hear voices coming from behind a heavy drape off to her right. The language she had been learning, became nothing but garble. And she didn't understand the size equivalents. The shopkeeper's Italian burst forth in rapid-fire dialect, her ruby-red lips smiling as if Prudence understood the importance of her words. Prudence's face was strained by her own fake smile. She was woefully underqualified for what should have been a simple task, but she'd be damned if she was going to cry in front of this stranger. The word *pronto,* came through the curtain. Whoever was back there was ready, for what, Prudence would never know. She hurriedly chose a cotton shift in two different colors, and red-faced, held out the lira she had brought, hoping it would suffice. Nick had handled their money the last time she was here and now it was all too confusing. Looking at the few lira left in her palm, she went in search of the bank where Marco would meet her. She didn't have to wait long. As soon as he spotted her, he took her elbow and ushered her down the street toward a busily populated corner—the location of the gelato bar.

"Thanks, Marco. I need this." She sat in the metal chair and placed her bundle on the small street-side table.

"*Cioccolato?*" Marco said.

"Si, grazie."

While she waited for him to return, a matronly woman passed by holding the hand of a toddler who was crying outrageous tears. Prudence could hear the Nonna-like whispers trying to soothe the little boy from his tantrum…no screaming, no anger, just a soft voice to coax a smile. Across the street, another woman, this time young and stylish, pushed a small stroller, stopping every few feet to show off the baby. Everywhere she looked, Prudence saw women and children. And just as suddenly, her eyes filled. It was all wrong; this was not how it was supposed to happen, with poor Lena stuck in the middle. Still, Prudence couldn't wait to get back to her counsel and to the comfort of Casa Bernoli.

"For *la signora,*" Marco said, presenting her with a plastic spoon and a waxy cup filled with the creamy gelato she had come to love.

She licked the spoon clean after each taste. "So good."

"We will finish and then Lena will be ready with the *grande insalata.*"

"That's more than enough on a hot day. I bet it'll be the *panzanella* with the leftovers of yesterday's bread and her garden tomatoes."

"Si, *magnifico,*" he said kissing his fingertips.

"You're a good man, Marco."

"Nico too, do not forget."

"I know, and right now, I wish he were here."

"Call him, tell him to come."

"Not until I know if I'm pregnant and if so, if this baby will make it; we've already lost two."

"Come, let us go and talk to Lena," he said picking up her parcel. "She knows about such things."

"You are very sly, Marco," she said getting out of the chair. Suddenly she was very tired. "You know more than you say, but you let your wife take the lead. Very smart indeed." She rose on tiptoe and kissed his cheek.

Marco blushed, tossed their empty cups and as if sensing her fears, took her arm protectively and led her to their parked car.

A week later, Prudence and Lena were seated in the office of *dottore* Giovanni Remo, a physician remarkably unlike Dr. Gordon. He was robust, clean-shaven but with a hint of violet shadow on his chin, which by dinnertime would require another swipe of a razor. His handsome face, like so many of the Italian men, seemed perpetually delighted. He spoke with Lena in their shared Tuscan lilt, and it seemed apparent by his dulcet tones that he could single-handedly coax the wine from vineyard grapes shown in the photo on the wall. Lena caught her staring at the picture.

"Giovanni and his brother Rinaldo. It is their business together, but Rinaldo works the vines so his brother can take care of the medicine."

"I was just thinking of a dear friend back home who would love to meet someone like Rinaldo," Prudence said, taking note of the hunter green sweater he was wearing. If she could, she would summon Vivien immediately to meet the Italian of her dreams.

And then, after examining Prudence, Giovanni announced to the astonishment of both women that Prudence was not only pregnant, but at least five months along. As shocked as Prudence was, the doctor seemed nonplussed by the fact that she hadn't known. While not common, he explained to Lena, who translated what was too difficult for Prudence, it sometimes happened this way; the mother under stress, underweight (having good hips apparently helped the whole process) and sad. Though how he guessed that part was a mystery. Basically, he was saying that she hadn't paid attention to anything and of course, this she understood. The Pill had kept her regular, which was great, but once off it, her body had reverted to its old pattern. At least she thought that's what had been said. Lena was having a bit of trouble translating how the effects of getting off birth control sometimes worked. Prudence listened with one ear. The one thing she had yearned for had arrived while she was in a state of oblivion.

"Such good news," Lena cooed as they left the office.

Prudence tried to feel the same reaction, but shock had already set in. How would she cope if she lost Nick? Not very long ago, she hadn't cared about anything but getting away, and now they were going to be parents. She began to shake—what if all her runaway emotions had impacted the baby? Lena was blathering on happily while so many what-ifs ran through her mind.

"We're not saying a word to Nick until I'm ready."

"This is no good Prudenza," Lena said.

"I need to be sure that he really wants this."

"How will you know if you do not tell him?"

"I need to think." Her mind swirled. Could he be trusted? How will he react? "Okay." There was no fight left in her.

In the following few days, Prudence began a dietary schedule set up by Lena; more food than she had ever consumed on a regular basis, loads of fruit and vegetables. The initial shock had only been tempered and she had started and stopped a dozen emails to her husband, finally deciding to post a well-constructed letter, designed to elicit the needed responses. But even that task proved difficult as the right words eluded her. Easier letters were sent to Kate and Julie, enlisting their advice, entrusting her feelings to the two women who knew her best. Allowing for her own adjustment to the news, Prudence kept her sentences light in her letters to Vivien, phrases meant to entice her toward a vacation to Italy one day—a footnote about Rinaldo had been included. But the more she wrote, the more excited she became; motherhood, to her astonishment, would happen. As she tracked the dates, she worried about her gallery commitment, and wrote a lengthy letter to Donny Bales, extending her apologies for failing to contact him earlier. There was no use pretending with him, so she summarized her time in Tuscany, couching the worst parts in simple statements. He had been generous and their relationship was a tie she cherished, but her pregnancy meant putting a hold on her art career. Underneath all that concern, she had an inkling Donny would thrill over a new addition to her family, a child he might one day tutor about fine art.

With new understanding of the changes in her body, there was a shift in her mental fortitude, especially each time she looked at the small ultrasound photo. Their baby girl would be cared for no matter what happened with Nick.

Prudence's skin glowed with good health, which she attributed in part to Marco's olive oil. And at night with her hand on her belly, she spoke the truth to the baby growing inside, repeating the prayers she'd offered last year at the Church of San Nicolo. The fact that she had prayed for a little girl.

As she awaited Nick's response, the weather changed; the evenings were cooler. The earth showed hints of the yellows and ochers that would soon lay the landscape and allow the viewer a small respite from the abundance of overwhelming color before the cold of winter took over. It was time for the harvests; the grapes, the olives, and once again the celebration of the chestnuts. The Bernoli kitchen was in constant use, as guests came and went with each new happening, the casa a mid-way point for events in the region. Marco's days were filled with tours of the press, and Lena dropped into a chair each evening to enjoy a glass of *limoncello* and share her characterizations of the tourists who drove her crazy, or left big tips as thanks for their fabulous experience. Prudence did her best to help in every way she could, even taking a few of the guests up to the grove. The doctor had assured her she should exercise moderately and the couples she guided were generally older and slower anyway.

She continued to write in her journal, but now the phrases were for her baby. Prudence wrote glowing sentences about Nick, things that she needed to remember, and in doing that, her love for him slowly overtook her mistrust. The anger that had fueled her began to be replaced by the images of a baby in the designated nursery on Thatcher Lane, a house filled with noise and toys, the way Hannah had claimed it should be. As soon as she spoke with the doctor, she would book her flight home.

"Come, sit with me," Lena said as Prudence entered the kitchen.

It was a windy Tuesday afternoon, the same day in September that Nick had surprised Prudence with their tickets to Italy. Nostalgia was in the air along with the ever-present fragrance of herbs.

209

"Do you want some help?"

"No...it was an easy morning," she said, swishing her hands through lemon scented suds.

"The Daltons in room two do not want the lessons, just a place to rest when they are not shopping. So many things they bring out of the car...a big car too."

Prudence had seen their check-in information with their stateside address. "Maybe they live in an area of Philadelphia called Main Line, where there are a lot of big homes and I imagine, a good deal of money."

"They are happy at least. Not so much the people in room four. These people, they make the noise, they argue, they are rude to little Carmen when she brings the towels."

"No one can be rude to her; she is very sweet."

"Si, but the season will slow and Marco and I will get a little time to see the *festas* in November."

"I feel bad that I have made more work for you and Marco."

"Nonsense, you have been a gift, and when the baby is born you will send pictures and Nilda and I will make the sweaters. It is cold in Maine, no?"

"Si, very cold in winter."

"Good. The knitting will keep her too busy to complain about me," she said, putting a huge metal colander into the soapy water. Compared to the one in the pantry of her own kitchen, Lena's was massive and studded with small holes that formed a large star beginning at the bottom and running up the sides. As Lena placed it on the drain board, Prudence marveled at the little feet that after so much use, had not lost their stability, even though dents and a few scratches attested to wear and tear over generations of meal preparations. It's like a piece of art, she thought, as she watched the loving way in which Lena caressed the form with a cotton towel.

"Wow, where did you get that?"

"As with everything, there is a story about the *colino*."

Prudence's pregnancy must have summoned the grandmother Lena hoped to become because after the doctor's visit, Lena continually remembered her own childhood stories.

"This was my Nonna's," Lena said, rinsing the suds away. She let me play with this on the kitchen floor when I was a *bambina.* I put it on my head to play soldier with my brother when I was older, out in the yard behind Nonna's house. "Gino never minded, but his small friends did not like playing with a girl."

"You must miss her," Prudence said.

"All the time, *cara.* I use the *colino* when I trim the beans from the garden, just the way she did. We would sit together in the big wooden chairs with the towel on our laps, and she would show me what to do. It has many uses.*"*

"I have one, but not like this," Prudence said. "Mine is much smaller and doesn't have those dainty curled feet."

"On my head, the little feet looked like horns—that is what Gino told me. But we must buy you a big one like this, to ship to Maine. You will drain the pasta, pick the beans and peas, and your *bambina* will play with it, and you will make memories like we do."

Prudence wanted to look ahead, but that was still difficult. "Si."

"Aldo will take you to see *dottore* Remo when he goes for the tools tomorrow; you will not mind?"

"No, of course not. I know how busy you and Marco are right now."

"Good. You will make him drive slow, no?"

"Si, si, don't worry, I'll be fine. I like riding in the Piaggio, but I won't drive this time. Aldo didn't like the way I made the turns."

"Aldo cares for the new truck like a baby. Marco said you drive very well."

"That's good. I would hate to think I don't have any redeeming qualities. Should I pick up anything for you while I'm in the village?"

"When Aldo gets the tools, he will get the parts for the plumber. There is still a problem with the lines in the back wall. Always the problem," Lena said.

Lena's hands were in constant motion and now she snaked a finger along the wall in the kitchen to simulate what was needed in the back of the house. Her hands, tanned from gardening, were never still; a concerto of words conducted for the benefit of her audience. Prudence watched in admiration, just as she had done when they'd met.

"You have such pretty skin, Lena. Is it really because of the olive oil?"

"I will tell you a secret. It is from the steam—how do you say, like a spa—when the water is poured from the pot into the *colino*. I put my face like so." She held the colander over the sink and placed her face over the colander.

Prudence imagined the pasta settling in the bottom of the colander and the hot mist rising; the idea was genius.

"Nonna's skin was like the *bambinos*," Lena said.

"What a great idea."

"The oil is good too, no?"

"Yes, I think I see a difference in my complexion already."

"The baby, and the skin, *brava!*"

The conversation was cheery, but there still hadn't been a response from Nick. "I'll call Nick as soon as I get back from town, I promise," she said to the silent question on Lena's face.

"Good. Now you go and cut the rosemary for the meat, okay?"

She smiled. Lena had become fond of that word. "Okay," Prudence said, picking up the scissors always at hand. She retreated to the garden and as she snipped the plant, tried to imagine Nick and what he was thinking.

Chapter Fifteen

Aldo arrived at the Bernolis' on Wednesday morning, dressed in his 'city' clothes—a tweed jacket and a cap so new, the shiny tag on the flap hadn't been removed. Lena rushed for the scissors as Aldo's cheeks turned apple red.

"You are only to buy the tools, old man, not to dance," Lena said clipping the tag.

"*Silenzio,* old woman," he said jovially, holding his arm out for Prudence.

She had seen their verbal dance before, the teasing that accentuated their deep friendship, grown from years of hard work and small successes. He led her to the red *Ape,* the newest Piaggio, according to Marco, to be seen on the farm for a number of years. The three-wheel vehicles were tiny workhorses and she had fallen in love with them.

"If only I could have one of these for Oyster Cove," Prudence said getting in and adjusting the seat for comfort.

"Si, si, it is a good *outtoe.*"

Prudence chuckled. Outtoe or auto, Aldo was a dear man, intent on getting her to her appointment safely, and that was all that mattered.

"*Bambina o bambino?*"

"*Bambina.*"

He carefully skirted another rut in the road and began to hum a familiar tune.

"Is that a song for the baby?"

"Si, *bolli, bolli, pentolino.*"

"Little pot?" She was positive the tune was the same tune as the one about the twinkling star. Aldo was not a talker, but when he did speak, his voice was gentle. His kind blue eyes and sturdy body, made him a comfort to be with, she thought, as the words of the nursery rhyme filled the small cab. On reflection, she had completed far more sketches of him than anyone else, using ideas garnered from their very first meeting in the Bernolis' great room, and floated to Donny in her last letter. A favorite sketch was Aldo in the grove, but when she tried to reproduce her idea with paint, the oils had made her nauseous. Her brilliant idea would have to wait until well after the baby was born. The ride lulled her worries, and she began to envision taking the baby to the studio with her on warm-weather days, her favorite music enveloping them and the scent of the sea casting its spell. Julie and Prudence had long ago woven stories of their future children playing together on Thatcher Lane, and now Addie would have her first Maine playmate. Everything else became insignificant as she imagined their children tide-pooling for small treasures or setting up their toys for inspection while Prudence tried to capture their likenesses. She felt the pull of home.

"We are here," Aldo said, pulling into a tiny slot between a motor scooter and a Fiat, the preferred car of choice it seemed, judging from those parked on the street. He jumped out and opened the cab door and helped her out as if she were made of glass.

"Grazie, Aldo," she said grabbing her tote. "I'll find you at the store when I'm done here."

"Si, I will wait."

Armed with her small dictionary and a new confidence about her overall health, she strutted into the clinic's waiting room. With a new sense of pride, she announced herself at the reception desk, and took a seat among the other patients just as a man with a bandaged foot walked in.

"Giorno." He spoke to the entire room.

"Giorno," she said, as he took the seat next to her.

He began to read his newspaper, and she picked up an Italian fashion magazine without paying attention to the words. The issue was two months old and there were pages of photos shot on the beach at Viareggio, a place she and Nick had not had time to visit. The article boasted glamorous bikini-clad women wearing gold jewelry and huge sunglasses. Page after page of high gloss photos, possibly touched up to accentuate the blond beach and aqua sky, showed vacationers or movie stars, she couldn't tell which, but the effect had her shifting the fabric of her sweater over her stomach. Would she ever have a waist again? Who knew how she would look in three months.

"Signora Pelletier," the nurse called.

"*Sono qui*," Prudence said, getting to her feet.

The nurse smiled politely. Prudence wondered if she had mispronounced the phrase, but she knew the drill. The table, the ultrasound machine and the doctor's final words before she was released. She removed her shoes and lay on the table while the nurse pushed up Prudence's blouse to reveal the rounded shape indicating small signs of growth since the last visit. Then she placed the cold jelly, sending a shiver through Prudence's body.

"*Momento*," the nurse said.

"It's okay." Prudence knew the gel would feel less cold as soon as the wand was passed through it. A picture formed on the small screen, and a baby's strong heartbeat luxurious to her ears. A delicate hand, an ear—was she smiling? Tears fell down the sides of her face. Mixed tears because Nick wasn't here to see what they had created. And worse. It was because of her need to flee that had caused him to miss such a special event. Now it was her turn to wonder where the burden of forgiveness lay.

Dr. Remo walked into the exam room, and without preamble, sat down and gently swiped the wand over her stomach. He nodded assuredly. She had gained weight and the baby's heartbeat was strong. Smiling paternally, he said, "*Complimenti, signora, la bambina e sano.*"

"Grazie," she said, attempting to hold back the flood of tears. He must have understood how emotional she was becoming, because he stood, resumed the brief conversation he'd started with his nurse, and quickly left the room.

Prudence sat up, dried her face with the tissue offered, blew her nose, and began putting herself together.

The nurse handed her two copies of what looked like a negative instead of a finished print. "You are okay?"

"*Va bene,*" Prudence said, staring at the black and white image of the child whose form had shocked her. Now she knew why she had begun to feel swollen and stretched and breast-heavy. This little girl with the kicking legs was going to be a big baby. Prudence's Italian was not sufficient to express the feelings colliding in her mind, so she extended the few small pleasantries she had rehearsed with Lena, and tucked the duplicate prints into her tote. At the desk, she handed over the correct lire, having been instructed on the amount before leaving the farm. Now she would go and find Aldo and share the good news.

The hardware store was two blocks over and one across. The street was busy as people scurried to accomplish their chores before the mid-day closures. The sun was warm and her thoughts all encompassing. Would this baby resemble the Stone's or the Pelletier's? Would she be tall and dark-haired, or take on the New England blood lines with their high cheekbones and square chins. The world around her had taken on a new prism of color. The only thing left was hearing the sound of Nick's voice and sending him a copy of the ultrasound. Deep in her bones she believed in his love. All that was left was his strength of commitment to their marriage.

Without preamble, she had the sensation of stepping off a curb onto rolling ground. At first, the people within her sightline stopped as one body, as though posing for a camera. Then within seconds, there were shouts and car horns and everyone scrambling in alarm. She heard screams, but couldn't tell where they had come from. Then she saw Aldo in the distance, running toward her, his arm raised in warning. She was frozen in place, her hands wrapped around the baby bump. A nearby sign dropped from its hanger with so much force, it splintered, and small cracks started tearing at the sidewalk to her left. There was a noise like distant thunder and glass breaking, but she couldn't find the origin. Standing where she was, a heavy-set man stood out in the crowd as he flailed his arms, his neon colored ball cap bright as a balloon going aloft.

Panicked, everyone scattered. Someone yelled, *teremoto,* the word for tremor. It was a word the Bernoli's had made familiar to their guests who were always inquisitive of Italy's earthquake history and its many fault lines. Within minutes the undulating sensation ended, but not before someone darted between the parked cars. She had to get out of the way, she thought, just before hitting the ground.

"Ah, you are awake?" Doctor Remo's voice sounded small. She was back inside the clinic.

Prudence hurt everywhere. "What happened?"

With a bit of difficulty, the doctor, his nurse and dear Aldo told her that she had struck her head and passed out, and they had carried her inside. There had been no warning. The temblors were not uncommon, but there wasn't enough news yet. Right now it appeared the center was a hundred kilometers away.

Aldo, visibly shaken, said, "We go home now."

"What about the baby?"

"She is good," the nurse said. "*Dottore* say only to rest; her heartbeat is strong."

"Thank God," Prudence said. "What about the street, Aldo, can you drive?"

"Si, si, the *Piaggio* she is good, can go around everything—you no worry."

"We get many tremors in Italy," Lena said after being told the entire story. "People are frightened and sometimes also careless, like the one who pushed you down. On the radio, the man said *categoria due.* Sometimes, the earthquakes are stronger and take out whole villages."

Aldo, seated across the kitchen counter, was staring into his wineglass, obviously shaken. His one big duty for the day—watching out for Prudenza—had taken its toll. *"Madre di dio."*

"Calmati, Aldo, she is safe," Lena said.

"Please Aldo, don't worry, I'm fine. And I'm calling the baby Nicola." Prudence announced in order to reassure him.

Lena clapped her hands. *"Meraviglioso!"*

"The name can be male or female, but I'd like to call her Nicki since we can't call her little Nico," Prudence said.

"Perfetto!" Lena said as Aldo crossed himself.

"It's four o'clock, so it might not be too late to call Nick," Prudence said.

"Go to the office where it is quiet," Lena said.

Under Aldo's piercing gaze, Prudence made it a point not to wince while getting out of the big chair by the hearth. "Grazie," she said as she kissed his cheek in passing.

She placed the ultrasound photo of Nicola on the desk and opened Lena's file on international codes, gathering her thoughts as she waited for the tenuous connection.

Nick shook himself awake; maybe he had imagined Pru's late night call. No, not so, he thought, studying the name he had written on a sheet of paper on the nightstand. Nicola—the name Pru had chosen for their baby girl. First it had been a shock—almost bigger than hearing Pru's voice on the line at ten at night. He had sent a brief email stating a letter would follow, but had dragged his feet out of anger because she had kept him in the dark so long. With her call, he had expected a brutal chastising and was prepared to state his case about going back to Denver. Instead, she told him about the quake, and that she and the baby were fine. Thank goodness she had called before he heard the news over the radio. He had been prepared to argue, about many things, but then out of pure guilt, he'd kept his mouth shut. After all, they wouldn't be in this pickle if he hadn't cheated in the first place. But the important thing was that she was anxious to come home, which was the best news of all. "Nicola." The name rolled off his lips and a tear fell. Pru had forgiven him. And even though she had said the words, it was up to him to prove himself worthy of that forgiveness. From what she said of her latest doctor visit, they would have a little athlete on their hands. A sailor maybe, he thought, as he headed for the kitchen. The *Mystic* hadn't gotten much use this summer, but now he pictured their little family day-sailing the inlets and coves along the coast, teaching Nicki to swim and tie knots and skip stones. Savoring his coffee, he remembered Pru's comments about the prayers she had offered before they had departed Tuscany last fall. He had nearly been undone when she said she wanted to name the baby after him, but he knew the choice had a lot to do with the Church of San Nicolo. She had picked the one name he would never have believed, and as he looked out at the view he began to cry. Wiping his tears, he grabbed up his coffee and headed out the kitchen door, his heart filled to capacity. The air was clear and the sea calm. Gulls soared and dipped as always; the world around him appeared unchanged though everything had. The Thatcher Lane house would be the home she had dreamed, he thought, remembering Hannah's final instructions. He had always secretly harbored a tinge of jealousy for the influence the old woman's words had on his wife, but he finally understood the term familial ties.

He thought of Lena, and how she had taken on the task of surrogate mother, where Rita had been lacking in that department. He had forgiven his mother, especially since she had paid him back from the monies made from the sale of the family home. There hadn't been time to tell Pru everything he'd found out while in Denver—the fact Charlie had walked out before Nick was born and that Rita's meanness was nothing but a protective barrier against the world and her perceived insults from its inhabitants. Rita had claimed through a barrage of tears, she had only been safeguarding Nick's interest by making certain that Pru was up to the task of wife and mother. Because she had failed so abominably with Nick. He had tromped all over the idea that Diana would ever again be in his life, and he would spend the rest of his days making it up to Pru.

With a jolt, he thought of the unfinished nursery, and rushed inside to phone his office. They could forward any calls to the house today; he was going to be a father. After saying the words out loud, he realized Pru hadn't said whether or not to keep the news a secret, so he called Vivien.

"Fantastic!" Vivien screamed into the phone.

"She'll be home in ten days, so I've got a lot to do."

"If you need anything, call; you know I'll help."

He was grateful Vivien hadn't mentioned their marital problems. A true friend, she knew the ropes, the boundaries and no matter what she and Pru had discussed, Vivien wouldn't throw it in his face. He would let Kate know about the homecoming later; there was too much to do than be on the phone all morning. Pru would notify Julie, the friend she missed most in the world. At the thought of all the dynamics, his heart swelled again.

Dragging the ladder out from beneath the porch, he realized he had dressed for the office and needed to run back inside. He changed his clothes, found drop-cloths in the attic, and laid them on the floor of the nursery. Then he ran back downstairs for more coffee and remembered he hadn't eaten. No time to fix breakfast he thought, taking the last of two doughnuts from their box. He'd gone into bachelor mode with Pru away, and as he studied the kitchen, he realized he had also let some old habits creep in. Dirty dishes, crumbs on the floor, sour milk in the fridge— discovered only this morning. Painting wasn't all that was needed, he realized, turning on the recently purchased Bose radio before rushing up the stairs. Fortunately, he wouldn't have to make a big decision about the paints; Pru had selected the neutral colors the first time she'd gotten pregnant, and then made him store them away in the closet as her dreams faded. The colors, he knew, would serve for many years, through the various stages of Nicki's childhood. He set up the ladder and checked the walls for cracks or cobwebs to clean. The room had lain idle for a long time. As he switched on the closet light, he saw the blue and yellow figures of the mobile. What a perfect creation. The artist had carved small bright-eyed fish and imbued them with shape and movement meant to keep a child's attention for hours. The tiny creatures would soon come to life as it floated over the crib, he thought, which they hadn't as yet purchased.

By day's end, his back ached and his stomach growled. He was in need of solid protein and a cold beer. He had been living on pizza and takeout food, but tonight he wanted to celebrate with a steak, grilled to perfection. That meant cleaning up in order to go to the store, but he was beat and he wanted to send an email to ask Pru if he could get the crib she had liked so many months ago. He thought of her journaling and was suddenly compelled to compose a short letter to his first child. He wanted her to know that he would be different than his own father, he would open up his heart to the tiny being he was to be entrusted with. So as the blue sky turned to gold on its way to orange, he emptied his heart onto the page.

As if by telepathy, Prudence had been writing to the baby as well. Playful notes telling her about her soon-to-be fairy godmothers, like the ones she would hear about in the nursery rhymes that would be read to her each night. Auntie Vivien would empty the shelves of North Sky Books, without question. But there was one letter she hadn't been able to write, though Lena had encouraged her practically every morning over coffee. The one to Rita Pelletier. Nick had promised to hold his tongue about the pregnancy, but as Lena pointed out, that was simply not a kind thing to do. The baby has a Nonna, she had said, tossing a look Prudence had never seen, an indication of what

221

Lena had been like with her own daughters. Without a mother of her own, Prudence knew the importance of those words, and with care, composed the letter to the woman who had a vested interest, the true grandmother of their child.

Dear Rita,

This letter probably won't heal everything that's happened, but I'm hopeful it's a start. I am not writing to cast blame since you know the entire story from all sides by now. But I felt you deserved to know that you will soon be a grandmother. I told Nick not to say anything until I was ready, and to my surprise, I am. No matter how much hurt we have thrown at each other, our baby—Nicola—must know her Nonna. Being in Italy has changed me, made me look at the world differently, and a Nonna is a high honor in this house in Tuscany. The baby is due around Christmas, and Nick and I will call you with more information when I return to Oyster Cove, which will be soon.

Prudence

Nick came home from the store with not only a steak, but some fresh sponges with which to clean up after himself, and a birthday card. The radio was a great piece of equipment, just as advertised, and had already been put to good use as he awaited Pru's return. Anything to fill the silences within the empty spaces. Now as the grill heated, he stood at the kitchen counter and surveyed their rockbound coast and the sea beyond. The wind had died and the horizon was backlit by shades of russet. He re-read the short note to the baby, elated with himself for the effort of writing to a being still in the womb. But it was a good letter, he thought, heartfelt, to the point, and substantial. He wondered, placing the steak on the hot grill, what Pru was doing at this same moment. Had nearly losing her made him a better man? Then with a pang of guilt, he remembered his mother— but a promise was a promise. Pru would make that decision when she was ready. And no matter how difficult Rita had been, he was certain that being part of her son's life as a grandmother would change everything for the better. Whether Pru understood or not, Rita's desire for grandchildren was real and deeply felt; their baby would be spoiled and loved.

Two days later, with the nursery smelling of fresh paint, he was back in his office in time to receive another surprise. Cooper and Julie wanted to reopen their cottage for the entire holiday season, which meant he had to hustle to get all the services in play before the heavy frosts. Pru had given him permission to pick up the crib and seemed genuinely pleased that he had figured out where it should go, telling him to hang the mobile over that spot.

Nick had never been an in-depth thinker, but this year the holidays would be as Pru had dreamed since the day he proposed. Her friendships with Julie and Kate were sacrosanct, and now with the addition of little Addie in their Thatcher Lane house opening gifts under their tree, Christmas would be near perfect.

He went about his chores and settled business matters, but his back became a little straighter with the thought of all the grown-up responsibilities he was about to undertake. Kate called. The Newcombs had just arrived home; at last the neighborhood would come to life after what seemed a long dormancy. Nick was anxious to see Cooper, and both of them would put up with Michael's even, though nerd-like, temperament for the sake of their women. It was the closest they would come to competing with the 'sisterhood' their wives boasted of, the one they had modeled after Hannah and her friends. As he poked around the house these days, Hannah's presence seemed less imposing; she'd been right to think the building was intended to be shared with love and laughter, the sound of excited children. Suddenly he was less afraid of fatherhood.

That evening after work, and to pass the time, Nick walked through the house in search of the Christmas lights. The stacked wood in the living room caught his attention. A perfect night for a fire, he thought, imagining the days and nights to come. Maybe they would get a pet. Did Pru prefer dogs or cats; he couldn't remember. What about childproofing the house? Did he even know what that was? Oh lord, he thought, what were they getting into?

Chapter Sixteen

"Prudenza, do not lift the bags!"

"I'm okay Marco; this one is not heavy."

"I will lift the bags."

"Yes, signore."

"Are you okay—no sickness, no pains?" Lena asked as they loaded the car for the drive to the airport.

"I'm fine, honest," Prudence said. Lena had been hovering for days and Marco acted as though the baby were his grandchild. At this moment, she didn't want to leave Casa Bernoli. She had been safe from hurt here, loved and nurtured and spoiled. It was turning cold, but it would be colder by the sea. She had begun to fret, as before, about everything, her appearance—would Nick still find her attractive—the baby's growth pattern and constant activity. She wished she could paint herself, cradling the baby bump as always, but she understood it had been right to come here, to obtain the security of mother love. Today Pru's ankles ached. However much she had gained to insure the baby's health, the excess weight provided her with an awkward walk. Going back to her room for her purse, she stood sideways in front of the mirror. Her body had become a complete stranger. "I ate a lot of pasta Nicki, what can I say."

Lena, walking into the room, overheard. "Do not listen, *bambina*, your mamma is sometimes a little *pozzo*."

"I am not crazy, just a little bigger."

"*Bellissimo* Prudenza, *bellisimo*."

Lena only called her Prudenza when she was out of patience. "You win, I give up."

"Grazie."

"Everything I did while I was here—the drawings, the photos—all packed up and on their way back to Oyster Cove, thanks to Marco."

"He is happy to help you," Lena said.

They had both indulged her every whim, and Lena had allowed her to eat whatever she craved, often making pastries after a long day of dealing with tourists, just so that Prudence could indulge her sweet tooth in the morning. Sundays with Nilda had been the biggest surprise. On more than one occasion she entered the house as always, ceremonial and pompous, but once she learned that Prudence was pregnant, her entire demeanor had changed. Along with the pasta, she often brought different colors of yarn with each visit, patting Prudence's growing bump as though trying to size the tiny wardrobe by touch.

Donny Bales had been the biggest surprise of all. He had hung the male portraits as planned, but would keep that show up until Prudence decided to come back. As to the other work, he would wait for as long as necessary, because in his words, she must attend to the most important creation of her life.

Tears of joy had been shared often since she first called Nick; his happiness was apparent and her doubts receded with each conversation. It was time to go home. A year ago September, the clouds never parted in Oyster Cove and her world felt colorless, and she and Nick had come to Italy to find themselves. A year later, she was returning to that seaside oasis at a time Nick said was ablaze with color, even after a long drought. And she knew, no matter the weather, nothing would be able to take away the joy she felt.

"I will mail the baby clothes," Lena said.

"Grazie, Lena, and I will send you pictures and Nick will call as soon as the baby comes. You'll see, we'll all be back one day. Nicki must know about Italy when she grows up. You and Marco will be her Italian family too."

They hugged, they kissed, they cried, and then Marco said, "Enough. We go before I cannot drive with all the water in my eyes."

After another tearful farewell, Prudence boarded the plane for the long flight home. This time, she had Nicola's safety in mind and found that her fretting was about to undo her equilibrium. She pulled out the knitting needles, a gift from Lena, and with newly-learned precise calculations, began the tiny sweater. As the strands of yellow lengthened into neat rows, her heartbeat returned to normal and a new sense of calm found a place within her body. Then a small kick, a nudge really, from the baby. She had been doing that more frequently in the last few weeks, Prudence thought, just letting her mother know she was paying attention. "Go back to sleep," Prudence whispered hoping not to disturb the sleeping teen sitting beside her.

Somewhere between knit one, pearl two of row eighteen, she had fallen asleep. When she woke, the robin's-egg blue sky above snow-white bunting made her squint. In just a few hours they would descend beneath that thick layering where Nick would be waiting to take them home. Stretching her legs, she headed for the lavatory with its accordion style door, grateful to still be able to squeeze through the opening. Her face was puffy, but she looked healthy, and with a bit of lipstick and blush, even more so. With plenty of time left before landing, Prudence placed a new entry into her diary.

October 16 – Darling Nicki, we're almost there. Daddy will be waiting to take us home to Oyster Cove, the place where I learned about love. The villagers will teach you about kindness and self-sufficiency. The seagulls will enchant you, the seasons will make you strong, and the spirit of great-grandmother Hannah will keep you safe.

Nick was running late, at least by his standards. He'd stopped for gas in the village and realized he'd left his wallet at home when he changed into better trousers. He raced back to the house, vaulted up the stairs and grabbed his wallet from the dresser. He hated the idea that she would be kept waiting on this of all days. He noticed the ultrasound photo that had recently arrived and jammed it in his pocket.

There had been a deluge the day before, a much needed rain, and the pavements around the village streets were slick with wet leaves. That part was reminiscent of the previous fall, except today the sun had come back and the rainwater polished rather than diminished everything it touched. He checked his watch as he hit Route 1; traffic was heavy and would be even thicker as he headed further south. RVs as big as buses rolled by as he waited at the intersection, then a small opening appeared and he cut in, his excitement building as he applied the gas only to brake as soon as he entered the line. He turned up the radio. He fiddled with the heater. He smiled at the surge of chivalry he felt, anything to keep his wife and baby safe. That thought led to the Jeep, which was getting old. They'd have to splurge for a new car, one that would safely hold an infant. By the time he had passed through Wiscasset, he'd run through a list of suitable vehicles, itemizing their qualities out loud as if Pru were seated next to him. "Listen to me, all dad-like." He heard a horn. Not paying attention, he had slowed too much. He slipped on his sunglasses against the glare of passing drivers, and dropped the window an inch. Clean fresh air. He loved October, at least when the month showed its true colors, unlike the pathetic fakery of last year. Actually, right now, he loved everything.

Finally, outside of Bath, the lines of traffic bled off in different directions. He checked his watch, pushing the accelerator higher. By the time he hit 295, he'd hit seventy-five and was keeping an eye out for flashing lights from the telltale police cars often parked on the side of the road. Instead, he spotted a black unmarked vehicle, the type used for surveillance. Dickie had only just warned him to be careful. Traffic was peak and Pru wasn't going anywhere without him.

The exits zipped by. In the distance, a line of rainbow-colored cars were hogging the passing lane, keeping the traffic from changing lanes to ease the flow. An auto club of some type, he thought, but too far away to make out the identical models. Parades of antique or low-slung sports cars were a welcome sight throughout the summer and fall, but in his anxiety to reach the airport, they now seemed a nuisance. He spotted an orange sign on the right shoulder—work somewhere ahead, more than likely the road crew doing seasonal cleanup, he thought, easing his foot slightly from the pedal. He switched the dial on the radio to the classical station, Pru's favorite. He could not even imagine how she looked, how different she would seem and how wonderful it would be to hold her in his arms again. He looked up from the dial—it had only been seconds. A silver vehicle filled his rearview mirror—like tinfoil reflecting the sun. No time to react. Nick yanked the wheel, and overcorrected. The truck struck his right rear bumper, the impact spinning the Jeep like a toy. A blur of color—the scream of glass and metal and his own voice. And then nothing.

The phone rang in Nick's office. The second one Dickie Bronson made that morning. He'd heard the scanner and called Portland Police headquarters first. He knew the drill. A few minutes later, the phone rang at the Newcombs'.

"Here she comes," Kate said. "I don't know how we're going to get through this."

"Me either," Michael said.

Prudence waited until the last minute to exit the plane; the fear of being bumped had remained since the tremor in Tuscany. When the path to the gate thinned, she picked up her satchel that Lena had provided along with the knitting materials and went to greet her husband. The baby had been aroused by all the activity too and kicked her mightily in the side. Prudence raised her arm at the doorway so as not to be missed with all the people milling near the gate, but he wasn't among them. He must have gotten tied up in traffic, she thought, searching for his face.

She spotted Michael first, then Kate, both unexpected and tired looking. "What a wonderful surprise," Prudence said embracing her friends. "Is Nick parking the car?"

"Come," Kate said. "Sit over here with us for a minute."

"You're scaring me."

"Dickie called us as soon as he heard. There's been a terrible accident. We came right away."

"Where's Nick?"

"He was in the accident, Prudence," said Michael escorting her to the nearest seat.

"Take me to him." Prudence's words came out in a hiss, Michael's arm nothing but a solid form to stop her from dissolving into a heap on the floor.

"Michael, get some water please," Kate said as Prudence's color washed away. "We'll know more in a while, but Nick didn't make it. There was nothing they could do."

"No, no, no! You're lying. Nick's not dead—he can't be, we're having a baby, Kate!"

"According to Dickie, it was a horrific crash. We need to get you home. He'll come by later and talk with you and answer all your questions, but we have to think of the baby, sweetheart. You need to be in your own home."

"No, I want to see him!"

"You're in shock honey, a brutal shock and when we get you home, I'm calling Dr. Gordon."

"I don't want to go home without Nick. Don't you see? That's why I came home."

Chapter Seventeen

The days swam by, blurred by grief, tears and longing. The only thing that made Prudence get out of bed each day was the movement inside her, Nicki throwing a punch here or a kick there. Had the baby sensed her own fears, Prudence thought, with each tiny blow. Was that even possible? To the dismay of her friends, she had begun to fret about the smallest details and now it seemed even the baby was taking notice. Dr. Gordon was keeping a close eye on Prudence's blood pressure, and her friends made certain she ate enough for the baby. If not for those office visits, she'd never have gotten out of her robe. It was cruel actually, that beyond the ledge, nothing had changed: the sea rolled forward and whispered to the rocks, seabirds rotated and greeted each other mid-flight, and boat engines droned under paintable Maine skies. She hadn't been near the waterfront and her studio and thought she might never again pick up a brush. She paced throughout the house and touched the objects that had only recently felt Nick's hands, her fingertips making ghostlike impressions on their dusty surfaces.

Kate had been by her side constantly, and right after the accident, Dickie had Nick's body transported to the local funeral home so that Prudence could say goodbye before he was cremated. That couldn't be the last thing she remembered, she had thought at the time, but it was. There was little consolation in having his ashes in the blue ceramic urn on the mantel. But alone in the house, their presence gave her a reason to summon aloud the words needed to keep the baby from feeling her angst, as if it could pass through the amniotic fluid like a broken record. But the words she spoke to him as she passed the hearth eviscerated her soul, made her want to find a suitable place to hide from the world. Like the small hermit crabs on the island of St. Thomas who lifted their natural burden—their protective shells—a second-hand home to tuck themselves away in safekeeping. Human burdens were not so easy to manage.

One day after the baby was born and the grass poked through the frozen earth, she would get a burial plot, a place to put a portion of his ashes, a marker for Nicki to visit when she was of an age to understand. Some of Nick's ashes had been sent to Rita, an agreement made after she and Prudence had shared the mutual grief over the phone. Even then, Kate had had to step in and finish the final arrangements and console a complete stranger weeping on the other end of the line.

The rest of the ashes would be scattered when summer came and they could all go out on the *Mystic*. The boat was a tangible expression of Nick's personality and for Nicki's sake, Prudence would do everything in her power to hang onto it. And if Nicki turned out to be anything like her father, she would one day sail the gleaming hull out along the shore all by herself.

Residents of Oyster Cove opened their arms as the news of Nick's death filtered through the phone lines and over the lunch counters. Food and flowers continually poured into the Thatcher Lane residence, with one of the largest bouquets sent by Donny. Nick's employees herded some of it back to their quarters and tried to keep a good front on a job they now hated going to. Letters and cards arrived from Italy with Mass cards enclosed— prayers for Nick's eternal soul. But feeling forsaken, Prudence could not bring herself to believe their meaning. As the end of October neared, the entire house was saturated with color and fragrance and sunlight that puddled warmly on the furniture, too much of everything for the mourning that was required. Waiting for predictable visits from Vivien, Prudence lumbered through the rooms, her mangled thoughts tearing at her while cooing words of encouragement to the baby. Prudence had forced herself to put up a front rather than openly hold herself accountable for the anger she harbored—Nick gone from her life just as they had found their way back. Such thoughts led to others—that she was nothing but a self-centered bitch—and the fretting went on. But none of her emotions seemed to fit the body she saw in the mirror. How much easier it was to soothe others. Just as she had done with an almost inconsolable Lloyd Tucker after hearing the news, allowing him the comfort of her arms as his taciturn spirit collapsed to sobs. But Prudence needed Lloyd as never before; there was no one else for Pelletier Realty to rely on as winter approached. It was up to Lloyd, who tromped silently through the old cottages, checking water lines and sealing up windows while trying to hide his sadness. The first thing she had him do was to ensure that the Smiths' house would be ready for their return just before Thanksgiving. Her oldest friend, Julie was needed more than ever now, and Cooper would help Prudence make the business decisions; to sell or not to sell the firm—the question on all their minds. If only the Smiths could stay permanently, Prudence thought, walking into the nursery as she did each day, taking small comfort in the stenciled work exclaiming the baby's name as the letters Nick had painted practically bounced off the wall around the coveted crib. She was about to sit in Hannah's old cane rocker when she heard the cringe-worthy clang of the ancient bell and the squeak of the front door.

"Come on up Vivien."

"How'd you know it was me?"

"Nobody uses that atrocity to announce themselves but you. Don't tell me you brought another stuffed animal."

"I couldn't resist."

"I'm going to need another shelf in here if you don't stop."

"How would you like to go out for a drive; maybe grab a bite to eat; you're looking very peaky."

"I don't really care how I look, thank you very much."

"That's the first time you've sounded like the old Prudence."

"Then you know how much I've bottled up. I'm sick with missing my husband, worried I'm hurting the baby with so much crying, and all I want to do is scream," Prudence said. "The mask

I wear for others is to keep me from totally breaking down. And yes, I'd like that drive now."

"Well, all right then."

Prudence had finally gotten out of her night clothes and was at least presentably dressed. But as she struggled into her coat, she studied her friend's appearance. Vivien had listened politely, but it was obvious she too had been crying before she arrived.

"You don't have to hide those tears on my account. You loved him too."

"I keep thinking you've had enough of tears, but sometimes I can't help myself. And I hate drinking alone."

"If not for Nicki, I'd hate to think of what I would have done."

"How about I bring you one of my jackets tomorrow, something that will keep you warm because you'll be able to close it completely."

Vivien's visits were a breath of fresh air in a world laden with sadness. "How can you sass me when I'm in this condition?"

"Because it made you smile, and I haven't seen one in a very long time."

Even without the mask, how could she tell Vivien that her days were spent waiting for the echo of footsteps on wooden treads? Or each morning shaking the cereal box to make sure there was enough for Nick's preferred breakfast. And how could she tell her friends the way she squeezed the tube of toothpaste in the middle so it would look as though he'd done it. Anything to savor his presence. The house rattled from the cold, and in the emptiness, she heard his complaints reverberating from the aging walls. The 'if only' rhetoric lodged in the space where logic met grief. On occasion, she reverted to Hannah's words for comfort, the letters written after losing Timothy. Pain was pain, but the ways of grieving were very personal.

"I'm trying, Vivien."

"I know, and I wish I could do more to help."

"You're here; that's enough. Now, let's go for that ride."

"How's the kicking today." Rita had begun making weekly calls to inquire of her health. A defrosting of sorts had been taking place when Prudence realized the conversations about Nick were also saving Rita's sanity.

"She's more active than ever," said Prudence. "I'll be glad when she makes her debut appearance."

"Me too; you're a comfort to me. Nick was a wonderful son, and he would want us to be friends. You're much braver than I'd have been in similar circumstances."

"Nick made me brave, and going to Italy did too. It brought both of us closer than we had been for a long while, and as horrible as this nightmare has been, I have to believe he's watching over us." She had taken strength from what she liked to call the 'Nonna effect' and with more long distance prodding from Lena, had gathered her courage and called Rita. They still weren't close, but at least hinting at being family.

When Prudence tired of talking, she would shut down, leaving Rita to ramble on with her own memories or simply cut the call short and rock herself to sleep in the nursery. Discomfort struck in every posture if she tried to sleep in her own bed. At least that's what she told herself when bad dreams woke her and she sought strength from the protective girdle surrounding her middle, all thanks to neighborhood friends and their oven-warm dishes. Who knew if the baby would react to the cold the way Prudence did? She read books on nursing, child rearing, and boned up on the latest methods for safety precautions, including the special car seat. When presented with that gift from Nick's staff, she realized she would have to part with the darling VW Beetle and had fallen apart. It was the type of decision they were supposed to make together, car shopping was Nick's domain.

"Are you all set for the hospital?" Kate said, as Prudence slowly maneuvered the rooms, her baby bump now too big to see beyond to her shoes. "Julie's on speed dial, and I'm able to do anything you ask."

"We have weeks yet, but yes, I'm prepared. And for someone who hadn't had a keen interest in motherhood, I see you ogling the little onesies and fuzzy toys. I think you're getting all broody on me."

"Don't be silly," Kate said as she leaned down and whispered to Prudence's tummy. "I'm more than happy to be Auntie Kate when the time comes—you're going to need someone with sound English reasoning to look up to."

"That she will, Auntie Kate." Prudence held back another flood of tears as she ushered Kate to the door. Not even the overwhelming kindness of friends made up for the longing to wrap her arms around her husband one more time.

Day and night, the scent of spice from proffered baked goods permeated the kitchen, but the former pleasure of rosemary was a distant memory. The once treasured plant had been left untended for too long. Another death, she thought, as she stared down the new Bose radio. Nick hadn't wrapped it, he'd said in what seemed an eternity ago, because he had liked the company of the broadcasters while he ate his meals. During one of their late-night calls, he told her he would put the radio in the nursery when she returned so she could share the sounds she loved with the baby. The Bose was a touching gift, but had remained silent since her homecoming because she couldn't bear the happiness it was meant to bring. Today, as the afternoon light waned, the silence screamed at her until she decided to put the unit somewhere out of sight. Picking it up, her fingers brushed what felt like a label that had come loose. Instead there was an envelope Scotch-taped to the underside—a place where it wouldn't get lost. It was a birthday card, but not for her. It was to their daughter. Startled, Prudence set the radio back down and opened the unsigned card. A folded piece of notepaper fell out.

Dear Nicki,

It is the beginning of October 2006 and today I painted your room. You can change the color when you're older if you like, but for now, we know you'll be happy the way it is. We (I) promise to keep you safe, love you and teach you how to play whatever sport you choose. But most of all, I will be here for you, to answer any questions you have, no matter how difficult they may seem. One day, you will meet your grandmother Rita. You have lots of godparents waiting to see you and auntie Vivien, who is a hoot, though you don't know what that means. I made your mother a promise that we would take you to visit Lena and Marco in Tuscany when you are old enough to smell the rosemary—your mother is crazy about the rosemary. I hope you are just like her. Wait till you see how much talent she has. You'll be here soon sweetheart.

Love, Dad.

Prudence let the paper fall to the floor as she dropped into a chair, her fist pounding the treasured wood of the breakfast table. The empty room was suddenly cold, the type of chill that might break in pieces if she moved from the seat. How would they manage without him?

Out beyond the ledge, spindrifts of white tendrils were limned by the rising November moon. There would be a very high tide, she thought, as Nicki punched at a vulnerable spot. The ebb and flow of life, guides that had always pulled at Prudence, a subtle reminder that caught her off guard and halted her breath mid-stream. The moonbeams angled through one of the windows and exposed the raw nakedness of her pain, forcing her to turn away from her reflection. In that moment, the voice of Hannah, the woman Prudence had aspired to emulate, caused her to question the strength of her heritage. Mistakes had been made. Laureates wrote about the healing of wounds and time that brings clarity. Prudence wasn't certain she would ever forgive herself as much as she had forgiven Nick.

The days grew shorter as Prudence's grief etched itself on the walls of her heart. And as predicted by time and tides, the seasons placed their mark on Oyster Cove. Halloween had been a cruel trick rather than the usual treat and Thanksgiving more about the people loved, than the food. For many, time had been skewed by losing a member of their community, but no matter the range of feelings, the clock never stopped for those on Thatcher Lane. Prudence's gang had come together, her pals, her confidants, those with whom she had shared everything now secreted within the walls of Hannah's house. She would always refer to it as that; nothing else made sense. With Nick gone, she was a very young widow—like Hannah. There was no pride in that truth, but Julie and Kate had taken on the duties of friendship and guidance just as Hannah's band of three had managed to do for each other a very long time ago. Prudence and Nicki would be somewhat better off financially than Hannah had been, since Nick had purchased life insurance after the first pregnancy, a fact she hadn't known until he died. But above all, Nicki would be part of a world family. Family, a word that until she moved to Oyster Cove, had not always had pleasant connotations. Now she knew better. Family came in every form, every circumstance, and best of all, here in Oyster Cove and its environs. Family now meant Rita and the Bernolis and anyone who cared enough about the Pelletiers to be part of their lives.

Christmas was a time of birth. The lights strung everywhere, a reminder of Christmases past. The medium-size tree set up in her living room, a gift from Michael and Cooper. The presents under the blue spruce were for Addie and Nicki—Prudence's friends had taken care of everything as they awaited Nicki's birth. She may or may not decide to arrive at that precise date, but Prudence was ready. And with all that had happened, *bambina Nicola,* of the prayers of San Nicolo, was now the only gift that truly mattered.

About the Author

Cheryl Blaydon is the author of the novels, *The Memory Keepers, Island Odyssey,* and *The Heart of Stone.* She lives in East Boothbay, Maine.   www.cherylblaydon.com